HOWS YOUR FATHER

HOWS YOUR
FATHER

ROSE BOYT

First published in 2014 by Short Books
3A Exmouth House
Pine Street
EC1R 0JH

10 9 8 7 6 5 4 3 2 1

A CIP catalogue record for this book is available
from the British Library.

ISBN 978-178072-147-7

Printed and bound in Great Britain by
CPI Group (UK) Ltd, Croydon, CR0 4YY

Cover design by Pep Sala

To my beloved father
1922-2011

DALSTON MURDER
MYSTERY

An unidentified young woman was found dead of gunshot wounds to the head on Saturday afternoon in a derelict basement premises well-known locally as a so-called *"shooting gallery"* or drug den situated adjacent to St. Anne's Church, Dalston.

Police fear the body of the girl will never be identified because of the circumstances of the crime and the extensive nature of wounds to the head and face. No reports of missing persons that could be linked to the victim have been received.

Detective Inspector Whitman, in charge of the investigation, expressed sorrow for the waste of a young life.

"In cases of this sort the family does not always miss the young person right away," he said. *"Even if a name was suggested, a check on dental records would not be possible because the victim had no teeth."* Detective Sergeant McMann, second in command, was not surprised by the lack of co-operation in the local community. *"As is usual in these cases no witnesses have come forward,"* he said.

As well as gunshot wounds to the head the girl had sustained a deep yet well-healed slash from the corner of her mouth to her ear, probably inflicted by a Stanley knife in a previous attack.

Detective Sergeant Mc-Mann admitted when pressed that on the streets this distinctive and time-honoured wound is still meted out on occasion as the mark of the "grass" or police informer, although he was keen to stress that he himself was not able to recognise the victim, nor was she known to other officers at Dalston Vale.

Rev. Brandon, vicar of St. Anne's, was deeply saddened by the circumstances of the death. *"The filthy cellar where the body was found is used only by those who have sunk to the very lowest level of squalor to satisfy their drug cravings,"* he said.

Kevin Hall, a support worker at the Hackney Chemical Dependency Unit, and himself a self-confessed former drug addict of heroin and crack cocaine, emphasised that lessons must be learnt from this tragic loss. *"The crime was probably a punishment killing carried out by a ruthless dealer anxious to protect his business,"* he said.

Mr. Hall pointed out that he himself is confined to a wheelchair as a direct result of his drug use. He lost both legs to gangrene through the collapse of veins and infection caused by dirty needles. *"That's what happens,"* he stated. Contact the CDU if YOU need help.

St. Anne's Dalston offers a range of services to local people including one-to-one counselling free of charge and yoga for relaxation. Each Tuesday evening a non-denominational narcotics dependency self-help group meets in the crypt for those who have decided to change the way they live. Everybody welcome.

Kyprious Kypriou, proprietor of Kip's Kebabs, an all-night cafe grill located near the scene of the shooting, said that people regard addicts as filth but the dead girl must have been somebody's daughter.

My mum got three months because some cunt left a pound weight of drugs on top of her kitchen cabinet. Everyone knew the drugs was nothing to do with her otherwise they would of thrown away the key but the judge reckoned she needed to be taught a little lesson. In other words that will learn you, you silly old cow.
– Take her down, he said, flap flapping his white hands like he was shooing her away.

She bowed her head in silence, waiting for someone to come for her. A court official touched her gently on the arm. The judge was shuffling his papers without even looking up as my mother was led towards the cells.

I couldn't see her face but from where they stuck me up in the public gallery I could see scalp through the sparse hair on top of her head. Her thin shoulders shook inside the brown coat she borrowed off of our Linda for her big day. The coat was too big and she was shaking with the effort not to show herself up in the court. She raised a hand to pat the hair at the back of her head. The ends of her fingers was stained orange brown and you could see a red tide-mark round the back of her neck where she put a rinse through her hair the night before her court case, to cover the grey.

Where was the cunt what hid the drugs when the old woman needed help? Nowhere. I thought my brother Alan might pop up at the back of the court like in church when the bride and groom are just about to tie the knot and the vicar goes like just impediment or whatever and someone at the back shouts IT SHOULD HAVE BEEN ME.

9

Afterwards I popped in the Macbeth to pick up my fags from the fag man. My sister Linda was playing darts with Shirley Irons and Julie and Julie's mum and who do you think was celebrating at the bar only our Alan with Alan's Sandra and that ex-copper what used to go with Sandra's sister and a couple of Alan's mates and his mate's cousin what was friendly with one of them from the social club over Green Lanes where they get the stuff off of lorries bringing boxes of tomatoes and coriander and those long hot green pickle peppers they put in kebabs.

Sandra was smiling up at Alan like he was god. Alan popped the cork on a bottle of fizzy wine and sprayed foam over Sandra. Sandra screamed and wiped her eyes. Alan's mates was back-slapping and hugging all over the shop and Alan started to sway with his arms in the air like we are the champions and the new landlord what's his name Ronnie something put in by the brewery after Mick and Maggie flitted back to Ireland wasn't he smiling and smiling behind the bar with his arms folded across his chest where he was waiting for it all to go off.

The fag man dipped in his bag for my change. Alan waved the empty wine bottle at Ronnie and was like same again my good man and make sure it's very and then he saw me.

– What you celebrating, Alan? I went.

– Maureeeen! he goes, opening his arms wide. – Another glass for our Maureen.

I put my fags in my bag. I slung my bag over my shoulder.

– I don't wanna celebrate with you, I said.

Alan moved towards me across the pub. He punched me in the upper arm. I rubbed my arm. He laughed.

– Have a drink, he shouted. – Relax. She'll only do six weeks.

– Only six weeks? Is that all? Oh that's all right then, I said.

– Don't be like that, Reen, he said. – Do her good to put

her feet up I reckon. You can keep an eye on the old man for her. Reckon I done her a favour. The poor cow could use a break.

– I knew it was your gear, I said.

– You only just worked that out?

His mates was laughing. He dug me in the arm again.

– Gotta laugh, he said.

I was like ha ha and poked him back, not as hard as all that but hard enough.

– That fucking hurt, he said.

– Good.

– Don't start, Reen, said Linda.

I looked at Linda.

– It's your fucking funeral, she went.

I turned back to my brother.

– Cunt, I said.

– You what? he said.

– I said YOU CUNT, I roared.

His mates stopped laughing. I thought he was going to nut me but he was like think about it Maureen, better for us all she spends a few weeks in Holloway than I do the best part of a ten stretch for possession with intent. Think all the mouths I got to feed. Think how she'd worry. The worry'd be a sentence for her in itself. She'd make herself ill over it. You know what she's like Maureen. She's better off inside.

– Better off? I said. – In Holloway? You sure?

– Whatever, he went, turning away from me.

I got my hands round his throat. His skin smelt bad.

– Fuck sake, Maureen, said Linda.

I let go and tried to shake his smell off of my hands. I tried to swallow my tears squeezing out before I mean I fucking hate myself sometimes I always let myself down like crying when I want to kill somebody I stop myself but I can't stop myself crying.

– Maureen? he said, in a different voice.

I looked up at him. I wiped my hands on my trousers. I thought he was going to say sorry but I was wrong wasn't I? I looked up and he nutted me. I leant against the bar and Linda fetched some bog roll and helped me to clean up the mess. The landlord was whistling, polishing glasses. Alan sipped his drink and lit up and blew smoke-rings at me.

– Nice one, Alan, I said, dabbing at myself.

– You want some more? he said.

– Alan, said Sandra, pulling at him.

– Fuck off, you. You want some more, Maureen?

– No.

– Well then don't start.

I swallowed blood and tears. Alan's Sandra tried to give me a sovereign pendant but I told her to sod off. I bowed my head and pressed the sides of my nose between my index and middle fingers to straighten it. The bone crunched, then clicked. My fingers smelt of Alan, of his skin problem and the skin cream like bad eggs he dabbed on to hide it and heal it. The front of my white top was splattered. I went in the bog to have a wash. When I lifted my head up to check myself in the mirror our Linda was standing behind me. She started to sing.

– Two lovely black eyes, ooh what a surprise…

On the steps of the court before my mother's case come up she got ten minutes to talk to her brief. He said if she gave a name to the crown prosecutor all charges against her would be dropped.

– I know who it belongs to, I said. – It belongs to our Alan. Doesn't it Mum? Tell him.

– Do you have proof? Asked the brief.

– No, I said.

I looked at my mum.

– Tell him, I said. – Tell him or they'll put you away.

– Steady on, said the brief. – That is hardly likely.

– No? I said.

– No no, said the man.

– Really? I asked.

– Really. Very little chance of a custodial sentence for such a small quantity.

– Good, my mum said. – Thank you. I don't feel so scared now.

– And yet, said the barrister.

– What do you mean and yet? said my mum.

– And yet let's not gamble, what? he said. – If you do know the identity of the perpetrator…

– I don't get you, I said. – I thought you said…

And then he was like well my dear the thing is I do understand family loyalty and I am conversant with the concept of honour amongst thieves but in a case like this I feel that a woman in your mother's position is unable to afford the luxury of such fine feelings.

– Fucking cheek, said my mum.

The night she got arrested it was the Lottery thing Midweek Draw with Dale Winton. She had her ticket in her lap and was squinting over the top of her big glasses at the telly and flicking through the pages of her weekly magazine. The balls spun out of the machine. My mum was acting casual to make out she was not all that bothered like she believed if she ignored the balls spinning across the screen her pretend lack of interest might shorten the odds of her numbers dropping. But she was on and on if her numbers did come up should she move out over by her cousin at Hainault or Epping's nice or Spain our Dolly and Butch got a marble pool out there on the coast with a gold dolphin fountain what the water squirts out of the dolphin's laughing mouth. Dolly sent me a photo, she said. I could lie by the pool all day in the sunshine and do fuck all. I just can't make up my mind.

Glancing at the screen out of the corner of her eye like when we was kids that time at the pictures eating sweets and glugging Tizer out of a big glass bottle in the front row of the Rex because no one clocked she found somebody's wage packet on the floor of the launderette and slid it in her coat pocket. We got ice-creams in the interval and after that I watched her watching through a chink in her fingers through mist in the graveyard the antics of the living dead. She made us promise not to tell the old man. She was hiding behind her hands. I nudged her with my elbow and she uncovered her face in the moonlight and said if you just peek at the bad bits round the edges a little bit at a time oh my god I can't look. She shut her eyes and was hugging herself in the darkness. I watched the living dead in their ragged nighties rising up out of coffins of mildewed stone in the moonlight what was terrifying in them days if you just peek through your fingers she said you don't feel so frightened.

The old woman looked away from the telly and pressed the mute button.

– Where would you go if you win? she said.

– Nobody wins, I said.

– I don't know where I'd go, she said.

– Don't worry about it, I said.

– But one thing I do know, Maureen, she said.

– What?

– I know that wherever I do go I won't be taking nobody with me.

– No Mum.

– I'll leave you all behind, she said.

– Yes Mum.

She took off her glasses and blinked and rubbed the lenses on the welt of her cardigan.

– I will, she said. – I'll leave you all behind.
– I know, Mum, I said, my voice sort of there there you
poor thing like some people talk in a special soft voice to a
child.

Not that what she said never hurt me whether she
was trying to or not even trying but I was used to how
she went on. The old man never heard nothing. He was
sleeping in his chair, his bad leg propped up on a nest of
occasional tables. He had not been out of the front door
since my Dawn's Natalie got christened and the old woman
had to wheel him out on the landing and half the flats
come out to help us carry his wheel-chair down the stairs.
Mother's boiled tea-towels and white swabs was blinding
on the string in the sunshine and the old man flinched and
covered his eyes. He was complaining because he wanted
to stay indoors. She was trying to explain to him what was
happening why he had to go out because our Maureen's
Dawn's Natalie is getting christened over St. Anne's
she said like he was too stupid to remember his own
daughter's daughter's daughter. The old man flinched and
hid his eyes because he was not used to such brightness.
Also I thought he was like a little kid, shutting his eyes so
that no one could see him. Half the flats come out even
Aggie's Mick as a rule what won't do nothing for nobody.

My mum was turning the pages of her book. The old
man coughed in his sleep. His circulation was bad. You
could smell the black toes on the foot of his bad leg poking
out of his dressing. It must of been at least two years ago
now since we got him downstairs on the morning of the
christening and I helped my mum load him in a cab. Then
I shot round Dawn's to take her and her girls to the church
what they hardly fitted in the car with the baby in her car-
seat and all the net petticoats and that where Dawn's Barry
was collecting his mum.

I got Dawn and the girls inside the church with Rev

Brandon his name was some new bloke in a cardigan
who took over from that Australian woman what went on
maternity leave and never come back. Dawn was carrying
Natalie on her hip. Bella and little Jess was giggling round
the font, all of our Dawn's kids in a froth of apricot satin
and white lace out of that bridal shop down Roman Road
where Barry's cousin used to work Saturdays and give
Dawn a discount. I kissed Dawn and the baby and went
outside to help my mum unload my dad. His legs was
wrapped in a tartan blanket and he was clutching his
tins on his lap in a carrier bag to keep his self going. As
she lowered the chair out of the cab to me his face was in
shadow. My mum said the new cabs was a godsend where
it was ever-so easy these days to take a cripple out for a
airing.

I hadn't thought of my dad like that. Mum patted him
on the head and said he don't half scrub up. Dawn in the
church with Natalie in her arms the spit and the other
two playing round the font and another one on the way I
cried she looked so proud and so happy. I was so proud.
But afterwards when my mum pushed my dad down the
ramp out of the church into the sunshine on the crowded
pavement his yellow face was red raw round the mouth
where she tried too hard to scrub the dirt off of him and
the kids screamed and ran when they saw him I mean talk
about the living dead.

My mum sighed and took her lottery ticket off of her
lap and placed it on the arm of the chair. She looked over
at the old man and tutted.
– He don't look well, Mum, I said.
– He won't take no solid food, she said.
– Since when?
– Since last week.
– Have you seen the doctor?
– We're waiting for another appointment.

– Take him up the hospital, Mum.

– My Tommy won't go near no hospital, Maureen. You know that.

– You gotta make him, Mum.

– Make him? She said. – Don't make me laugh. Doctor Patel come up and give him the once over a couple of weeks ago and after that the silly sod said he don't want no more quacks poking him about.

– What did Doctor Patel say?

– He said he wants the old man's leg off.

– Jesus.

– But Tommy said there ain't no point.

– He said what?

– Well, said my mum. – Where he don't feel no pain no more? Doctor Patel give him some tablets for the infection. He's gonna take another look at him after clinic next week.

The old man was snoring. I felt angry. A pair of slippers was tucked side by side under the nest of occasional tables, the worn hairy toes nudge nudging together so I had to look away. I'd only popped over to sort out my mum's catalogue money.

The slippers belonged to Victor what she let him move in after our Susan never wanted to sleep over home no more. Where he was always welcome over my mum's to keep her company or keep an eye on the kids if she popped out and she was so grateful to him when we was kids looking out for our Alan over the Scouts and the Territorial Army and he was her friend. And helped her out with his board and lodging what was a miracle she even give him a bit of dinner since my dad never ate no dinners no more and Raymond fended for his self she reckoned it weren't worth her while to put herself out. But she sighed and tore her lottery ticket in half. I watched her shred the torn halves into the ashtray. How she buys jeans

and boots and that for our Billy what is the third youngest
of her kids above Susan and Raymond she is always
getting herself in a state over her catalogue payments. And
bits for Billy's kids what he takes off of them and sells in
the pub because them kids is her own flesh and blood she
can't stand to see them go without. So she skints herself
over Billy and the old man's tins even though Victor bungs
her for his room and that and our Raymond pays her
wages every fortnight out of his giro on top of her cleaning
money on earlies over Shoreditch School off of the cards
and the rent paid and what she gets off of her book for her
and the old man.

So I had to clear her debt for her didn't I? Where
my Tony had lifted that bit of plain Wilton out of the
warehouse for his mum when she had a small windfall
after her aunt passed away, a sort of reddish brown
chestnut colour looks lovely in her front room what I
seen the self-same colour in the window of that shop
on Kingsland Road they wanted twenty-seven fifty not
including underlay if my Tone done out his mum's front
room a ton all told with fitting or so he told me and I had
the money off of him because I knew he must of charged
her at least double what he owned up to with her windfall
and her brother left her a few bob over that cold spell he
got a cold on his chest what done for him what my Tony is
like.

Although he did do me the off-cut for my stairs
and passage with those shining brass stair-rods out of
Homebase I always wanted what finished the job beautiful
I don't care what nobody says. With an abstract border
and heavy paper embossed caramel below and above the
lovely soft colour of that whippet pup my sister Maggie
lavished so much love on that dog some toe-rag had it
away outside the Co-op where the silly cow only went and
left it tied to a tree when she popped in for a pint of milk.

I don't care what nobody says my Tony done out my stairs and passage lovely with the abstract border although when you run up the stairs the rods rattle and you bang your toes how things turn out sometimes if you ain't careful what you wish for.

I can hardly believe when I think how we used to live in Dunstan Court in arrears so bad we didn't even have a telly. A pair of crates on the bare floor to sit down before we got that black leatherette three piece Pakis dumped in a skip the spicy smell coming off of it once we got it indoors after dark hoping no one wouldn't notice that woman upstairs thought she was better than us because her daughter worked in a bank. The floor in the front room worn in patches to the bare concrete underneath what was breaking up to small stones and grit and baby Dawn and Craig perched on the table screwing winkles out of the shell with a couple of bent pins even the nutter what had the flat before us never wanted that table. Although she lugged the stove out of the kitchen and sold it to the Pakis for ten bob what she didn't need no stove no more where they was taking her. And left me with a dirty great gap. And I do mean dirty. If she'd only of said I would of bunged her a quid and saved her the trouble.

The winkles on the yellow and black table in one of them white enamel bowls with the dark blue rim all chipped to fuck makes me feel sad. One of them memories I don't even know if it's a real memory because I got a photo of it to remind me as if I wanted reminding. And it couldn't be helped the fumes of the glue of my outdoor work to make a few bob sticking shoes for a shoe factory where some bubble from Old Street dropped off cartons of uppers and soles once a week even the kids was out of it. Our Craig in his underpants it was so hot in that flat right next to the boiler for the whole block and the glue fumes in my eyes and Dawn in a napkin and vest. I do remember how ashamed I don't need no one to remind me where I can't believe I give my Tony the rent money every week and he made out like he was off down the housing but he never got past the bookies what I had no idea until I got the final eviction notice intercepting the mail. I can't even remember who took the picture. I didn't even get a chance to comb Dawn's hair.

So that told the catalogue woman on the understanding I mean I wagged my finger she was not to let my mum buy no more stuff. I told my mum if Billy wants jeans he should fucking work for them. And his kids sell their dinner tickets you know how they spend the money the poor little fuckers off of the old block ain't it? And where is Lorraine? I mean you reap what you sow you know that Mum.

Well she had some squashed boxes of cakes off of that Brenda down Hoxton stacked in the passage and after the catalogue woman fucked off we was dunking cake and Mum goes like this is nice and I'm like tum ti tum.

Because I know she misses me because I don't often stop for long when I pop up to her no more because of Victor what lodges over home ever since our Susan went and Billy and Lorraine in and out for a bath and a bit of anything what they can get out of the old woman home comforts like anybody else my mum knows how I feel. But our Linda told me Vic was on Scout Camp over Potter's Bar with his troop and Billy had cashed his giro that morning so why would he come home to her until it was all gone.

She said to take a few cakes over Dawn's for Dawn's girls. I asked her how much but she goes on the house which was. So I just flopped down next to the old woman on the chair and the old man was nice and quiet. Although there was the funny smell off of him he was nice and quiet. So I just flopped down next to my mum on the chair. I could hear the click click of balls from upstairs where our Raymond was in his room playing pool against his self on his little pool table he got squeezed in up there next to his bed. What no one would ever believe was twins with our Susan seeing as one of them was so big and slow and smiling and the other well the less said about our Susan the better.

So I sat and ate cake to kill the half-hour before my Dawn was waiting for me to sit with Bella and Jessie and Natalie and Baby Charley while she got herself dressed and went over the Winnicott Centre for her parenting course. Seeing as her Barry was on lates I said I would sit with the girls. What I done for Dawn whenever she needed me like she was attending ante-natal clinic or post-natal support group or taking the baby over the baby clinic or she just needed to go for a walk sometimes on her own and think about things or a darts match if she was picked and I was passed over.

She is such a good mum all the things she does for her kids over the park or swimming down Whiston Road before the baths shut down or Britannia if I lend a hand even the baby goes in the water and making puppets over the Geffrye Museum out of bog rolls and felt.

Dawn said not to worry because Barry would pick up some chips on his way home for their tea and a couple of savaloys to go with it and a wally on the side. I remember how hard it was sometimes with just my two let alone what she's got on her plate.

– This is nice, Maureen, said my mum.
– Mmm, I said.
– I wish I saw more of you like we used to, said my mum.
– Mmm, I said.
– You could be more of a daughter to me, said my mum. – What with the old man the way he is and that.
– I'll get the door, I said.

Detective Sergeant McMann and Detective Inspector Whitman pushed me out of the way and went smirking straight for the kitchen. I was after them. I watched Whitman climb on a chair. He reached for the biscuit barrel on top of my mother's kitchen cabinet. He took off the lid.
– Bingo, he shouted.
– Show us, said McMann.
Whitman held the barrel under McMann's nose.
– Must be a pound weight there at least, I reckon, said Whitman.
– Bingo, said McMann.
My mother just sat in the chair and stared at the telly. Whitman sat down next to her and showed her the biscuit barrel half full of brownish powder.
– Who's been a naughty girl then? he said.
I kept my gob shut. Mum hardly even bothered to fake surprise. She was like oh blimey, oh no, of course not mate, ain't nothing to do with me.
Whitman couldn't stop smiling. He didn't seem bothered where the stuff come from. He just sat down next to my mum and watched the telly for a bit with the biscuit barrel cradled in his lap. He didn't ask no questions. He just sat there grinning and hugging the biscuit barrel while McMann in the kitchen made a show of examining the old woman's battered saucepans, her set of olive-green mugs what I give her for Christmas. I could see McMann through the serving hatch tweezering fag-ends out of her ashtray and rummaging in the fridge freezer. Mum and Whitman was watching Oprah on cable what Alan got her wired up some big fat people shouting at each other my father fathered my daughter's baby or my son fathered my mother's baby or something while Mum tut-tutted at the people on the telly like animals they are she said and I watched McMann half-heartedly turn the place over.

She wanted me to go with her down the nick but I didn't want to go and anyway I was looking after Dawn's kids.

– I'm sorry Mum, I said.

The old man started shouting in his chair. Whitman went out to the kitchen with the biscuit barrel.

– Ponce, the old man roared, shaking his fist.

– Go back to sleep, Thomas, said my mum.

The old man closed his eyes.

– Please Maureen, said my mum. – Please.

– No, Mum, I said. – I can't.

– I can't do this on my own, she said, and started to cry.

– Where's Alan? I said.

– Him and Sandra went down Julie's caravan Clacton to see about a pub down there needs a lot of work but it could be a nice little…

I sighed and phoned over home for my Tony but there was no answer. Craig was at the warehouse, unsocial hours, driving his fork lift truck. Linda was at bingo. My sister Georgina was taking her Steven's boy over the doctor's. Frank lived out at Beckton, too far away. Raymond was too slow. Susan was just Susan, like Billy, like Lorraine, no good to no cunt. My sister Maggie answered the phone but when I asked her to help she shouted at me.

– Mother made her fucking bed tell her to lie in it. You want to help her, you help her. Don't get me involved. I can't be on with all her dramas. Tell her from me it's her own stupid fault the company she keeps. I hope they throw away the fucking key.

Maggie was shouting at me and my mum was staring at the telly. Maggie was still angry since she lost her old man that Christmas when the bad gear was going round. I was holding the phone away from my ear and watching the police in the kitchen through the serving hatch. The police

started messing about in the kitchen with the drugs.
– Bye, Maggie, I said.

They thought I couldn't see what they was doing or they was not all that bothered but I saw what they was doing. Whitman took a little shovel and a set of scales out of his pocket. He scooped a spoonful of the stuff out of the biscuit barrel, weighed it, bagged it up, labelled it and put it in his case. Then he split the rest of the drugs between two evidence bags, stuffed the biggest bag in his own jacket and gave the other one to McMann.

– Come on, love. Time to go, said McMann.
– Let's be having you, said Whitman.
– Go on Mum, I said. – I'm sorry. I feel bad. You'll be all right. I'm sorry.
– Shut up, Maureen, said my mother. – You don't want to come with me.
– Yeah well, I said.
– Come on love, said McMann. – Move it.
– At least look after the old man, she said.

I followed them outside. Down below in the grounds an unmarked car was idling, keys in the ignition, doors open. I heard the old woman joking with the police as they led her along the landing towards the external staircase.

– Surprised no one ain't nicked your motor, she laughed. – I mean round here, you know what they're like. But can I ask you something?
– It's a free country, said McMann.
– How did you know about the stuff?
– A little bird cheeped.
– What bird?

McMann looked at his watch.

– A dead bird, said the copper, tapping the side of his nose. – With a gob on it. And no teeth.
– That'll learn her, said my mother. – Should of kept it shut.

I leant over the landing and watched McMann and Whitman take my mother away. They led her past the wheelie bins towards the car. Before she got in she drew deep on her fag and looked mournfully at the long butt before flicking it away across the broken tarmac. Out of the back window of Alan's flat Sandra's kids was pushing and shoving, trying to gob on my mum's head.

```
Dear Maureen,

Encl. one V.O. for you and one for Dawn because
I know what your like you lean on that girl
thats if you come at all. But if you do come get
me some tobacco PLEASE Maureen and papers and a
pair of them glasses for short-sighted out of
SUPERDRUG only 3.99? I'll pay you back. and tell
that fat lump Barry from me to look after the
girls and let Dawn get out.

This is circumstances beyond my controle and not
of my own making. You don't know the half of it
what happened what I go through with them boys.
I'm sorry if I upset you but Billy is my own son
and Alan likewise what if your Craig would you be
able to turn your back on him. Look after the old
man Maureen. Please don't waste this V.O. from
your mum.
```

What she had let herself come to. What put me in mind of that old bag down Hoxton with them from the hostel on the bench and Little Dave and Shirley Iron's dad over the road from the Queen's Head where they planted that little scrap of grass and shrubs was like Knees Up Mother Brown and mooning her skinny arse behind a bush I seen her squat and shit and wipe herself on her hand.

How I clocked the old woman first what was my own

mother stood by a small table peering half-blind through
the smoke where she was trying to make me out in the
crowd without no glasses nor teeth and tugging at her
shrunk cardigan over her tabard if it wouldn't meet in the
middle because they must of boiled it in the washing or
stuck it in the tumble dryer.

Her knees was bare. She never smiles when she ain't got
no teeth in so she never smiled but if she had of got her
teeth in when she saw us she would of smiled. I give her
a big wave. She waved back and covered her mouth with
her hand. She had a dirty great big yellow crimson purple
yellow bruise on her bonce. Dawn started to cry. My mum
sat down on one side of the table and me and Dawn sat
down on the other side. I give Dawn's hand a squeeze
under the table. I lit up and handed it to my mum. I lit one
for Dawn and one for me.

– Fuck sake Mum, I says.
– Cellmate trod on me teeth, she says. – You got me them
glasses?
– I give them in at the desk, I says. – Who bashed you up?
– Cellmate trod on me glasses, she says. – So what? What
are you gonna to do about it?

Meaning that there weren't fuck all I could do. She
was on her own with her own troubles what was the
consequences if she lived how she lived with all them
people she was more at home in her life than she felt with
me. And she thought I was blaming her for the state she
was in. Dawn took a toilet roll out of her bag. She unrolled
a length of pink paper and blew her nose so loud every
cunt in the place turned to look.

– How's the old man? Mum asked.
– A bit better, I says. – He's eating soup and that. Dr. Patel
give him some new tablets. Alan's been up to see him with
some Special Brews.
– He's a good boy, says Mum.

– Yeah, I says.
– I worry about Billy though.
– No need, I says.
– That's easy for you to say, she says.
– He's gone down Lorraine's mum's.

My mum blinked and leant in towards me and went like let me tell you what happened about the gear and that I will have to whisper and I yawned. Because I was bored. So fucking bored like when you watch something *A Touch of Frost* or *Morse* on the telly and ten minutes in you realise it's a repeat and you know exactly what's gonna happen.
– My keeping you up? my mum asks.
– Sorry, I says.
– Sorry? she says. – You're sorry? You fucking hurt my feelings, Maureen.
Dawn looked at me. I shrugged my shoulders. My mum sucked on her fag.
– Don't you want to know what happened? How I ended up in here?
– Not really, I says.

My mum blew smoke slowly out of her mouth and stared at me. Dawn reached across the table and touched her on the forearm.
– I want to know, says Dawn. – Tell me what happened.

Where she was encouraging my mum because she wanted to make amends over my lack of interest because Dawn never felt comfortable when I showed my mum disrespect if my mum pushed me too far or maybe Dawn wanted to hear my mum's side of the story and my mum never needed much encouragement. Dawn was too fucking polite.

But I could not make myself pretend. I looked down at my feet and felt angry and bitter against my mum like it was me what was suffering her incarceration and unable to rise above it like Dawn what put me to shame how I

weren't bringing my mum nothing but more pain if that
was cruelty under the circumstances and not fair on
her. I felt a heavy weight on the back of my neck and my
shoulders like my mum put a yoke on me. What I weren't
able to shrug it off until she was finished telling her story.
So I just had to endure it.

– Well, says my mum.

– Tell me, says Dawn.

But without no teeth it weren't all that easy for the old
woman to speak. She was mumbling and turned down
the volume so Dawn had to lean in to hear her. And all
them other people in that recreation hall or visitor suite
of unlucky girls or women doing time if they deserved it
or never deserved it and screws screwing us out and the
nearest and dearest never heard nothing over and above
that babble of noise we was making to pass the time before
the end of the visit when we could go home and get on
with our lives on the outside what was freedom of a sort.
Of tears and laughter if a person could find something to
laugh at without causing offence what weren't easy where
we was all tense and angry people gathered together with
our own problems to visit our loved ones and my mum
was flicking her eyes at me sideways to make sure I weren't
tuning her out.

– Where Alan and Alan's Sandra come up to me
a few days before I got nicked about three o'clock I
remember like yesterday what they don't do as a rule, she
says. – Where she lets her mouth run away with her?

– I know, says Dawn.

– She just can't help herself, says my mum. – Wondering
where he puts it about when he do put it about if he do put
it about what I don't think he do. What ain't nice hearing
about your own son like that.

– I know what you mean, says Dawn.

– Whether it's true what she says or all in her head. But

you watch if she carries on pointing the finger she'll end
up driving him to it.

– What must be hard for them both, says Dawn.

– Because it's either him to get away from her if he gives
her the slip or her if he goes out on his own she can't stand
it so she comes up to me. What proves there's a first time
for everything.

– What do you mean?

– The pair of them popping over home both together?

– Oh yeah, says Dawn.

– What was just a social call they said. But they was both
out of breath trying to make out like nothing was wrong if
they think I was born yesterday but I ain't silly.

– No, says Dawn. – Of course not.

– Where Alan was all over me how he goes on yeah yeah
to make out like everything was you know but I could
hear nee-naw nee-naw in the flats. But I thought they just
wanted to wait until it was all blown over. I mean Doreen
works in the launderette remember her boy got in the way
last time the flats was turned over in the cross-fire he was
lucky it lodged itself in an empty space in his brain.

– What was a miracle really, says Dawn.

– You'd think they'd warn people to stay indoors although
you could say it's your own look-out if you want to wander
about and get yourself shot where they taped off all our
little bit of grass I'll say that for them.

– So what did Alan want? Dawn asked.

– Well Sandra was on about some tom the usual sale or
return she wanted rid but will she take no for an answer
or do you know anyone who wants to buy some or to
sell some for me how Sandra was speaking so fast gobs
of white spit was flying out of her mouth. Where she is
on something off of the doctor three a day Temazepam I
think she said but if you ask me they should up the dose.

– For her nerves?

– Yeah, something like that. But while Alan was in the toilet
I wasn't taking no notice of Sandra the way she goes on
waving the gold about and blocking the door of the front
room because out of the window the grounds was swarming
with armed police and a man was shouting through a
megaphone although you couldn't catch what he was on
about it was obvious didn't I? And then I twigged all the
palaver about the gold was just a blind. Sandra was trying to
keep me out of my own kitchen. So I said I was gasping for a
hot drink and she tried to go in the kitchen and make it but
I can't stand her coffee me where she puts the powder in and
the sugar and the milk then pours the water on it without
stirring so it's all lumps. And if you don't drink it all to the
last drop she's like what's wrong with my fucking coffee your
royal highness and all that so I went out and there was Alan
up on a chair pouring some stuff out of a split freezer bag
into the biscuit barrel on top of my kitchen cabinet.
– Fucking bag burst, he says.

Dawn tried to look surprised. My mum looked down at
her hands. Her ring finger was dented white where her
ring had never been took off of her before. Even when we
never of had nothing. She'd of sooner seen us starve.
– You should of grassed him, I said.
My mum rubbed her finger.
– No, Maureen, she whispered. – How could I? Not my
own son.
I closed my eyes. I didn't want to make her cry.
– Bollocks Mum, I shouted.
She started to cry.
– Stop fucking crying, I shouted.
– I'm sorry, she says. – Alan is my son.
– You love it, doncha? I shouted.
– Don't Mum, said Dawn.
– You love it. You make me sick. You make me fucking sick.

I got up and my chair scraped across the floor, toppled, crashed.

– What you fucking looking at? I shouted.

– Please Mum, Dawn hissed. – Sit down.

She picked up my chair for me. – Please sit down.

I sat down again.

– What? I shouted.

– You don't understand, said my mum. – What he says. He does my head in.

– He's full of shit, I says.

– But he reckons you all feel the same. Even you Maureen. You all blame me. He said you said I was weak.

– Weak? I says.

– He says he's only trying to make his way in the world the only way he knows how some mums would be proud the home he and Sandra all mahogany and leather and glass her kids ain't even allowed in the front room. He says what chance did he have the way he was dragged up. Where it was dog eat dog in our house and nobody never give a fuck.

– Bollocks, I says.

My mother was still crying.

– Is it all my fault? she says.

– Oh Mum, I says.

– No it ain't, says Dawn.

Mum blew her nose.

– But it makes me sick you let Alan shit on you, I says.

– I wish I never of caught him, Maureen, she whispered.

I lit up again and fiddled with the ends of my scarf.

– You know what his Sandra did? she says. – Well I'll tell you what she did. She poured all her rubbish gold on my kitchen table and pulled off her rings and chains trying to get me to take them for nothing as a gift she said to buy me but I turned round and told her you can keep it I mean identity bracelets with the wrong name on and baby rings

and all that if you bumped into the person what owned
it in the first place talk about egg on. I don't know why
Alan takes it in kind maybe a soft heart. Maybe if a regular
customer even that shop down Bethnal Green for smelting
most of it only nine carat you'd not make much more than
your bus-fare over there not worth the aggravation ta very
much all the same.

– A soft heart? I says.

– So Sandra swept it all back in her holdall all huff and
puff you know the way she snorts down her nose if she
thinks you ain't giving her her due. Then she pushes
past me out of the kitchen into the passage. Alan is still
standing on the chair wiping his prints off of the biscuit
barrel with a tea-towel. Well Sandra's oldest you know that
poor Kelly what is a grass everybody reckons when Sandra
was with that other bloke he got done for whatsitsname
feedopilia against her kids anyway that poor Kelly well
Sandra just let her walk in on Alan in the kitchen. Not
that my front door ain't always on the snip where I can't
be arsed to get up and answer it every time someone pops
up to me but I mean her own daughter the woman's not all
there half the time she just didn't oughta of let that Kelly
anywhere near our Alan on that occasion.

– You ain't wrong there, I says.

– Jesus, says Dawn.

– And he was on at me the way he goes on wheedling and
whining to get his own way and in walks poor Kelly right in
the middle and clocks what Alan is doing of. So she says she
wants a tenner off of him to get a new top down Hoxton.
Alan bungs her two ten pound bags out of his sock. One for
now and one for ron, he says. Don't do it all at once. Don't
say nothing to nobody. Now fuck off. So Alan carries on
cleaning his prints off of my biscuit barrel and turns round
to me and he's on and on at me to give him a break just this
once until things blow over mum it'll only be a few days oh

don't be like that mum please don't go on. And I am telling
you Maureen I wanted to slap him like when he was a kid I
had to slap him sometimes to shut him up. Not that when
I slapped him he did shut up. He just never stopped. I'm
only talking about my hand up the back of his legs Maureen
I mean you had to do something. You remember what he
was like. He was a right little fucker.

– I know it was a struggle in them days, I says.

– But Alan reckons I done him damage. He says he can
still remember how frightened he was. When I put him in
the cupboard for his own good what I ain't proud of what
I done. To keep him safe Maureen when he just would not
shut up I got so wound up you know when you just can't
trust yourself?

– I remember, I says.

– Well Alan reckons he still gets nightmares what I did to
him when he was only a baby. So after I caught him with
the drugs in my kitchen it was just like when you was kids
he come out of the cupboard wiping his snotty face on
his sleeve all angry blaming smiles looking at me where
he knew I knew I done wrong. He turned round after I
caught him with the drugs in my kitchen and smiled at me
and said he was sorry if any of my behaviour causes you
inconvenience he said but it was dog eat dog in our house
ever since we was only tiny little bits of kids how we was
dragged up. What can you expect? He said I'm sorry you
find it hard to accept me as I am. Did you think I'd go to
college? I'm sorry you can't offer me unconditional love
without judgement you know how he carries on since he
was under that doctor or whatever was it in the Scrubs last
time for his anger management thing he said I'm sorry you
can't find it in your heart to be proud of me.

– What weren't fair, says Dawn.

– Well I wanted to say I am proud of you son just to stop
the bad mood coming off of him. But the way he was

waiting for me to say it I hate it when they do that like he was trying to milk me. So I just stared at him. Then he turned round and said if you touch it Mum even one gram even for Billy however bad he gets or Susan or sell it or say anything to anybody even Maureen how you talk to Maureen I will fucking kill you. I saw his gun poking out of his trousers about an inch in front of me nose and he put his hand down to touch it. He said did you hear me Mum? I'll kill you. I will.

– And what did you say? I says.

– I never said nothing, says Mum. – I just sighed and filled the kettle. Where I had all them boxes of cake in the passage I thought we could have a nice cup of tea and a box of cake. And then you come up to me, remember?

– Yeah, I says. – To see if you was all right. When I see poor Kelly fly out of your door and down the landing like she was on fire. What nobody can't say her life weren't worth nothing. Where she was human just like the rest of us and weren't to blame for nothing what happened to her if Sandra never looked after her properly when she was a kid and should of protected her from our Alan.

My mum rubbed her eyes and stared at me.

– You can judge me, Maureen, she says. – But there ain't no point in getting all aeriated on Alan's account. You know what he's like.

Where I was down in the flats with my Tony's dog when Kelly flew out of my mum's front door. I never seen her move so fast. So I went up to see what was going on. The dog yapped in the front room. I told him to lay down. He lay down under the nest of occasional tables and chewed on Vic's slippers what I let him chew to his heart's content. Alan was sat with Sandra and the old man was asleep in his chair. Mum come through with mugs on a tray.

– What does she want? says Alan, cocking his head at me.

– Charming, I says.

I sat down and flashed my fags.

– Ta, says Sandra.

– Ta, Mum says.

– Don't tempt me, says Alan. – I give up, remember?

– Sorry, I says, lighting up and blowing smoke at him. – I forgot.

I knew they was all hiding something. Mum smiled and looked over at the old man. Alan picked his mug up off of the floor and took a slurp. He balanced the mug on his knee.

– Mum, he says.

– What mate, says Mum.

– Do you want a new coat?

She looked at Alan. I looked at Alan.

– What do you mean? she says.

– Well Sandra reckons I oughta get you something sort of thank you like for all what I put you through.

Mum looked at me and grinned.

– Why, what's been going on? I asked.

– Nothing, says Alan.

– A new coat? says Mum, sniffing.

– Yeah, says Alan. – A new coat.

– Yeah, says Mum. – Ta ever-so.

Alan picked up the paper. Mum was on about whether something a bit different in olive suede she's seen down the Roman with a belt or leather's always nice in black or dark brown classic like the one our Maggie's wearing only not with that hood on it I mean who does she think she is.

– I'll send a couple of the boys round, says Alan. – With a selection for you to choose from.

– If it ain't too much trouble, says Mum.

– If it ain't too much trouble, I says.

– Shut up, says Alan.

– Trouble? says Sandra. – Them boys owe him, Nora.

Everybody owes him. If he wants something done he just whistles. You know that.

– He's a good boy, says Mum, turning to Sandra. – Thinking of his old mum.

I was rolling my eyes and Sandra looked at her watch.

– Although he has been moody since he packed up the fags, she says.

– Well, says Mum. – That's understandable, ain't it.

– Yeah, says Sandra. – But it ain't bin easy for me, Nora. Where I'm on these tablets off of the doctor? I ain't supposed to suffer no stress.

– Shut up, Sandra, says Alan.

– And since he knocked it on the head he do like a bit of something sweet with his coffee, says Sandra.

– He's a good boy, says Mum. – The extra bit of weight suits him.

– You think so? says Sandra.

– He looks well, says Mum. – Wish I could pack it up.

– Tell me about it, says Sandra. – But they do say it's gotta be the right time.

– They do say that, says Mum.

– He has put on a bit, says Sandra. – Eating cake and that.

– He looks well on it, says Mum. – Funny, he never used to like any of that.

– Where he packed up the fags Nora? says Sandra. – Eh Alan, she says.

– What, says Alan.

– A nice slice of cake goes nice with a coffee ain't it? What ain't cheap, eh Nora?

– Nah, says Mum. – But he do want to watch his self.

– You can't say he don't look well on it, says Sandra.

– No one ain't saying nothing like that, says Mum.

– That walnut cake out of Marks's is dear, says Sandra. – I don't know how they can…

– I just seen your Kelly in the flats, I says.

– My Kelly? Says Sandra. – Never!

– I just seen her, I says. – Out of here like her arse was on fire.

– Nah, says Sandra. – Can't of been. Eh Alan? She went down my sister's last week and she ain't come back.

– Funny, I says. – I could of sworn…

– Well he's big boned, says Mum. – Takes after my Tommy's side.

– Battenburg or whatever, says Sandra. – Madeira. He ain't fussy. Eh love?

– What?

– You ain't a fussy person, Alan.

– Shut up, Sandra.

– I was just saying.

The old man shouted in his sleep and woke his self up. My mum got up and went to him. He turned his head away and closed his eyes.

– Where he do like a bit of cake with his coffee since he packed up the fags, says Sandra.

– He must of had a bad dream, says Mum, straightening the blanket in the old man's lap.

Alan looked up from the paper.

– Fuck sake, Mum, he shouted. – You gonna fetch me a bit of that fucking cake you got out there in the passage or what?

– Tell you what though, says Alan, through a mouthful of cake. – We're gonna get ourselves a new three piece. You might as well take the old one, Mum.

I looked at Alan.

– The Italian leather? my mum gasped. – Oh thank you son.

– No problem, says Alan.

– Aah, that's nice, says Sandra, her head on one side.

– Pleasure, says Alan, looking all round the room and smiling. – I'll send a couple of the boys round with it.

– Thank you, says Mum.

– Aah, says Sandra. – That's nice.

– And if she don't want it I'll have it, I says.

Alan laughed. I handed round my fags again. The old man grunted. Sandra took a sip of her coffee. Mum was beaming. Alan looked at my mum's yellow ceiling, the bald greasy carpet.

– State of this place, he says.

– I know, says Mum.

– It's a shame, says Alan. – It's a shame on you living like this.

– You what, says Mum.

– I ain't comfortable coming up here no more the way you live.

– You what? I says.

– Like I'll have to think twice next time before coming up, he says. – I mean how did you let it get so bad?

I thought my mum was going to cry. She coughed and looked at the stained wallpaper and dirty carpet like she was clocking the state of her home for the first time.

– I tell you what though, says Alan. – How about as a favour I get your place done out for you?

– Oh Alan, says Mum. – Do you mean it?

– I wouldn't say it if I didn't mean it, would I? says Alan. – You deserve it, Mum. I've got a load of paint and that in my lock-up. I'll send a couple of the boys round. As a special treat. That will keep her sweet, he says, winking at me.

What was a big gesture on Alan's part and made my mum happy. But was all talk I suspected at the time and turned out to be all talk. Not that being right about all that never give me that smug feeling I TOLD YOU SO and no pleasure at all when he let my mum down. What she never needed any of that on top of everything else what was insult to injury and you know that.

But all that crap bandied about over home instead of talking sense what was never gonna happen with them people. I still weren't none the wiser why Alan was up there with Sandra offering my mum the world like that was compensation even if he did come through on all of them promises what weren't the same thing as love and respect. But I weren't able to take no more of all the crap what they was bandying about. So I went back down in the flats with the dog. The armed response units was clearing out. The dog goes on the patch of grass and my mum's front door opens. Alan is still eating cake when he comes out. Then Sandra comes out. Sandra is stood on tiptoe trying to brush the cake crumbs off of Alan. Alan pushes her off of him. My mum comes out and is telling Alan I do love you son I do love you and I heard every word what happens when all of us used to live on top of each other in those flats you couldn't fart without.

Alan and Sandra go down the outside staircase. My mum hangs over the landing and waves at them as they come out by the wheelie bins but she don't notice me. She takes off her glasses and polishes the lenses on the cuff of her cardigan then goes back indoors. I see Sandra hugging Alan so tight she is getting on his tits where she can't read him at all what is not safe for her.

Sandra's Kelly is behind the wheelie bin injecting herself and Sandra is squeezing Alan Alan Alan give us a kiss Al give us a kiss until he slaps her off of him. Sandra puts her hand up to her face and sees her Kelly float out from behind the bins.

– Tell him, Kelly, Sandra whines.

– Tell him what? says Kelly, blinking. – Tell him not to touch you?

Sandra grabs Alan again. Alan shoves her off of him and gives her a dig.

– Tell him, Kelly.
– You want me to tell him not to touch you? You're having a laugh ain't ya?
– Just tell him, Kell. He's hurting me.
– Old bill, I shout.

An unmarked car skids across the broken tarmac and stops at the bollards. Alan and Sandra let go of each other. McMann flies across the grass, jumps Sandra's Kelly, drags her between the bollards and bundles her into the back of the car. Whitman puts his foot down and the car shoots backwards out of the flats.

– You talk I'll do you, Alan shouts after her. – I'll do you.
– She won't bite the hand what, says Sandra.
– Maybe I oughta move the stuff, says Alan, looking up at Mum's landing.
– Nah, says Sandra. – Don't worry about my Kelly. She won't say nothing. She ain't stupid. Come on Alan. Come on. Give us a kiss.
– Fuck off, says Alan, and runs after the police car.
– Al? Alan? Wait for me, Sandra screams. – I love you. I'm proud of you.

She screams and tries to run after him but she snaps the heel off of her shoe. Some of her kids is kicking a ball about in the road. The police car is forced to stop. The kids clock Kelly grinning out of the window of the car and wave. Sandra limps back towards the wheelie bins. Alan catches up with the car. Kelly lifts her hand and zips her toothless mouth.

– I'll do you, he shouts, as the car pulls away.

Dear Maureen,

Tell me how is the old man. Ta for the letter last week, I hope Dawn is feeling better. Please don't tell me that arsehole ain't gone and

knocked her up again. I don't think that would be
fair on her after all what she went through the
last time with the infection what she suffered
leaching through into the front part and the lump
of scar tissue was it or what we go through after
she split the first time where they sewed her up
too tight because they ain't got no idea Maureen
even if she do end up in a three bedroom.

But the young girl they put with me reckons
Holloway is a holiday camp compared to the life
she leads on the outside with five kids on her
own over Canning Town and on the stuff what is
rife in here and two of her kids is like it an
all what is why most of us got nicked in the
first place and ended up in this shit-hole. But I
do not find no comfort for myself where they say
there is always some poor cunt worse off. What
she told me her old man just pops up to her if
he wants anything off of her or her daughter what
is only fourteen if he is her real dad or what.
Or if one of his mates wants to and if she won't
her old man gives her a clump and makes her do
it for a rock. And watches them at it with his
mates what he makes her on all fours like a dog
in the front room where all them poor girls will
do anything if the little kids is playing out or
he locks them in the bedroom she says her life on
the outside is harder by far than in this shit-
hole we both ended up. Because there ain't no men
in here what she sees as a good thing to get away
from all that even if some of the women is just
as bad if they think you are weak. And they took
her kids off of her in care half way she done her
time what she left with her mum. But her mum said
she weren't coping with them they all got so big.
And she ain't sure whether or not she will get
her kids back. Unless when they sling her out of
here she can stay off of the crack and that where
all her neighbours is like it she says it ain't
easy and she is dreading the day she goes home.

But they ain't got enough staff to organise
nothing or your education joke if you want to
better yourself. They do us two dinners a day
without lifting a finger and cleaners from
outside to swab out the cells and the toilets
what the screws keep on telling us is the life
of riley whether you like it or you ain't got
nothing to do all day but think and worry and go
back over and over all what went on. Or play ping
pong sometimes if you are lucky. I mean for the
first time in my life I ain't got no work.

What they get up to in here cutting their selves
with broken glass. Or anything else they can find
of metal or plastic they pick up in the yard to
sharpen and use against their own selves what is
worse than lashing out to cut others what you
can't blame people now we all find ourselves in
difficult circumstances sometimes. Like it ain't
bad enough in here without bleeding and crying on
top of everything we suffer of missing our family
and how it makes you feel when the door slams and
they turn off the lights. Where even the young
girl they put in with me ended up in hospital
wing.

But they never knew she was on. I knew she was
on but nobody never asked me was she or weren't
she. I couldn't of touched her, Maureen, how some
people you just couldn't bring yourself even
before she slashed herself. So I called them
and they took her and I heard they put her under
for four days for her own good. So I never said
nothing, it was her time of the month, if I had
of spoken up, because I never thought and the
tampon up her went bad, Maureen. Over the shock
of it was toxic where she weren't all that strong
to begin with, somebody said they saw her went
in the ambulance when we was in the yard with
a blanket over her head. They tried to keep it
quiet. I never hardly knew her but I cried when

word got out, like she was one of my own. If you
share a cell there ain't much you don't know
about a person, if only I had of said something
but I never thought. Before she harmed herself
she said I was a good listener what was worse in
hindsight after all what happened.

What was a nice letter you wrote to me. I'm back
now after the bell rang for assoc not that you'd
want to assoc with many of them what end up in
here. Although some of them from round our way
like that mate of Lorraine's if you remember what
was a bridesmaid at the wedding got five years
for doing what she done? And little Brandy what
used to be in your Dawn's class at Burbage. Not
that I recognised her at first but she recognised
me and greeted me like a long lost friend. And
the only one she's got in this place where she's
all over the screws like flies round shit. How
she is teacher's pet trying to get attention or
some-one to love. Where the lights just went out
whether you like it or not and I don't like it.
It's too dark to write no more. The noises start
up all them women banging

Now I'm nice and clean what feels better washed
hair and cleaned my nails because it is filthy in
this place. You get a shower once a week whether
you need it or not. Ha ha

But Brandy is out of here next week. And promised
me she'd bring this letter to you. I don't
know where how she is going to hide my letter
down her knickers because you ain't supposed to
take nothing out of here but she said she's got
friends in high places if you give her a couple
of packets of fags for her trouble what I'll pay
you back when I get out. Where I am missing you
Maureen and you know it.

To mask her disappointment my mum said it couldn't be helped the furniture man bunged Alan a ton for his nearly new Italian leather suite when they delivered his new three piece. And she never blamed him because he did get her a nice new leather coat after her first court appearance when she was remanded on bail for reports. But by the time her second court date come up after she never said nothing to nobody what Alan told her to keep it shut or else the sleeve was hanging off of it and we all knew it was Alan what should of been going down. Where some kid tried to grab it off of her back in broad daylight by the bus-stop outside the Geffrye Museum so my mum had to lend the brown one off of our Linda.

Still, at least she's got something to look forward to. Where she is making the time pass on her bunk in her cell dreaming of Alan up a step-ladder peeling the polystyrene tiles off of her yellow ceiling. While our Alan is parked on his fat arse in the Macbeth with his pint and two packets of Bovril crisps.

– Eh Alan?

Without a speck of paint on his jeans Sandra ironed for him with a crease down the front of each leg so clean he smells of fabric conditioner since he give up smoking.

– Eh Alan?

And ain't bestirred himself even once to see his old mum in Holloway where she is doing time for him.

– Eh Alan?

What looks up at me over his pint.

– What, he says.

– You bin over home lately, Al?

– Fuck off.

– You ain't done nothing over there. Not even started on it.

– What's it to you?

– You promised the old woman.

– You having a pop at me?
– Someone's got to have a pop at you, Al.
– You poking your nose in?
– I'm poking. Watch me fucking poke.
– Get off my back will ya?
– I ain't on your back. When I do get on your back you'll know about it. Don't worry about that.
– Do what?
– The old woman thinks she's coming out to a nice new home.
– She'll have to think again.
– Times hard, Alan?
– Leave me out.
– I thought you was doing a roaring trade.
– I got a big dent in my capital that new shuttering over all my windows and over my front door in case like next time they want to turn me over or some black cunt tries to move in on me you know what I mean?
– That shuttering must of set you back at least a day's takings, Alan, I says.
– Business is business, Maureen, he says. – And don't forget getting the stuff back off of McMann and Whitman to put myself back where I was on turnover I had to dig deep. Although they done me a good price. Not that they didn't have much choice ain't it? What with things the way they was I got them over a barrel selling me back the gear they had off of me in the first place when they turned over the old woman. Ha ha. Over a barrel? Biscuit barrel? Get it?
– Who's laughing? I says. – I ain't laughing, Alan.
– You never do, Maureen.
– You give me something to laugh about.
– Do what?
– You know what you gotta do, Al.
– Remind me, Maureen. I've got a lot on me mind at the minute.

– You said you'd sort out the old woman's home for her.

– Or what?

– Or I'll get on your back and I won't get off of it.

– You and whose army?

– Just me, Alan.

– I ain't scared of you, Maureen. You sort her place out for her if you're so bothered. I can't be fucked.

– That's where you're wrong, mate, I says.

– Do what?

– Watch me, Alan, I says. – Just watch me.

– I'm shaking in me boots.

– You will be.

– What you on about?

– You seen your Kelly lately, Alan?

– She ain't my Kelly.

– I ain't seen her about.

– What's it to you? says Alan. – Who gives a fuck? I ain't stupid Maureen. I got pulled in over that weeks ago. They ain't got fuck all on me.

– Your Sandra must be missing her, I says.

– Dream on, Maureen, he says. – Sandra ain't never had no time for her. She ain't like you, Maureen. Where she always puts me first over and above her kids.

– Poor Kelly, I says.

– I wouldn't waste no tears over her, says Alan. – She weren't no good.

I blew my nose.

– Does Sandra know what you did? I asked.

– Yes and no, says Alan.

– What's that supposed to mean?

– She ain't as stupid as she looks. She never made me confess. She don't want to talk about it. For my sake as well as her own.

– You ain't a very nice person, I says.

– No, says Alan. – They do say that about me. But

you know what? I got other good qualities.

Because I was laughing my head off over the presentation
box with ribbon and tinsel in the palm of his hand for the
joy of it and the stupidness in front of our Maureen my
cackling or sniggering and coughing what I remember
last year or the one before that he brought in the cold with
him in his khaki jacket and took off his boots and slid it
out of his zip pocket all pink and red and silver what made
Maureen look out of the window if it was a necklace or
bracelet not that he disappointed me when I slit the tape
with my nail and took off the lid because nobody can't say
I ain't a greedy person.

– Thank you, Victor.
– My pleasure, Nora.

Because he wanted Maureen to see what he had bought
me. When the old man must of been over the pub for a
Christmas drink and it was snowing then, all whiteness
in the sky what made a nice change out of the window
where my nets was in soak in a bucket after Maureen come
up to help me get all my home ready for the morning as
long as you didn't have to go out in it because I never had
no boots at all when she was kind to help me like that
where the soles was all come unstuck and I never had no
glue. When you could smell it in the sky. Of top quality
leather gloves with a soft lining like silk to the touch and
fitted me lovely how he knew my size or is just clever
not like my Tommy over anything like that what weren't
knock-off if he got it gift-wrapped in the shop or done it
his self what was unlikely even for him. But he always gets
me something nice. Even Maureen asked me if she could

try them on once he was up the stairs and out of the way because she never of wanted to give him the pleasure. So I switched on the fairy lights and Maureen said I done my tree nice what was high praise coming from her.

To get a feel of the inside after I went on about the lovely softness of the lining and all that but her hands was too big. Where I only got him a card. I was glad he never of bought me a necklace. She told me to put the gloves back in the box and stick them under the tree for something to open in the morning.

But then he come down again. With a jumbo pack of sliced ham he had off of the Territorial Army he just done them a Christmas disco over the community hall and so what if they only give him a pound of cured shoulder for his trouble! So I agreed to swap it for the Festival Assortment out of the biscuit barrel on top of my kitchen cabinet our Maureen said was a fair exchange and no robbery even if she never of had no time for him and weren't best pleased to see him again before she was on her way to get her own home ready at the last minute what couldn't be helped. Where I could see he was hurt over the ham. And she thought he would of stayed upstairs until after she was gone. What Festival Assortment was a gift off of Lorraine's mum where I never said nothing but everyone knows I don't much like biscuits. So Victor had them off of me. And let me have the ham. What was his idea and weren't none of mine if you could of put a value on what we had off of each other not including the gloves, where I lost the gloves over the bingo. But that weren't the point. And he got two or three slices back in the sandwiches I done him before he went out again at that time of night but I ain't got a clue where he was going not that Maureen said nothing snide over it or nothing like that.

And I kept the ornamental tin and put it back on top of

my kitchen cabinet. Where he just had the contents off of me in a plastic bag for the boys in his troop he said when he took them on camp in the New Year and they slept in a hut because of the cold and cooked on a fire in the woods made out of branches they gathered under the trees and piled up in a pyramid like he taught them to keep warm.

I give Lorraine's mum a bottle of bubble-bath. But it was biscuits for the Scouts my arse where Victor gobbled up all them custard creams and Viennese with the jam and white stuff holding together a swirl of crumbs in his room what our Susan moved out and thought I never knew what he was doing of over the holidays. He tucked himself up with a hot drink and one of them books of a night-time of jungle survival and the outdoor life all what he was into since he was a kid. I know because of the jam smear of the same duvet cover our Susan had out of Argos when she was twelve with the pink hearts on it and crumbs the comfort of it for him on the bottom sheet I understood because he gets lonely so I never said nothing and he is my friend.

What sometimes feels like the only one. When he used to rub my feet for me when my feet hurt what was a gift in itself. He made me take off my socks and holding my poor feet in his lap and stroked firmly not to tickle me and dug in with his fingers and thumbs until I had to tell him to stop.

Not that I wanted Maureen to start after our Alan stashed the drugs in the biscuit barrel and ate two boxes of cake to calm down where he had packed in the fags and upset his self. But I knew it costed her to hold back. And she never even knew what he done to me. Where a part of me wanted it all to kick off like somebody needs to tell Alan since my Tommy ain't well and he give up on all that. But I never said nothing and Maureen went down in the grounds with that little dog what her Tony loves more than his own mother.

Where Alan couldn't help his self once he got stuck into the cake. And Sandra never shut up what was doing my head in. Because I just wanted to get on with my work. If I never felt no sympathy where he was off of the fags what I have not tried to pack it up myself what he was going through but I could see it weren't easy for him.

So I followed them out on the landing to say goodbye to my son what was not before time. I thought they would never go. Then filled my washing bucket with water and powder and bleach and heaved it on the stove no sooner to boil my whites than Maureen popped up to me again.
– Oh it's you again Maureen what do you want.

Where I was on my knees in the toilet with a scrubbing brush because they splash what drips down and over the floor even Vic who is not like that and I was trying to forget about the drugs in my biscuit barrel. What never had no biscuits in it not since that Festival Assortment from Lorraine's mum.

So I was thinking about new wallpaper and nets, I mean I was thinking about scatter cushions after our Alan promised me a new home on my knees in the toilet on a folded towel what I thought about when I was not crucifying myself over Billy and Tommy and wondering if I was going to go down. Scatter cushions and a new carpet. And a pair of lamps with fringed shades in dark red and a round mirror and display cabinet of shiny wood with gilded ornaments behind glass to take my mind off all what I had on my mind of my troubles.
– Hello.
Maureen was smiling at me.
– What do you want?

Not that I weren't glad she come up to me. But the toilet and the kitchen floor wanted a quick once-over with the mop and ironing a few bits my work if you keep at it I

don't let it get on top of you. Where I was over Shoreditch
School every morning at five even if I never put all that
much into it when I was over there because I never had
the heart. So Maureen and Georgina and the rest of the
girls got to pull extra weight where we was all on the
same team off of the cards what they denied because they
thought my age was catching up with me to scrape gum
off of the bottom of the desks and that but it weren't that.
I just couldn't be arsed to slay myself. With the scrubbing
machine slopping about in the dirty water I mean what
good did that place ever do for me? Seeing as most of my
kids drifted out of there at fourteen or fifteen worse than
when they went in. What the teachers never even noticed
or they was glad to see the back of them. And they never
even learnt Alan and Billy to read or spell or nothing like
that. They never learnt them nothing.

So I was trying not to dwell on what our Alan dog eat
dog and that he said when Maureen popped up again for
a minute. With a top for me she got me up Ridley. With
Tony's silly little dog what yaps and yaps. I don't know how
she stands it. If it was me I would ring its neck.

That top was a nice thought, Maureen. I seen them tops
two for a tenner off of that stall sells nice bits like what
you get out of Marks's the odd thread pulled or a hem
down needs a stitch but quality one fitted her perfect she
said but the one she give me she said was too tight under
the armpits on her well she is a big girl. So she thought of
me. The colour was good on me she reckoned I suited it
perfect. I'm not silly I knew why she come up. But I never
told her nothing and put the kettle on.
– I do worry, she said.
And give me one of them looks. A silent lecture will you
never learn to stand up to them you stupid old woman.
But at least the lecture was silent not shouting at me what
happens when Maureen loses it sometimes like WILL

YOU NEVER LEARN YOU STUPID OLD WOMAN.
What I do hate it when she is like that.

I cope with it all what is our Alan selling it but he don't
never touch it and Billy well the least said about him the
better and Susan and all the rest of them what are like it
or if they ain't like our Frank on the buses out at Beckton
takes a drink like the old man or over the betting shop
like Maureen's Tony what nobody reckons she's a right
one to talk. Looking down her long nose. Or shouting
at me like they got answers what they ain't because there
ain't none. Not that I know of. And the old man don't
know nothing and if he did I don't know how he ain't got
room in his head the things he don't know what goes on
in this family. I don't know how I keep going. It's a case of
having to.

Don't get me wrong I was glad she come up to me. She
only ever stays five minutes anyway ain't it? She can't wait
to get away. In case Billy pops up for a sandwich or his fags
if I treat him off of the fag man ain't any of her business
because it upsets her to see him like it. And she ain't even
civil to Victor what ain't fair the harm he never done her
even where he is my friend she can't bring herself. But I
wanted her to go because she made me feel so what do you
call it?

Although the top she got me was right nice. Something
hot choked up in my throat. Like she can see straight
through me and thinks I ain't done right by her but she
don't want to say nothing. I know that but still. She do
get so angry exploding sometimes when she's trying to be
nice. What is her other way of carrying on. When she can't
do enough for me.

But she was in and out so quick I never of got a chance.
But at least she still come up to me not like some of the
others I might as well be dead. And don't think I weren't
grateful. Not just for the blouse what she give me but how

she come back to me. She knew Alan upset me. She sat
with me and never asked me why I do what I do like I got
a choice or making me look at things all sideways upside
down makes me so dizzy I can't think of the answer where
she wants to know from my point of view how I pretend
everything goes on the way it goes on.

Well let me tell you. Where I turn a blind eye. Like I
told our Maggie nothing makes no difference no more. No
amount of pamphlets telling me how to think and feel.

Because it's all right for Maureen seeing as her kids is
good kids. But she never said nothing. She just sat with me
for five minutes before she had to go somewhere and see
someone about something she said and neither of us said
nothing much. But I felt how kind she was just not saying
nothing sometimes. Not digging. I was so grateful. When
I needed her she was holding my hand and I wanted to
say THANK YOU for that. Where it was lucky she never
asked me all what had gone on in case I told her about
Alan. Then she would of gone after him. And opened her
big mouth.

She reckoned I looked right nice in my new top. What
got hung up in my bedroom where I tried it on and took
it off again after she went home to save it for Friday if
we was out on the piss for Georgina's birthday what
was coming up and a kebab over Bethnal Green how it
turned out in the Venus wasn't it what does a nice bit of
halib. And I was smiling she was so good to me when she
wanted to be.

Then I done out my front room and passage and
swabbed the kitchen floor how I do enjoy the true stories
in my book when my work is done on the chair in the
front room when the old man is asleep and Victor off to
a squadron meeting he said where I snatch a few minutes
with my feet up? Oh no. Because our Billy come up to
me before the floor was dry in a right state because

Lorraine sold his medicine.
– I ain't well, Mum, Billy said. – Lorraine sold my
methadone.

What a cow. I mean she got him into it in the first place
didn't she. Seeing as she was going with a mate of Alan's
who sold it when she was still at school. And her little
brother was like it even before she met Billy what my son
would never of dreamed of nothing like that before she
come along. And it is hard to believe when she was sixteen
she worked up the West End in Dorothy Perkins now she
looks older than me.

But on her day off from the shop Lorraine was outside
the Queen's with her mum talking to that Doreen and
some other woman and her mum had a couple of bags of
bits off of the market leaning up her leg for Lorraine's nan.
What got left behind when they moved out over Barking
way where Lorraine and her mum used to come up once a
week to tidy up and see to all what the old woman needed
out of the chemist and that. Not that they never offered
her to move out with them. But she wanted to stay down
our end where she was born and bred.

Well Billy was carrying my spuds for me off of Des. He
used to do all that for me. And Lorraine was flicking her
hair and laughing and Des and Big Sid and all them down
Hoxton was looking at her how she was licking the red
juice and sprinkles off of the pointy top of her ice-cream.
Them blonde streaks what her auntie worked in a salon
by Murray Grove and fancy sun-glasses on top of her
head like jewels twinkled and flashed in the sunshine I
asked myself if she knew what she was about or was it just
natural, how she was in herself if she was too pleased with
herself or I thought she was too pretty for her own good.
But if she loved herself like I thought she loved herself
she would never of let herself go down the pan what was

the life she led herself if she done all them bad things.
What you don't need to read one of Maggie's pamphlets to
understand that.

Where I ain't being funny or nothing but I never
understood why she chose him. Billy used to reckon
himself but I thought he looked stupid. Those skinny
cap-sleeved t-shirts he used to wear in them days. But they
was all wearing them what he said when I asked him did
he have to go out like that looking like I don't know what
like Leo Sayer? His soppy eyes like his dad. His ringlets
was golden. I preferred it how they used to wear what they
wore before the baggy trousers and that caught on. Before
the pegs. When they used to look hard.

But who Lorraine was with before. I mean his own
place and that out over Braintree was it and a good car she
could of had her pick. I remember them sundresses she
used to wear before they all started wearing them. When
she come up from Barking with her mum on her day off
to see to her nan. Or white pedal-pushers and a halterneck
with a bolero and hairslides how she used to tart herself
up?

I thought our Billy was having a laugh. He never had
a lot to offer. Where Lorraine was a right sort. And I
wonder what did happen to that other one she was going
with before Billy? Teddy Lucas. The one what got away.
Maybe if Lorraine had stayed with him Billy would never
of got dragged down where she dragged him down.
What nobody can deny. Where her brother what died of
it and her sister's on it and even her mum dabbles where
Lorraine used to pay her in gear to drive her round where
she buys it and sells it and that. Until her mum got to
know all them people. Then Lorraine was sending her
own mum on errands in her car. And her mum got in
with all them people. On the tablets she was under the
hospital after Lorraine's brother died and no one thinks of

themselves like that when they start. A couple of rocks on the house to make you feel better of the misery of losing a son and a ten pound bag of the other stuff to ease you out of it when the time comes. What you keep on telling yourself is your little treat if you don't use needles what it is all about Lorraine's mum reckons. Where it don't cost her much more than a night down the pub.

So I waited for Billy while he was cashing his giro. He come out of the post-office and slipped some notes and change in his pocket and bounced right up to Lorraine in that skinny yellow T-shirt what looked a bit girlish on him in my opinion not that I said nothing to him with his mop of curls and those high-waisted trousers they used to wear with all the buttons up the waistband. And off they went together down the market, arm in arm.

Lorraine's mum was gawping after them. She called out but Lorraine made out like she never of heard nothing. My Billy had left me with bags of spuds and onions and that off of Des what I thought he was taking me home. Lorraine was wearing a gold chain round her ankle with charms on it and wedge sling-backs made out of pink canvas. Billy bobbed on his heels the way they used to walk like Jack the Lad what makes me feel like crying how he shuffles now like all them people shuffle or rush about in panic you can tell them a mile off. And went out and got his self a job on the buildings or was it packing I can't remember now. And Lorraine moved back up to her nan's to be near him.

Then we was all over St. Anne's three months after they met because Lorraine thought round our way as home she said the place she was born. In a long white dress her auntie got her a staff discount where she done a perm for some woman worked in Berketex and Lorraine sold it the following week to a mate from work and made a small profit where she said it took up too much space in her cupboard and she would not be needing it again with any luck what I thought she was too cute for our Billy and was running rings round him already. And the reception out at Barking her Mum had to hire a charabanc was a proper knees-up.

When we come in the hall across the coach park and it was all spread out on long tables against the wall in oval dishes rimmed with gold. Where Lorraine's Dad fucked off after they lost their son and shacked up with that fat girl in the hotel catering from the coronation chicken to the whole ham what Lorraine's Dad was flourishing over a big sharp knife was all beautiful. The fat girl was chatting with Lorraine's mum if she was trying to take the sting out where she stole her old man from under her nose while Lorraine's mum was still in mourning what she would never get over. Like it weren't bad enough where Lorraine's mum blamed herself for his death. And was smiling all over her face and laughing to keep her chin up some fat cunt taking over her own daughter's wedding what she never wanted to ruin by punching the girl if she felt like it. Where she had just cause. And I don't think nobody would of put the blame on her if she had of done it.

But the show-up of our lot never surprised nobody. What was all pushing and shoving over the buffet and coming away with plates piled high of eels where the jelly was starting to melt and ham and sausage rolls and dollops of pickle and bleeding beetroot and salmon mousse and potato salad and the chicken what chunks of breast swimming in curry mayonnaise. To get their money's worth all that way on the coach. Missing the pub and the football of a Saturday afternoon when the Arse was at home v Tottenham. No wonder the vicar never had no other bookings. Like we never got nothing decent to eat down our way. I didn't know where to put my face.

And crusty white bread and butter and a cheese board with little bunches of red and white grape on each corner and fruit salad for afters in fancy dishes topped off with pink cherries makes my mouth water. What was before the old man's dancing days was over. Where it was thirsty work all Lorraine's aunties and cousins from Bethnal Green in their glad rags how I felt sizing us up what they're like from over that way if you come from where we come from you ain't worth shit. But our Frank brung me a large port and lemon and another port and lemon and a couple of bottled lagers and I felt a bit better.

Until out of the corner of my eye Tommy's hands crawling up and down Lorraine's back. There ain't no point making out like the old man was anything different from what he is. I turned a blind eye but that don't mean. Not that I wouldn't magic him back to health if I could magic. But at least I don't have to suffer all that no more. Where I used to smile to cover it up people never understood how I got shamed just as much as the next person. Like we got that grant off of the council to enjoy ourselves for beer and food and a tea-urn outside in the flats over the Silver Jubilee the old man up and down the long table in a Union Jack apron and a bowler hat after that young girl what was Aggie's niece over from Ireland in hot-pants never had no business doing what he done. And don't think for one minute he never knew what he was doing of. People must of thought I got used to it.

Not that Lorraine couldn't handle herself. And her mum what was next after Lorraine on the floor with my Tommy was fair game in that dress with all her wares on display what weren't mutton I don't know what is. Where that woman do like to set her stall out since her old man shacked up with that fat girl. Not to my knowledge if it never went no further than that. Where my Tommy never meant nothing by it what men are like once you let them get the whip hand. It was like the song says. *Save The Last Dance For Me.*

And I had my eye on Maureen and Tony. How the pair of them jumped up when it was their song. Craig and little Dawn wanted to follow but our Linda gathered them up in her arms and held them back. Even she wanted our Maureen to enjoy herself.

Tony was holding her and grinding on the floor under the mirror-ball that record what was on the jukebox the night of their own wedding playing over and over if it sent shivers up my back the mood of it was so dirty. Maureen was smiling. She has a lovely smile and looked nice in her outfit. And Georgina done her hair with a pair of combs like I used to wear mine when I was a girl. And Tony turning her round slowly on the dance-floor. I was watching them. If Maureen was happy. He was holding her tight and her hair looked right nice from the back all them loose curls cascading over the collar of her jacket. Tony was stroking her back like they was still courting and breathed in the smell of her hair what was a handsome devil in them days, beard or no beard. What she saw in him. He was holding her and his eyes closed if we was alike as two peas what people said about me and our Maureen. Still smiling after all the hard times I was thinking whatever happens our Maureen and Tony still got each other. Even if he do give her a hard time and nobody reckons him round here where he ain't never tried to stand up to our Alan or no cunt on her behalf. What ain't easy for Maureen he is like that. But she should think herself lucky if he weren't there no more. At least she's still got somebody indoors to come home after all the years go by so fast not like our Linda what ain't got nobody. And I don't care if Linda says she's better off. Maureen chose Tony. We don't live in cave-man times no more where nobody ain't took her off of her mum and dad by force. She made her own bed. What weren't a big do when he made an honest woman of her. I never done nothing for her. I couldn't. Only one of them mauve pot-plants in the ceramic pot-holder how I live my life hand to mouth what ain't of my own choosing. If I say I'm sorry. I ain't never got nothing left.

Because Maureen was eating for two wasn't she? But it never showed. She looked slim in that cream trouser-suit. In Mick's Cafe over the road from the town hall afterwards and Tony's mum wore that hat with the flowers on it. She treated Maureen's Craig to an ice-cream float and egg and chips all round and tea and two slices what she put her hand in her pocket for me and the old man and Linda and all them on our side what bothered to show up what was for the best if we was thin on the ground as Maureen and Tony had been living together since before Craig was born and never wanted no fuss because they was skint.

But Tony's mum never ate nothing. Like she couldn't bring herself to eat with the likes of us what her precious son was marrying into. Or just losing her boy what she wanted all to herself how it had been the two of them since he got slung out by that other one he was with before and come home to his old mum.

She never thought she was gaining a daughter. She never wanted any of that, not with our Maureen what baggage they call it meaning me and the old man and all my kids what ain't turned out no better nor worse than her Tony and the rest of his lot but she thinks their shit don't stink. She never took to us. How she felt she weren't getting nothing out of it, of what she wanted. All what she got in her head to upset herself over she was losing a son.

And leaning across the table with a paper napkin to

wipe little Craig's mouth for him every two minutes. Weren't no grandson of hers with muck on his face she spat on it and rubbed until Craig couldn't take nor more. – You just gonna sit there mum and let that 'orrible old cow hurt me? Ain't you gonna do nothing?

So Tony took him outside. Tony's mum was crying in her handkerchief. She wouldn't look at me. But I thought to myself if she wants to be ignorant. Who does she think she is? The boy was her own flesh and blood, not just our side of the family. It was no good just blaming us. He was only a kid.

And on the night-time over the Queen's where Tony's brother stuck a ton behind the bar. What was enough in them days to have a good drink. I don't know how many packets of salt and vinegar crisp Maureen ate. She should of listened to me. By closing time she was doubled over. We all thought she was losing the baby. Our Linda took her up the hospital. Tony sat in the pub with his mum. All that seems so long ago now. But it weren't the baby. The doctor said there was nothing wrong with the baby. It must of been the crisp. We was all so happy.

Where Billy and Lorraine had a cake with five tiers. Just a bit of puff at first and Lorraine used to help herself to her mum's tablets. I blame it on her. She knew all them people Teddy Lucas and them what was into it a long time before we knew anything about it or anyone round our way was like it or sold it or any of that. Her brother was one of the first. Billy and Lorraine was so good before. Their wedding was so lovely. Lorraine's lot done us proud.

– Mum, said Billy. – You gotta help me. Lorraine sold my methadone.
– I ain't got nothing for you, I said.

So Billy made me phone over Dr Patel to see if he could give me something. Like that other time Dr Patel wrote me a script for Diazepam when I got myself wound up that trouble last year with Susan a couple of tablets was enough to knock me into the middle of next week. With two or three lagers in the Macbeth with Alan and them you gotta get out sometimes and live a little.

Billy had the rest of them pills off of me last time he got ill to take the edge off but this time when Dr Patel phoned me back after I left an urgent message he said no no Mrs Thomas no more for you not without a consultation very habit-forming and the next available appointment let me see now is the week after next. While poor Billy was crying in my kitchen, pulling out the drawers in my cabinets, rummaging through all my bits and bobs. Absolutely not Mrs Thomas. And just a couple of feet above Billy's head the biscuit barrel overflowing more than enough to finish him off.

So when I come off of the phone all I could think of to tell Billy was what about Lorraine. Where we all know Lorraine is the one what ducks and dives out of the two of them and Billy is supposed to keep their place nice. And keep an eye on the kids.

Billy said Lorraine was down her mum's for a few days. Well what about Alan then? But Billy said he'd seen Alan already. What did Alan do? Alan kicked Billy down the stairs. He called Billy an arsehole and said he would never sell gear to his own brother even if Billy had cash up front which he ain't never got cash up front where he reckoned I would kill him if he sold gear to his own brother. He wanted to know what Billy took him for. He said he loved Billy too much.

Through my kitchen window I could see Billy's kids outside on the landing, all three of them the spit of their dad when he was a kid. Them boys was watching their dad through my looped and scalloped nets what Aggie next door. I didn't know what to do. They was breaking my heart my own flesh and blood suffering like that where my Billy was so ill it was no good for them kids seeing their father like that.

Billy said he felt like he was going to die. Usually I got something for him a few quid if he gets bad see he don't ask me unless he's a good boy not unless it gets very bad. And I was trying to think but all I could think was do not let your eyes wander up to the biscuit tin you silly old woman. Otherwise he will be on to it. Up on a chair in no time expecting to find a couple of bob put away like my catalogue money or coins for the telly. Wouldn't he get a nice surprise?

But I never had a pot to piss in. Not even for chips for the boys see Billy had my money off of me outside the post office Thursday some bloke was going to do his knee-caps. Otherwise I know I know but the bloke was standing there waving a baseball bat. I had to have a fiver off of our Maureen that night to get the old man his tins.

– Go upstairs Billy out of the way with the door shut. That's what I told him. So I could let the boys in and get them something to eat. I mean it's not fair on them when he's like that. I had a couple of tins of soup in the cupboard but Billy said he would not let his sons anywhere near me he reckons because I am evil.

– The boys are hungry let me make them something to eat. And hand it out to them on the landing? A bit of cold meat in the fridge left over nice with some pickle and a packet of crisp and one of them cakes I got out there in the passage? I bet they ain't had no dinner.

But Billy told me to fuck off out of it and leave his boys alone.

– You are always trying to feed everybody, he said. – What is your problem? Why are you always trying to feed people? Stop fucking trying to feed me.

What was wishful thinking you can ask anybody where

I never even cooked them nothing of a night-time for my kids once they was on the school dinners and Tommy never come back from the pub until after closing unless he ran out of money.

And I ain't proud where they went without. But Billy was crashing round in my kitchen with the drugs in the biscuit barrel on top of the kitchen cabinet if he only knew enough stuff to kill him I felt like smiling a couple of feet above his head. And then he got me in the corner. He took my purse off of me. And give me a clump.

Because my purse was empty. He dropped the empty purse on the floor. The kids was watching through the window but when they saw him do what he did to me. They ran away like they knew they was next.

He hit me again and I thought if only our Maureen popped back up to me at a time like this because Maureen is pretty tasty putting a stop to him with her right hand when he starts on me. Tommy used to say she has got a punch on her like a man and he should know. I thought of screaming so loud Maureen would hear me all over the flats and come to my rescue. But then I would have to suffer afterwards how to run my life on the receiving end of her pity and concern I'd rather get my head kicked in. At least Billy doesn't think he's better than me.

He hit me a few times then he sobbed and said he was sorry. I offered him a cup of tea. I put four sugars in and a lot of milk to cool it down in case he flung it at me. He took a sip and flung it at me. He said it was too cold.

He got the shakes bad like they do that horrible empty retching and cried like a baby. I had nothing left to give him except what was in the biscuit barrel. He was so ill I thought he was going to die. I looked down at him barking on all fours on my kitchen floor. I looked up at the biscuit barrel. There was enough stuff in the barrel to kill him. But I didn't want to kill him. He is my son. And I

didn't want Alan to kill me.
– Help me, Mum, Billy cried.

He was curled up on his side on the floor, his hands
jammed between his thighs. The smell coming off of him. I
couldn't hardly.
– Mum, he said. – Help me. I'm so cold.
He was lifting his arms up to me.
– Hold me? he said.
– I'm covered in tea, I said, and ran up the stairs.

You'd of thought he'd wear long sleeves. I just couldn't
of done it. I changed into the new top Maureen give me
and sat on my bed. I could hear Billy crying in the kitchen.
I wanted to give him some of Alan's stuff, just enough
to tide him over. Alan would never notice. I thought a
teaspoonful or so would be enough. What about when
Billy goes in the toilet then I could climb up on a chair.
That was it. Just a teaspoonful. Alan would never notice.
I could put it in a matchbox and tell him Alan dropped it.
Alan would kill me if he found out. Maureen would kill
me. That's what I was thinking. Everybody wants me to
turn my back on our Billy like I am trying to kill him with
kindness. Kindness? That's a laugh. I don't feel very kind.

When I come down again Billy was trying to cram
his self in the cupboard. He got his head tucked in the
cupboard with the old man's holdall and overalls and that
and crouched hunched hugged himself into the dark hole.
But his bad leg dragged out behind him and he couldn't
shut the door.

I saw my chance. I moved a chair across the kitchen to
the cabinet and was just about to climb up when Billy shot
backwards out of the cupboard. I sat down quick as you
like on the chair, humming a little tune. Billy was on the
floor, his cheek squashed against my nice clean vinyl. I had
a stupid thought I'm glad I washed it. The dirt on Billy's
face was streaked with snot and tears. He was making my

clean floor dirty with his face. It's not often you can say that. I was going to tell him to go out to the front room there might be a couple of quid down the back of the chair and I was going to climb up and get him a spoonful of Alan's stuff poor sod I couldn't bear to see him suffer no more but when I reached out to pat his shoulder he flinched and shouted at me leave off of me you fucking cunt.

The hurt he done to me then calling me all sorts it's not like I wanted to touch him. I was forcing myself to touch him because I thought that's what he wanted. Can you believe his own mother what give birth to him how do you think he made me feel? Nobody speaks to me like that. Well they do but you know what I mean. He hurt my feelings them things he called me. Usually he's so nice most of the time I don't even think about it what he gets up to I suppose that's the trouble most of the time as long as he's had what he needs I just take no notice.

And that weren't the end of it with Billy once he gets going there's no stopping him. In my own kitchen he was calling me all the cunts and blaming me for everything what went wrong in his life. Even Lorraine going with some other bloke like that was anything to do with me. Where she bought their gear what I didn't even know about it. Not for money nor nothing Billy said she was at it because she wanted it of off some other bloke he felt so worthless and it was all my fault. What I did to him how I didn't oughta of looked after him the way I never looked after him when he was a kid. Because I neglected him and hurt him so much I made him go and choose Lorraine who was nothing but a bad mum because I was nothing but a bad mum to him it was all my fault he chose Lorraine. He was saying he chose her because she was like me.

Until they was just words pouring out of his mouth what meant nothing to me no more and it was like I was

seeing him rattle on my floor from a distance for the first
time where he had pushed me away how he went on until
I was sort of numb like he never belonged to me no more.
Like he belonged to some other poor cow what neglected
him when he was a kid and didn't know how to love him
and make him feel loved. He got that voice on they use
when he is angry what is self-righteousness whining like
they whine at you if you won't buy all the old baloney they
feed you how well they are doing and how their life is so
good compared to yours.

Until I felt all my mothering side of myself whither
or soured by what rubbish he was trying to poison me.
Like he was nothing to me I was some old woman with a
stranger on my kitchen floor from Adam who had picked
me out at random for punishment what was a good
feeling. But it didn't last.

– Mum, Billy cried.

– Son, I said, holding him.

I held my son in my arms. He didn't have much flesh
on his bones. And what there was of him riddled with
burns how they pick at the burns on the crack and itch all
over the holes from the needles. I felt his bones poking out
of him. The smell coming off of him I held my breath and
his crusty ear-holes weeping and I remembered he was
trying to turn me over because I am his mother.

Don't forget I am wearing my new top. I got all Billy's
snot and that smeared up the front of it. Where his face
was pressed against my chest. He was trying to turn me
over because he can't get enough out of me however
hard I try he just can't walk away from me because I am
his mother and although I done my best when my kids
was kids nobody is trying to pretend I was fucking Mary
Poppins he is making me pay. He never had enough off of
me then so he wants it all now.

Billy broke away and picked my purse up off of the

floor and looked in it again. He unfolded a receipt I kept for Maggie's dog meat she sent me over to get it when she had a cold. And stared at the little piece of paper in his swollen palm. I just sat back and watched him like some one had turned all the lights on all of a sudden. Where he was milking me like what suited him best on the gear he was never short of an excuse to be round me. What I could see was the whole point of it.

I watched him limp across my floor and open the fridge. There weren't much in there just a tub of soft marge and a pint of cow's milk. And a bit of cold meat sandwiched between two plates. But Billy pulled out the salad drawer and found the two tins I had hid in there for the old man. Billy opened one tin and drained half of it.

– That was for the old man, I said.

– Yeah well, said Billy.

He pocketed the other tin in his trousers with all the arse hanging out of them.

– Where you going? I said.

He never said nothing. He shuffled away from me into the front room.

– Ssh. Don't wake up the old man, I said.

I watched Billy balance the half empty tin on top of the telly. He unplugged the telly and tried to lift it but he was so weak I grabbed the telly back off of him and put it back on top of the cabinet. The tin of beer slid off but Billy caught it before it hit the floor. He took a mouthful. I went to sling him out but he was like I am out of here anyway you evil old woman so I followed him to the front door and opened it for him.

– Goodbye son.

– Yeah yeah.

Well I was not going to let him get away with it. So I dipped him on his way out and shut the front door properly and put the tin back in the fridge. Before he went

out Billy said I might not see him for some time what
was supposed to hurt my feelings. I heard him sling the
empty beer tin over the landing and waited for him to
start shouting when he discovered that the other tin was
gone. He started shouting. He banged on the front door. I
ignored him. He tried to hurt my feelings.
– I will go away and never come back, he said. – I will
never come back.
But it didn't because I peeped out of the kitchen window
and watched him lay down on the landing right outside
my door.
– I'll never come back and then you'll be sorry.
    I know I shouldn't but nobody knows how I feel when
he disappears how I am in the night blaming myself all
what I done wrong and picturing him what he is injecting
his self on the needles five times a day and can't get
enough. I get so tired I can't sleep. How dirty. How bad he
gets I need to see him or I can't sleep for the headache and
gutache and heartache of not knowing.

But Billy howled on the landing for about twenty minutes.
Poor Aggie next door was banging on the wall SHUT
UP SHUT UP SHUT UP then it went quiet. Peace and
quiet. The old man was sleeping in his chair. Victor was at
some Scout do over Edmonton. Raymond went with him
to carry his records. I was grateful to Vic how he made
Raymond feel useful, giving him a little job. He was good
to our Raymond and he was my friend. I made myself a
strong coffee, white, two sugars, just how I like it. I smoked
a couple of fags and ate a box of cake.

I was praying nobody trying to take nothing off of me just
for five minutes.

I'm not saying Billy was born like it but he was kicking and wriggling so hard in the midwife's hands she was laughing at him and turned round and said she was after thinking he would go back in. He screamed blue murder when she cut the cord.

And his first Christmas I had to do the whole dinner with him on my hip like it was yesterday. Not that the dinner was all that. Because the treasurer ran away with the club money I had been putting in two bob a week all year so as to have enough for a nice turkey and sausage meat and bacon and that and a piece of beef for over the rest of the holiday in my Christmas club what I lost out all what I put in and never had nothing. What felt like a disaster at the time.

The spuds we got through that year I had washerwoman's fingers by the time I had finished peeling them. Maureen cut them up for me and turned them in the hot fat in two big trays and put salt on them and kept an eye on them in the oven until she went over to our Dolly and Butch before dinner to see what they got for the kids where me and the old man was on our uppers. Dolly done all she could to help me.

Tons of spuds for my kids what was always hungry and some for the old man when he come home from the pub if he weren't legless and never passed out on the chair in the front room. And a couple of small ones for me and Auntie Violet what was my mum's sister and never had no kids of her own. What Auntie Violet perched on the stool in the kitchen and kept on trying to grab the baby off of me. But every time she went for him he screamed.

And was upsetting herself all over me thinking it was something about her. And wanted to know what it was about her. When Billy wouldn't even go to Maureen what was good with babies and knew how to change babies and feed them and settle them if they was fractious and making a fuss over colic or any of that. I was trying to do the spuds with Billy on my hip. What was hard enough not to cut off his fingers if he grabbed for the knife. And all I got out of Auntie Violet was tell me Nora, what is it about me?

Maybe because she never of got married herself. Because no one never asked her nor even looked at her twice what my mum used to say she just couldn't understand it when there was always queues at the door when she was a girl but no one never knocked for Auntie Violet.

What got the miseries all over me. What would make you cry at Christmas, not having nobody of your own. But even when she weren't crying she was no use to me. Because her hands was claws where the arthritis got in them and her feet was paining her every time she put weight on them. She just couldn't get up off of her fat arse.
– Tell me Nora, what is it about me? Why won't the baby come to me?
On and on begging some soothing words off of me she wanted to squeeze out of me but it weren't half tempting I had to bite my tongue what you don't say to your dead mum's sister what was an old maid what never had nobody of her own.
– Put your teeth in at least, Violet. Put a rinse through your hair, Violet. Have a wash. Wipe your nose, Violet. I don't want to speak ill but you should of seen her when she went. What weren't cheap I'm telling you the size of the coffin what costed us extra. She just let her self go.

So I got little Billy wedged on my hip and held him in the crook of my elbow and managed to do a good twenty pounds of spuds at the sink not once letting him slip or cut him with my knife. And don't forget a couple extra to mash up with a spoonful of gravy for him what was my baby whatever Violet said I was making a stick to beat myself.
– You got to let him know who's boss Nora. You got

to put him down, Nora.

Until I nearly said some of them things what you don't say.
– I wish someone would put you down.

To your mum's only sister when you lost your mum.
What only spent Christmas with us one year and with
Dolly the next before Dolly went to Spain and Violet come
to me every year after that until she kicked the bucket.
Where you had to feel sorry for her. I mean she never did
get herself a man. She never had no kids. She never had
no one. What must of been no life for her at all.

Although I thought what my mum would of said if
she'd of seen me. How thick peels turning I pared and
pared the eyes out in her grave but needs must and I done
my best. With Billy on me all the time and the peelings so
thick my mum's voice in my ear-hole scolding me like after
the war my dad hardly cold in his box and me doing all
her work for her while she was enjoying herself with Uncle
Johnnie I was all the little sluts. The knife was blunt and I
could hear Johnnie sing in the shed in our yard. She said
I got enough spud on them peels to keep a pig for a week.
Carry on like that and you'll end up like our Violet. What
will die an old maid you watch.

And to make it go a bit further I roasted and boiled
some bones for the gravy. What the butcher give me for
the dog he said very loud he was so nice so as not to show
me up where all the queue was staggering out of the shop
under the weight of their Christmas meat what was lovely
great lumps of sirloin and birds the size of our Alan who
was going on two. And I used up a whole packet of gravy
browning. So we got a lot of nice thick brown gravy each
on our potatoes and a mouthful of scrappy pork on tick
off of the butcher what took pity on me when I told him
what some heartless tealeaf went and helped his self to
our club money. The old man got a couple of big slices not
that he was all that bothered by the time he come home.

And I thought I would have a go at the leftovers off of the plates but there weren't none. Not even a bit of fat our Alan ate the string the butcher tied round the bits of belly slices and shoulder and that to make it look like a proper joint.

Still Dolly popped over with the pudding lovely and hot what Butch's mum sent up for her every year stuffed full of red and green glace cherries as Dolly had not got the heart to tell the old woman she can't abide. So at least we had a bit of that each nice and hot. And Aggie next door let us have two tins of evaporated milk what she got a crate-load off of her Mick and a packet of plain biscuits not in the first flush of youth I mean to say but beggars cannot be choosers.

All that kindness of neighbours when you find yourself potless at Christmas made me feel sick to my stomach even though we was all more or less in the same boat and I'd do the same back if it were Aggie what was down on her luck one year. And I would enjoy helping her even more than she enjoyed helping me.

Except something bad did happen as I remember. Baby Billy got hot grease splashed up his leg what poured off of the meat and I cried running the burn under the tap and put butter on it they used to say because he weren't perfect no more. The exact same place when he had been on the gear for a few years his left shin got eaten to the bone some bug in a big sore hole he packed with gauze and ointment and taped over what will never heal now. Where he showed it to me like it's a war wound he thinks he's good if he was living on the edge bleeding me dry and letting his kids run wild sleeping on Maureen's floor I don't know how that Lorraine can live with herself wherever they found somewhere warm and safe.

I sipped my coffee. Billy was as quiet as a baby on the landing. I made myself a sandwich out of that bit of cold meat left over from Sunday Victor cooked us a nice dinner and we all fell asleep in front of the telly. I don't know what I was hoping. Billy was as quiet as the grave. I don't know what I was hoping. I peeped round the door to see if he was dead or what. I sort of tested myself how I would be if he was dead. I mean would I feel glad? A part of me might feel glad. If he ever does knock it on the head I know I won't see him for dust. If he gets off of the drugs I mean what would he want me for?

I peeped round the door to see if he was going cold out there on the landing on his own when I could of give him a bit of Alan's gear to tide him over. Just a spoonful to make him better. Like Lorraine told me her mum stuck her brother in her nan's lock-up under the railway over the back of Dunstan Road so no one could hear him with some sweets and snacks and that and left him to rattle with a dirty great big padlock on the door. With some of her pills off of the quack what must of backfired. She thought she was helping him. She was at her wit's end with him. That woman ain't never gonna forgive herself now.

But Billy weren't dead. He was gone. I looked at the swept mark in the dirt where he must of been thrashing with the pains you know what they're like when they get like that sometimes if he vomits or shits himself. I looked up and down the landing and over the side of the railings. I heard the old man shouting at me in the front room.
– I'm gonna shit myself.

I went indoors to help the old man get on the toilet. I knew Billy was hating me. I should of given him some of Alan's gear, just to tide him over. I love my son. You can't just sit back and watch your own son in agony. I wanted to go back outside and shout out over the landing to tell him to come home you can have the telly sod the old man come back but by the time I got the old man on the toilet I knew Billy was long gone.

– I love you Billy.

Still, maybe I was right not to give him nothing. He did get up and walk away didn't he? He couldn't of been as bad as all that.

Before my mother got sentenced for possession a social worker was called to address the court. I never knew her from Adam but she told the judge that after talking to the defendant for some time and in the light of all her hard-won experience working with drug-related crime and the families of those involved in drug-related crime she had come to the conclusion that the addict could be brought back from the brink of total self-destruction and be helped to find a new life for him or herself and even the dealer could be rehabilitated but that in her long and painful experience she said that WORKING WITH THE MOTHERS OF DEALERS AND ADDICTS IS A NO-HOPE WASTE OF ENERGY, TIME AND RESOURCES. Because these women have been so confused and demoralised and corrupted they just can't tell right from wrong any more. That's what she said. They can't tell the difference.

I jumped up out of my seat in the gallery and whooped before I knew what I was doing like I was going to give the social worker a standing ovation. My mum looked up at me then quickly looked away. Not that I don't feel for her because I do. My heart aches for her if she is too stupid or broken down to deal with her true feelings head on what ain't easy I know that. Or she was too hurt. My face was red hot. A court official sitting right behind me thumped his hand on my shoulder and made me sit down.

LOCAL WOMAN WINS BUS
GARAGE CANTEEN CONTRACT
FAMILY EAT THEIR HAT

LINDA THOMAS, a member of the large and locally renowned Thomas family, was up against big firms and chain operators when she tendered her bid to run the canteen at Leyton's Parkvale bus garage. Miss Thomas, 50, a private caterer, of Chaucer Court, Haggerston, is well known in the area for her celebration buffets and wedding cakes.

"I managed to undercut the big companies in spite of the fact my family put the mockers on me," she said. Miss Thomas will offer traditional fare such as cooked breakfasts, roast dinners and a selection of her famous pies.

Miss Thomas's sister, Mrs. Maureen George, also of Chaucer Court, expressed her warmest congratulations. Her brother, Frank Thomas, a bus driver who works out of the Heathside garage, said that Linda was always determined to better herself. *"Good luck to her,"* he said.

"The canteen is a vital refuelling station for the men and women who keep our buses on the road," said Miss Thomas. *"My mother and my sister Maureen will be working for me. Ironic, really,"* she added, referring to their alleged lack of support for her bid. *"Still, they are family. And they know which side their bread is buttered. Talk about eat your hat!"*

Over the back of Kingsland Waste they pulled down that tower block my Tony used to live up there with some woman. In case you're thinking even before I come along it never did work out the two of them and her kids before I even set eyes on him he was back with his mum. All them homes to rubble and dust I never got that sick feeling no more down Queensbridge Road he was up there with that woman and kids like there was the big boom of the demolition and they was wiped out.

I was young then. Tony was not from round our way. He had a beard like a Brillo pad what used to scratch up all my face. I loved his big yellow dog. What died not long after I fell for our Craig and we was shacked up together over Dunstan Court living off of chips and biscuits what was all I could run to out of my own money where I never saw a penny off of my Tony. Before I even got a chance to find out what he was like.

Even when he had a win or earned his self an extra few bob over the carpet warehouse out the back door it was in the bookie's pocket or running errands out of the cab office in his brother's motor like a kid he got paid in sulph what didn't help one little bit with his moods. Still he was all the world to me then and he still does now I suppose when push comes to shove but times was hard what he put me through.

Where there might as well of been three of us over Dunstan Court even before our Craig was born. What was me, my Tony, and Terry Harrison. What my Tony could never let me forget. Even though it was dead and buried between me and Harrison long before I even clapped eyes on my Tony it was like I was on the bash the way he went on. I was all the cunts and whores of a night-time after he ate his little bit of tea what I eked out for him when he done all his money in the back of the pub playing cards or over the dogs however long it took until he never had nothing left but the clothes he stood up in what weren't worth fuck all to no cunt. And no one wouldn't never borrow him nothing so he had to come home.

What was all my husband thought of me. Because Terry Harrison got to me before him where we was courting when I was fifteen and Terry was seventeen. Although I didn't know Tony from Adam then and he was with that woman and the kids at the top of the tower block. He still reckoned I should of saved myself.

And I never said a word about her to him. I never asked him questions why she must of slung him out because if she never of slung him out why would he of gone back to his mum? Not that I'm saying nothing against his mum. Nor that woman he was shacked up with before me. But he don't think every time he takes off his shirt a beating heart pierced by cupid's arrow and her name Mary he got tattooed at Margate after a few beers one bank holiday they had a day out with their kids.

Tony says I make him sick. The thought of Terry Harrison touching me. Terry's fingers inside of me and kissing me his tongue making me wet. If only I had saved myself. Tony is tortured the thought you dirty cunt let that Terry Harrison went up me first.

Yes I did. I loved him and he loved me. Not what I endured like me and Tony still together after twenty-five years but Terry Harrison was kind. He was kind to me.

Terry Harrison. Terry Harrison. Terry Harrison. Terry Harrison on remand in Ashford the last eight months I was supposed to be going with him for manslaughter what his brother only stabbed some bird in the chest at a party where the poor cow went and died in hospital a couple of days later and Terry's brother pointed the finger. My Terry wasn't even at the party. I missed him so much when he was away it was like a poem. Some of what I writ out in my letters to him and sent to him how much I loved him and how much I missed him and some I binned. He did eight months on remand waiting for reports then the judge threw the case out of court.

And Terry Harrison went on the buses. What was a good job for him because he was very calm and very patient with people. And he had been driving a bus for years over the bus training ground with his dad what was a bus driver and trainer his self, round and round on his Dad's knee or when his legs was long enough his dad let him do it all on his own.

But something happened to Harrison inside what I loved more than I have ever loved anybody not including my kids. He never sent me the last V.O. I was expecting to see him in there one last time before he was due in court. Instead he sent all my letters back to me. He returned all my poems on the crinkly paper where I had cried. He never writ to me no more. All I had to read was his old ones and my ones over and over what he sent back, looking for a clue where I went wrong.

I showed one of his letters to Linda what was all I had left. I wanted her to read how he felt about me in his own words because she was laughing at me where she never believed no one could of loved me like that. I watched her unfold the sheet of lined paper and I was beginning to wish I'd never of give it to her the way she was smiling.

– And they say romance is dead, said Linda, fluttering the letter at me.

So I tried to snatch it back. She held it just out of my reach.

– You prat, she said. – You ain't got the sense you was

born with. I can't believe you swallowed all that what he
come out with. Don't you know nothing Maureen? When
they're banged up they always go on like that. Where it's
all just stories to fill up the boredom. None of what means
nothing. When they're inside they can say what they like.
– Gimme back my letter, I said.
– You can have it, she said, flinging it at me. – It's a load of
old wank. I mean what the fuck do you think they do all
day?
I refolded the letter and put it back in my pocket.
– Wanking, she said. – Wanking over you under the
covers. That ain't love, Maureen. Why are you so fucking
stupid?

I never got invited to his welcome home do over his
mum's. His mum blanked me and my mum down Hoxton.
They never went over the Queen's Head no more. What
I am saying he come out where I had waited for him and
visited him every two weeks and writ to him poems and
letters telling him every minute of my day, every second
like I went over the shop for my mum and then over
Dolly's to help hang her new curtains and who I talked to
on the way like I bumped into Julie outside the pub with
her nan and I looked in the newsagent to see if my mum's
book was in but it weren't where the delivery van broke
down in the Blackwall Tunnel and we made beef cobbler
in domestic science and all that so he wouldn't worry
about me what I was getting up to while he was away.

Well, I was stupid. When he come out he didn't want
to know me. He never even give me the elbow to my face.
He told our Alan to tell me. Like I hadn't already got the
message. I got a pain in my chest so bad my mum took
me over the doctors. Even I got on his bus to Liverpool
Street for my mum to pick up her glasses from the optician
for her on the 149 he pretended he never saw me. But he
looked small at the wheel like he had shrunk into his self

when he was on remand protesting his innocence and nobody was listening what never helped it was his own brother fingered him for something he wouldn't never of done nothing like that however much he was provoked what must of done his head in. And two years down the line outside the pie shop his mum told my mum he was moving over Victoria Park some nice girl called Tina he met on his bus what worked in a building society and had a nice little place down the back of Cassland Road overlooking the common.

And my Tony just would not let me forget. Pestering me when he come home buzzing and skint after the kids was in bed all what he done to his self shouting and crying and shedding betting slips and little pens out of his pockets all over our home and the porcelain slipper with cherubs perched on the instep I displayed in the glass cabinet what he smashed off of Linda when she got them teak units and my carriage clock and school photos flew off of the walls I splashed out on quality board and frames what looked antique behind glass shattered in pointed shards on the floor because I was proud and it was worth it to keep up with my memories.

And a nearly new onyx ashtray on a stalk off of some bird in the pub for the front room where small things can go a long way to making your home when you ain't got fuck all. But you are doing your best to make things nice what is the beginnings of something. So you ain't ashamed the health visitor poking her nose in where you ain't got no home to speak of just big greasy marks on the bare walls how someone else was living life in Dunstan Court before you painted over it in pixie green what you found half a tin in a skip and was not a nice colour. To check my babies ain't wet or dirty or losing weight or bruised or burnt or cut if she would have them off of me quick as you like and you know that. What terrified me if I lost them however hard I tried in my home with my Tony was just as bad for me as you would feel if they took yourn. What never laid a finger on them. And come home and went in the kitchen where the health visitor was in the front room thinking what she was thinking how can that woman live like this? Until she fucked off what ain't got no kids herself and don't know fuck all however careful they trained her to judge me. Then he's spitting like no cunt ain't looked twice at you now Maureen not for years on a plate up your fat arse where you lot all take it even your mum you fat cunt because Terry Harrison never wanted you then and he don't want you now.

Until his mum had to bale us out of arrears and we got rehoused over Chaucer Court right opposite my mum it took me years of hard work to put my home back together every fucking time when my Tony got a temper on him over Terry Harrison what dumped me he just could not let me get over. What is just the sulph talking he reckoned in the morning when he was sorry what he done to my home but that don't mean it never hurt me as much as the next person would get hurt over anything like that.

Where we was all over the Macbeth with my mum the night she come out of Holloway our Alan put a few quid behind the bar was the least he could do. And the landlady done us some platters like on a darts night of ham on white and scotch eggs and thick slices of pork pie and sausage rolls with mustard and cress sprinkled over and crisp and pickles and that to respect my mum what done her time and survived more than you could say for most people and nobody thought any the less of her where she told them it was all a mistake and never took no responsibility for any of what went on.

Except my dad what stayed indoors with his cans. You should of see my mum eat. And who can blame her she got pissed what she suffered belting it out on the Karaoke I Will Survive with Tony's Sandra and our Georgina and Shirley Irons and Julie and all them off of the little stage stumbling in floods even Billy and Susan for the free drink and poncing fags and what they could get off of Vic where they wanted to belong when it suited them and Mum hugging me over and over thank you ever-so what I done for her over home.

Come on Mum it's only a bit of paper on special out of Woolies with a pastel garland pattern and a lick of new gloss after work and on the weekends and that with Craig and Dawn's Barry what ain't as useless as he looks eh Barry. Where I had to pop up anyway ain't it to see to my dad. What I shrouded in his chair when I was having a go at the woodwork and all that with sandpaper folded over a block of wood like a ghost under the dust-sheet to protect him.

And Victor out of the way in Susan's room while I was papering I told him to keep out of my sight or I'd chin him.

Them ceiling tiles my mum glued up a stepladder when we was kids I remember brightened up our home in a couple of hours what was so yellow now and all peeling. So I reckoned they'd come off easy but I was at it the best part of a weekend where they was stuck fast. And half the ceiling come down on the back of them tiles what crumbling craters so big I wished I had never of started and my dad coughing under the dust sheet I lent off of Aggie next door. Then Polyfilla in the craters and over the cracks why she must of stuck the tiles up there in the first place and sanding and more Polyfilla and papering what is hard upside-down up a ladder and a couple of coats of paint. No, Vic, I told you to stay upstairs.

With nice new nets in the front room in a leaf pattern although I say it myself where no one else ain't gonna say it for me if they was gutted they never of lifted a finger when they went up to the old woman's and saw all what I had done. What weren't a bad job. Where Aggie's niece works in the curtaining shop down Mare Street she made out like them nets was for her mum. And even my Tony got a bit of carpet out of the warehouse what weren't all that but he said I could pay him later when I was able to pay him if he remembered or he might end up out of pocket if he was expecting me to remind him.

Our Linda in the pub in a pale silky blouse and navy skirt and court shoes and matching bag with gold padlock clasp plonked on the table mouthing off about the vacancies over the bus garage not that I blame her all the graft she put in to get where she's going. They'll be queuing round the block she said when it gets out seven or eight catering assistants required over the depot shift-work where she won the contract hands down if we wanted the work or didn't we? Seeing as they'll be queuing round the block off of the cards and that like she was doing us a big favour joke the money she was paying.

And I wouldn't of given a thought to Terry Harrison on the buses if it hadn't of been for my Tony over the years telling me like it was yesterday Terry dumped me because I am a fat cunt and I take it up the arse.

Terry Harrison what talked and talked afterwards and stroked my hair when I was looking out the window where his aunt let us kip in her front room on her own of a Saturday night in a one bedroom if I told my mum I was kipping over Julie's.

The sky was yellow in the night out of her window and the high walkways criss-crossed from block to block above the carpark and the empty playground what drove his aunt mad the voices of screaming kids all day long caning her ear-holes until she felt like jumping off.

When the yellow sky turned blue. He let me take the settee and he kipped on the floor. He told me I was beautiful. He listened to me how I felt the mood what come over me how he was too nice for me where I was used to be treated like shit. He never said nothing but I could hear how he was breathing, thinking about what I had said. I could hear pigeons jostling outside on the window-ledge and cooing what the housing was trying to evict his aunt where she called them her little friends. And fed them twice a day on peanuts and stale bread and all down the windows underneath where she lived was streaked with shit.

I was on the settee in the dark, waiting for Terry to answer me. If I had gone and said something I should of kept quiet.

– Tel?

– What?

– You all right?

– Shut up, Maureen.

I could tell by his voice he was smiling. He pulled me off of the settee. We rolled about on the floor then he held me on top of him where his aunt had made up a narrow pallet for us out of folded blankets. His eyes was shiny in the dark, like he was trying not to cry.

– Don't feel sorry for me, I said. – I don't need all that.

– I ain't, he said. – I just don't want to lose you.

But Tony calling me all the slags and cunts over the years did not make me feel like it was Harrison what lost out but me myself what got lost finding myself married with two kids to somebody what kept on shouting at me.

So as soon as Linda mentioned the job over the bus garage, before I even had the chance to think about Harrison and wonder if he was still on the buses and ask myself what I really wanted to know why he dumped me chewing over in my head when I felt like shit after a row with my Tony you know how you imagine your life if you had of taken a different turning not to end up where you ended up.

Well there was Tony shouting the odds first thing Linda opened her mouth does that cunt work out of that depot because if he does work out of that depot then you can take your new job Maureen and you know where you can stick it.

But Linda was quick off of the mark spelling it out to my Tony Terry Harrison was not still on the buses in fact he fucked off to Spain on the Costa del Sol. Best place for him if you ask me she added off of the top of her head like she had something against him where his mad brother ended up running a pub. So my Tony let me and I said I wondered how Shoreditch School would get along without us girls killing ourselves at dawn to scrape the shit off. And my mum raised her arms above her head and swayed from side to side and smiled and sang Shoreditch School Up Yours into the mike to the tune of I Am Sailing where she did like a bit of Rod because something about him put her in mind of the old man in his prime she said what was going back down memory lane a very long way and weren't nothing like how I imagined it.

The wardrobe door dragged out of a skip with her own hands Linda propped in the yard outside the staff toilets for us to check in the mirror when we was headed back in the canteen like she thought we would come out of the bog with our knickers down or trailing bog-roll or to make sure me and my mum never forgot we looked a right pair of prats in the hairnets and paper caps she made us wear like a white bird on your head working long shifts for shit money while she was coining it.

Where Linda is one of our own cracking the whip and blood is thicker than water and all that my mum said she wanted to do all she could for her like any mother would feel proud. And I never saw my mum work like that without sparing herself. She wanted to graft so that Linda would prosper even more than she was already prospering off of the back of her own family where we was all pulling together and that was family for you like in the old days when people was supposed to look after their own if you can believe that.

But three weeks out of Holloway the work was knackering my poor mum like no old woman ever worked so hard nor felt so tired. Because she was worn down before she even started over the canteen after her sentence and never managed to get off of the back foot. And nobody likes to be shouted at.
– Mother!
And wanted Linda to recognise her work. What was not to say she never complained about it all day long because she did complain. But she wanted Linda to praise her. What made it worse for her because Linda was not like that.
– Mother!
Where my mum was slumped in an arm-chair outside the back door of the canteen kitchen so deep her bony arse almost bumped the ground. And nobody was going to tell her that tea-break was over when she had never even managed the whole of her first fag. And never moved a muscle in spite of all her good intentions.
– Mother!
And her eyeballs through the scratched lenses of her glasses loomed in the half-moon at the bottom to look at her weekly book full of true life miracles and misery out of the sweetshop over a quarter of sherbert lemons she knows how to live. If the puffy bags under her eyes was magnified like the blue-white pearly pockets was full of her tears. Where we all got the same look round the nose and eyes and cheekbones off of my mum and Dawn and her kids and their kids when the time comes and their kids after I'm gone made me full of wonder.
– Meat pie!

What the racket was our Linda still shouting at my
mum through the back door and whacking the steel
serving counter with a steel serving spoon. Bang bang. But
my mum lit up again. Because she reckoned the noise put
her in mind how she suffered after lights out all what the
girls done to their selves head-banging in the cells and that
she looked so tired.
– Mother! Meat pie!
My mum took a last drag on her fag.
– Reen? she said, offering it to me.
– Just put one out.
I watched her dock the cigarette on the thin sole of her
shoe and slide the long dog-end back in her packet.
– Come on then, she said.
– Yeah, I said.
– Meat pie! Linda shouted.
– I'll fucking meat pie her in a minute, said Mum.

The pie was three feet long, and two feet wide give or take
a few inches either way in one of them aluminium trays
like school dinners somebody must of had it away from
the kitchens at Shoreditch once Linda knew she got the
contract and none of us would go back there no more
except Georgina what was stuck cleaning the classrooms
she used to sit at the back with the boys and never learnt
nothing where she never liked change. Well it weren't me
what nicked it! What was camaraderie between me and
my mum where our Linda pushed us closer together how
it does make you feel you are in it together and we never
was all that close but we had to laugh. With Linda on top
like that and don't she know it.
    But when my mum tried to get the pie out of the
oven she wouldn't let me help. Steam gushed out and
her glasses steamed up. I watched her wrap her hands
in cloths and take hold of the metal handles. The gravy

was bubbling out of the sides of it.
– Fuck me, she said, trying to stand up.
– Come on Mum! shouted Linda.
– Wanna hand? I said, shaking chips in the chip basket.
– Nah. You're all right.
– Where's my pie? Linda shouted.

My mum carried the pie out to the serving counter and
I followed her with a tray of chips, thinking why she would
fall down sooner than drop her burden for Linda and I
was behind her just in case where she was staggering and
the strain showed in her back and her hips.
– About fucking time, said Linda, and never even said
thank you.

So my mum folded her arms across her chest and
watched Linda set about the pie with her knife. Her face
was not a good colour and her breathing was laboured
where she had strained herself and now she was getting
riled how Linda thought she could speak to her own
mother like that. Although none of us was all that
surprised.
– What? Linda said.
– What? said Mum.
– What? Linda said.
– The pie was too fucking heavy, said Mum.

We all looked at the pie. The cut pastry was wet white
underneath and the gravy flowed over lumps of meat and
disks of soft carrot.
– Don't say a lot for my pastry, Linda said.
– Well you said it, said Mum.
– Don't start.
– Start?
– I said don't start.
– I'm not, said Mum. – I wouldn't.
– Oh wouldn't you?
– I'm too tired, love.

– Tired? You're too fucking old.
– What?
– Do you want me to write it down for you?
– I'm sixty-six, Mum said. –What is no age.
– Eight.
– What? Mum blinked.
– Sixty-eight, said Linda, wiping the knife on a
cloth. – Work it out.

My mum looked down at her hands and began to turn
her ring on her ring finger.
– I must of lost count, she said. – I lost two years of my
life.
– What you won't never get back, I said.

I don't know why I said that. My mum took a few small
steps backwards, looking over her shoulder to see where
she was going, and leant up against the fridge. She closed
her eyes. Linda shrugged.
– What feels like a fucking tragedy, said my mum. – Where
I ain't got all that much time left?

I never said nothing. The drivers and conductors
shuffled the length of the serving counter, shunting their
trays along the steel shelf. I served chips, mash, peas,
beans. Linda doled out slabs of pie.
– I said don't just stand there, Mother, she shouted.

Then my mum wouldn't take nothing after they all ate
their dinner and Linda told us to have ours when it went
quiet. My mum wouldn't eat where she never wanted to
give Linda the satisfaction. But I had the pie with mash
and peas was a lovely dinner why Linda won the contract
over the bus garage what nobody never said she weren't
much of a cook I'll say that for her. But I wolfed mine
and went out the back kitchen to see how my mum was
doing. Where we washed the pots out the back her skinny
forearms chafed against the front edge of the deep pot

sink. Her forearms was all red and she was scrubbing scabs of burnt pastry and burnt gravy off of the big trays and scraping pale marks with the wire wool in the aluminium. She rinsed a clean tray and racked it up on the drainer. I took it off of the rack, dried it and put it away. Her hands looked sore.

– Fuck me, she said. – Sixty-eight, Maureen. No wonder I feel tired. And I ain't had no dinner.

– What ain't nobody's fault but your own, I said.

Where she was up to her elbows in dirty water and I was waiting for her to hand me another wet tray I was feeling what I was feeling, if I could help her because she was my mum but she brought it on herself and I had my own work to get through. I knew she wanted to talk. So I wiped down the splash-back so as to look busy while I was waiting for the clean tray in case Linda popped her head through the double doors. I wiped down the empty drainer.

– Must of been fifty years ago then shackled since we, she said.

– Fifty years! I said.

– Yeah, she said. – I can't believe I lost track.

– So it's your Golden this year Mum, I said.

– Yeah, she said.

– Congratulations, I said.

She blinked and stood at the sink, letting the dirty tray slide back in the water.

– Here, I'll finish that for you, I said.

– Go on then, she said.

I fished the tray out of the water. Mum was drying her hands. The swing doors flapped where Linda had just pushed through.

– Who done them cups? she shouted.

– I just done them cups, said Mum. – While you was having your dinner. Them cups is all clean.

– Clean? Linda shouted, holding a cup up to the light.

– Honest, said my mum. – I just done that lot.

Linda passed her the cup and folded her arms across her chest.

– Ain't what I would call clean, she said.

Mum looked in the cup.

– Where I was trying to get it done too fast so I could get on with the floors ain't it Maureen? Tell her. Ain't I been grafting? That cup is stained.

Linda sighed and turned on the tap. Mum squirted neat washing up liquid in the cup and took a brush to it under the running water.

– I'm gonna get this cup clean if it kills me, she said. – You better check it again after to make sure where we don't want nothing like that risking your good name what is at stake if people was saying you don't run a clean kitchen.

She handed the wet cup to Linda.

– That'd be all you need, she said. – People can be so cruel. You can't be too careful.

– Shut up, Mum, said Linda, examining the cup.

– What was a close shave if you ask me if the Health and Safety had of come round. What is sod's law, said Mum.

Linda put the clean cup to drain.

– Well, said Linda.

– Well what?

– You'd better do all them cups again.

– Do what, said Mum.

– Them cups is all rotten, said Linda.

– I'll do them, I said.

– No, said Linda. – I want you on spuds for tonight. You know that. Them spuds won't peel themselves.

– You're telling me to wash all them cups again? said Mum.

– All of them, said Linda.

– Or what? Mum asked.

Linda ignored her.
– Or what, Linda?
  Linda put her hand on the back of Mum's neck and pushed her head down over the pot sink. Mum's paper cap fell off and dropped in the greasy water.
– Or I'll fucking drown you, said Linda.
– You what? I said, and pulled Linda off of her.
– Only mucking about, said Linda.
Mum rubbed the back of her neck.
– You didn't oughta of done that, she said.
– Well, said Linda. – I'm sorry. All right?
  She went outside for a fag. Mum took a sherbet lemon out of the pocket of her overall and put it in her mouth. The water ran cold. I topped up the sink with scalding water carried across the kitchen in a bucket from the urn and topped up the urn with cold water carried across the kitchen in a bucket from the sink. My mum started again on the cups. The washing-up liquid was rubbish. The rubber gloves had perished. The brushes was worn and balding.
– I hate this fucking job, she said. – I done my best.
– Yeah well, I said, starting on the potatoes. – Take care. You don't want to break nothing.
– Yeah yeah, said Mum, rattling the cups under the water.
– Don't forget she will fine you, I said.
– How could I fucking forget? she said.

Meaning her fourth day over the canteen a glass cracked and slashed up all her left hand under the water. She was white round the mouth and where she never liked the sight of blood curling in the sink her legs went from under her and as she went down she cracked her head on the corner of the deep freezer. Her glasses flew off. She was lying on the floor with her head in a heap of peelings by the sink where Aggie's cousin had made a mess scraping carrots.

I knelt down and patted my mum's cheek. Her mouth was wide open.

– Mum, I said.

But she was spark out. Linda slapped her round the face. Mum closed her mouth and blinked.

– Maureen, she whispered. – Fetch me glasses. Can't see a fucking thing.

I give the old woman her glasses and lugged her into a chair. Linda held a cup of hot tea to her lips with four sugars in it for the shock and picked a piece of carrot out of her hair. I tore strips off of a clean tea towel and bandaged the flapping cut in the old woman's hand, trying to staunch the flow of blood.

– I can't make it stop, I said. – She needs a stitch.

– I got my new Merc, said Linda. – You hold the fort, Maureen. I'll take her up the hospital.

– Nah, says my mum. – I ain't going nowhere without Maureen.

– What is a blessing and a curse for both of yous and a pain in the arse for me, said Linda.

Her new car was lilac. My mum sank back in the back seat and closed her eyes, cradling her cut hand in a kitchen cloth. The cloth was filling up with blood.

– Over the auction the man said to go with the mauve where you get more for your money, said Linda. – He reckoned the car was feminine what men bought if they wanted to get a special something for a special someone. Well I put him straight on that one, didn't I? I opened my bag and showed him my money. I earned every penny of that, I told him. You gonna give me a discount for cash?

The way Linda was driving she leant back in her seat and pushed hard with her right hand against the steering wheel like it was down to her powering the car to surge forward. I patted my mum's arm. She opened her eyes and looked at the bloody cloth in her lap.

– Nearly there, I said.

– There's a box of tissues on the back shelf if you need tissues, Mum, said Linda. – You be careful of my upholstery. Fuck sake don't get no blood on it. I'll fucking kill you if…

The nurse cleaned the wound and stitched it up. Mum was apologetic where the nurse never took enough care and I thought she was a brute manhandling the old woman like she never deserved no better. Then they decided to keep her in overnight on obs after the X-ray the doctor thought questions was raised where he never knew my mum like we did what was babbling a little bit of the shock and they was worried she was silly in the head after the knock she took but we never noticed nothing out of the ordinary. But the nurse went away before my mum even got settled. So I drew the curtains round the bed and helped her strip off her bloody clothes.

– Me and Maureen's gotta get back to work, Mum, said Linda.

I done up her gown for her with the white tape at the back like I was her mum and that was my job to look after her now she needed me whether I was happy or not with that arrangement. Her back was greasy grey. And red where her bra was rubbing and I thought I could not remember the last time I seen her in her knickers of white interlock with faded flowers on it almost washed to fuck.

Once I got her in bed. I opened the curtains again.

– We ain't got all day Reen, said Linda.

– You want me to stay with you, Mum? I said.

– Nah, said Mum. – You're all right. I just wanna sleep.

She lay back on her pillow and closed her eyes.

– Must be the shock, I said.

Linda patted Mum on the leg.

– Bye, she said.

Mum sat up suddenly.
– Pass me purse, she said.
She winced and fumbled with her purse. I took it off of her
and unzipped the zip.
– What's this? said Linda.
– A pound, love, said Mum.
– What for?
– Where I already had my wages off of you for today
remember you subbed me last night for Daddy's tins so
there ain't nothing you can dock the glass money off of,
said Mum.
– What? said Linda.
– Like you would of forgot I owed you, said Mum. – For
the glass what I broke.
She was holding out the coin in the palm of her hand.
– Go on. It's yourn, she said.
Linda looked at the coin.
– Seeing as I ain't even earned what you paid me already
for today, said Mum. – Where I'm in here ain't I? Not
grafting over the kitchens like what you paid me for.
– Give over, Mum, said Linda.
– By rights it's yourn, love. For the glass what I broke.
Where I was clumsy you told me to watch what I am doing
of? Not to break nothing or else?
Linda leant her head to one side and looked at my mum.
– What do you take me for? she said.
– But I owe you.
– Don't want it.
– Don't be like that.
– Like what?
– Just fucking take it will you?
    Linda took the coin and put it down on the bedside
cabinet.
– See you in the morning, Mother, she said. – Not that
you'll be no use to no cunt the state you're in. You better

make sure they give you something for the pain.
– See you, Linda.
– Ta ta.
– Mum? said Linda. – You know you can hop on the bus
right outside the hospital takes you all the way to the
depot?
– I got me pass in me purse, said Mum.
– I'll fetch you home in the morning, I said.
– I need you in work, Maureen.
– She ain't got no clean clothes to put on, I said. – Them
ones is rotten. And she needs rest. The doctor said. You
heard him.
    Linda sighed and moved away from the bed.
– Pop in to Daddy tonight, Maureen, said Mum, as I leant
over to kiss her.
– I know, I said. – Look after yourself. I'll phone you over
later on the ward phone.
– Cheers, Maureen, said my mum.
– Come on, said Linda.
    So me and Linda started to walk along the ward
between the double row of beds towards the nurses'
station and the exit.
– You forgot something, Linda, Mum shouted.
Linda turned back. Mum picked up the coin in her good
hand and flung it in Linda's face. Linda raised her hand
and caught it just in time.
– Cheers Mum, she said, sliding it in her pocket.

But cleaning Shoreditch School was a doss compared
to this for an old bag like me. Where our Maureen and
the rest of the girls was covering for me or shoulder to
shoulder in the same boat and equals cutting corners and
paring as much as possible off of our work right under the

nose of that bullying cow above us the supervisor but what did we care was a fair fight and she never meant nothing to none of us? Where we was taking the piss when we never owed her nothing. Not like under our Linda.

But I can't believe I lost count since me and my Tommy till death and after they stack us up or side by side where we buried my mother as long as they don't set me on fire like I have told Frank what is my oldest boy and I trust him to carry out my wishes. Fifty years! What feels like a lifetime and no time at all if it's nearly over. But you wouldn't go back if you could but you can't so what is the fucking point of even thinking like that?

After the war effort picking potatoes in Wales my mother looked over my shoulder and wanted to know why I never brought lover-boy home with me because people was all talking and she was disappointed he must of bottled it and never followed me home after the hostilities was all done and dusted and they let me go back where I belonged. What gossip was thanks to Doris from round our way on the same farm as me sending dirty letters to her cripple sister waiting for the war to end in the webbing factory with Dolly and them because Doris was a cow and stuck her nose in where it was not wanted. And my mother had a sharp tongue.

All that time on my knees in the mud was hard graft in the war when my mother was keeping the home fires burning I could hear her sharp voice in my ear having a pop what made me even more lonely where the fields was so fucking bleak on the rim of the valley. Some of the girls sang as they worked to keep their spirits up but I never felt like singing. Where we was dragging our sacks behind us through the furrows on our hands and knees and my fingernails was all broken. And when I stood up to dump my full sack on the cart I was frightened of the horse and I never wanted to look over the dizzy edge of the field in case I fell down in the dark dirty valley full of water and mud and behind me the wind was singing in the fence of thorns and barbed wire and black sticks. I was afraid of the trees and the open sky. And on the hill behind the fence I could hear the steep forest was full of wild animals what foxes and wolves prowling out of the forest like they tore apart stray sheep and there weren't nothing left but bloody scraps of bone and bits of bloody wool caught on the fence and smeared on the ground and I was afraid it was me next where I weren't much bigger and never had no more sense than them dumb animals what never knew no better and weren't familiar with nothing like that where I come from.

And it was what you fucking looking at just like down Hoxton if one of us dared to stare at any of them what was born and bred in that place. I was used to all that but never on the receiving end where it was my first time I never belonged when they deployed me. The Welsh women trudged past the fields on their way to work. They wore boots like us. And head-scarves and heavy coats and gobbed at us and laughed and threw stones.

But he went and picked me. He was miming love over the edge of the field in his own arms melting how he courted me what was the first time I saw him and he was a clown. I was on my knees in the mud but I had to smile. The white sky behind him was all birds in circles waiting to swoop once we turned the soil over. He was trying to be funny but I was crouched in the mud under a potato sack tied with string on my back to keep out the cold wind and the cold rain and I felt too sad. Because my father topped his self in the war. They let me go home in the train to bury him and I come back straight after and went back to work. But I tried to smile and asked Tommy why he was not in the war. He never understood. He never spoke a word of English. But when I stood up at the end of the row to empty my sack into the trough he heaved me over his shoulder. I could feel the heat off of his big hands inside my work jacket and I felt my sides paining me where he held me too tight round the ribs and would not let go. The tears was welling up out of me where I had never even started to shed all I had to shed over my dad so they just spilled over. My muddy legs scissored over his head and the combs fell out of my hair. My hair uncoiled and trailed in the mud what I could see the ends brushing the bloated stems of the potato plants and the girls looked up from their work and smirked and Doris clocked what was going on. I did scream but no one done nothing. They must of thought I was laughing. I was laughing and screaming. Tom kicked open the barn door and laid me down in the straw. He pulled down my trousers. The weight of him on top of me I could hardly breathe. He closed my mouth with one hand and opened my legs with the other and afterwards I bled and was hurt underneath like somebody went and kicked me there for no reason.

He turned away from me to buckle his belt. I saw he was crying and I didn't feel anything for myself where he was unhappy all my own feelings for myself just sort of drained away. That was the first time I'd ever see a man cry.
– Mae'n flyn da fi, he said.

I knew he was sorry. I pulled up my trousers and shuffled towards him through the straw. I felt sorry for him. I wanted him to stop crying but he pushed me away. I hobbled out of the barn and back to work in the dusk trying to act like it was nothing. I was pretending that nothing had happened. But the girls was all silent when I come out of the barn. They was working in silence and ignoring me as the darkness crept over the field like they knew I had gone too far. Because we was all warned if you give yourself to a man that don't mean nothing binding where he is concerned if he don't want nothing binding we was fair game in the war. So I never saw Tommy on the farm after that and I tried to forget him. Like you make yourself forget if you know you have lost someone what is a sad ending and you just go numb. But in my ear my mother's voice kept on at me until I felt dirty. I only had myself to blame where I wanted him because I was happy he chose me. I got what I wanted.

My mother bought me a posy of late chrysanthemums from Ernie Sullivan's allotment he raised from seed and I borrowed a cardigan off of Auntie Violet it was so cold in the church it makes me think where your life went. And Tommy was late! I shivered in my dress and heaved over the carbolic the church women scrubbed out the nave some soapy water was still puddled on the tiles and Uncle John looked at his watch and laughed and went like ten bob says he don't show and he thought that was funny.

But on my big day in the church I needed my dad. Not Uncle John standing next to my mother on my big day with the flat of his hand up the small of her back. My back was aching and I felt ugly. And I hated my mother then, the way she was laughing, and she was on at me like it's no good crying, you can't say I didn't warn you, I said if you can't be good be careful.

But where she had run up a dress for me out of a bit of a parachute she bought off of some woman in the pub she said it looked nice. Empire line under the circumstances, she said, and called me a slut – she reckoned I should of waited.

What was a bit rich where tongues wagged over my mother was no better than she should be if that makes sense to you because I never understood it when people used to say that about people. When I got home from Wales and she looked over my shoulder I clocked a pair of boots parked under her table only eight weeks after we buried my dad. Not that I said nothing. But she must of saw my face. She blushed and told me that after my dad did what he did she needed somebody where she was afraid of the bombs and the nights was so dark and cold and Uncle John lost his wife before the hostilities in a fire she fell asleep smoking in bed and no one could save her.

My mother said they was both lonely and her heart went out to him and I understood that. And don't forget I was still waiting to come on. What made me even more confused what was the nature of love. Because I was only a young girl and my mother never thought much of me and was distracted by her own feelings. And my Tommy was not with me to protect me what was the whole point. Because they used to reckon you can't fall unless you enjoyed yourself. And that is all lies. I never enjoyed myself. It was the worst thing that ever happened to me in my whole life. I couldn't believe no one never told me what he was doing me I felt sick the shock of him ramming me and I felt myself turned inside out.

What weren't a good start. And when Tom did show up down Hoxton the talk was like I was going with a black. Mother said she could not believe I'd lower myself where he never even spoke the same language and the girls was behind my back when he had a drink in him in the pub to see if they could get anywhere with him but I knew their game. But why should I care? Because it was me he come after. All the way from Wales for me like a fairytale I mean why bother unless it was me he wanted. He found me! And Dolly said to take no notice in the pub if he's only after a bit of a laugh with the girls what don't mean nothing. Men do like to enjoy their selves, she said. You don't want to try and stop them from enjoying their selves.

And my mum poked me in the gut and said no daughter of hers weren't to bring forth some bastard into the world to shame her out of her neighbours' good opinion what was the pot and the kettle all over Haggerston and Hoxton where they was talking about

her and Uncle John. What must of had a word with my
Tommy. Until Tommy went down on one knee what is
the same in any language. Then I stopped caving myself
in trying to hide what we had gone and done. I asked
Tom what took him so long after we done it that one time
and he never wanted to do it again but he just smiled and
shrugged where he never knew what I was on about. And
by the time he had picked up enough words to explain
his self he told me his old woman had made him go up
in the mountains for weeks and weeks to help his aunt
with her sheep and when he come down I was gone. And
Uncle John got Tom something working casual on the
demolition. He looked a big strong lad in spite of his weak
chest why he was out of the war. I saw him over the pub
after work Friday nights with my mum and Dolly and
all the rest of them and at the end of the night he said
goodnight and trudged off coughing and coughing with his
torch in the dark to kip where he was kipping in a room in
Martello Street over the other side of London Fields with
some of the boys of off the buildings what John fixed him
up and at church on Sundays to hear the banns read and
all that and afterwards over home where Mother did do us
a lovely baked dinner I'll say that for her since she took up
with Uncle John we never went short in that department.

Of course in them days there weren't no question in
spite of the fact we was engaged I never even got a look
at where he was staying if he had of wanted to do it again
where there's a will but he showed no sign. What Dolly
thought was maybe out of respect but I said don't make me
laugh.

But it was all frolics and fun over home with Mother
and Uncle John. She waited on him hand and foot on
account of the shrapnel in his leg and he was flogging
horsemeat and cold cream what we weren't to let on how
he boiled the skins and bones and skimming off the fat in

a tin bath out the back by my dad's shed in the night what
smelt so bad it made me vomit in the morning when I
had to go outside in the yard to use the toilet. I can hardly
believe my mother used to smear it all over.

John lodged in the spare room what was supposed to
keep up appearances and Mother was happy. I'd never
known her happy like that before. And she didn't much
care what they was all saying about the sequence of events
where it was our Dolly what started it. She was spoiling
for a fight after she put away a couple of pints in the White
Horse and said you want to ask yourself what happened
first. Uncle John was playing the piano, singing his heart
out, and my mum was singing along with Auntie Violet
and them and our Dolly behind their back whispering
you wanna ask yourself Nora was it the telegram the old
man on his way home in his box first or Uncle John got
his boots under our mother's table and news travels fast so
the old man done what he done. What don't make no odds
now but I still blame her for what happened.

Tommy was late for the wedding. My heart was sinking
in my boots. Then there was a bit of commotion at the
church door. Mother turned to look. She was like that's
ten bob you owe me and held out her hand. John felt
in his coat pocket and fished out four half crowns. You
could hear the money jangling in the church. Tommy was
flushed and squirming on account of the beer and the
suit he borrowed was too small and he was half strangled
by his tie. I took one look at him and wished he would of
fucked right off back where he come from. That's why he
never of touched me since he turned up. He was bricking
it what he had got his self into. We was both young. But
Uncle John took me by the arm and steered me up the
aisle. It wasn't that I never liked him but he weren't my
dad. I felt angry towards my dad for the first time for
leaving me. I had the idea standing there by the altar in

my white dress I would never of got myself in this mess
if my dad hadn't of gone and topped his self. I mean like
topping his self he was running away from me. Not just
he went and died in the war but when he went he took
away something from me because he did it on purpose not
just dying like people died in the war. He went because
he didn't love me enough. After that I just let bad things
happen to me. I wanted to run away out of the church but
Uncle John stopped me.

– I can't do this, I said. – Let me go.

– You ain't going nowhere my love, he said.

So Maureen was up the cash-and-carry in the new van as
soon as she done the spuds and the dirty water gurgling
in the drain after I pulled the plug and I am sweeping
and swabbing the bog floors where they dump their fag
ends and the cardboard applicators off of their tampons
and clumps of hair and fluff combed out of their dirty
brushes and left it for me to sweep up as if I ain't already
got enough to cope with on my plate without all that on
top of everything. And smeared paper when they wipe and
miss the bowl instead of dropping it where it belongs you
can hardly believe the stubborn shit off of the toilet bowls
where I am bending to go down the U-bend with the
brush I know what our Linda weighs me up and finds the
harder I work the more stupid in her eyes even when it is
her work what I'm killing myself over. But I scrape out the
sanitary bin of the dried blood smell like rotten bananas
and unblock and wipe out the sinks where they block up
the trap with sodden bog-roll and swollen soap and gob
and piss in the bowl when they can't wait for the toilet if
both the cubicles are busy and throw up the morning after
the night before or a bun in the oven and I have to put my
hand in to pull out the plug.

Then I wash my hands and light up and Linda comes in

and she's like no smoking in the toilets Mum if you don't mind. So I give the mirror a bit of a rub with my cloth. Linda pulls the pins out of her hair. Her hair falls down. She bends forward and bashes herself up the back of the head with her big brush where she ain't all that kind to herself for all her talk. She made the back of her neck all red from the brush. But she has got nice hair. So I tell her.
– Your hair is nice.
What is not what I say to my kids if I can help it but I just said it. And she's like you what? And tosses her head back and lets her hair fall to her shoulders.

I tap ash off of my fag into the clean basin. Linda gives me a look. And she goes I thought I told you already Mum. No smoking in the toilets. Do you have a problem with that?

I smile at her and turn on the tap and wash the ash down the plughole. She is my daughter. What come out of me with black hair puffed up in a quiff over her forehead like Elvis. And I was playing dollies out of her baby bath to warm by the fire wrapped in her own towel, the white bristles of the baby brush so pale and soft stroking her scalp from my new-born gift set all in lemon off of Dolly what never believed me I was carrying a girl. I wanted the pink one but she knew best.

The dummy and yellow brush and tiny scissors for her nails and a comb and soap laid on a white towel with a yellow duck under cellophane in a baby bath with lemon ribbons like what you give a little girl to play with her dolls where Linda was my first and I had more time to see to her until Frank come along. Her back and shoulders was downy when she come out like she was a new animal, so fuzzy I just stroked her what I thought the baby was for, where she was my first, I thought she was put on this earth for me to play with her.

And I go a bit quiet in the toilets thinking when they

was nothing but little bits of kids remembering my babies if I ain't done my best for them Linda turns round and pokes me in the chest what none of it weren't my fault.

– Got the hump? She says.

– I ain't got the hump, I says. – I'm tired, Linda, that's all.

– You gotta eat, she says. – There's pie left if you want it.

– I don't want no pie, I says.

– There ain't nothing wrong with my pie, she says.

– I knew you was gonna say that, I says.

– Well you wasn't disappointed then was you? she says.

– But I am disappointed, I says.

– Do what?

– Don't take it so personal, Linda.

Where she twists her hair into a knot and pins it up. I take a last drag of my fag.

– I said no fucking smoking in here, she says. – What's wrong with you? You deaf?

And I flick the dog-end down the toilet. Linda smiles at herself in the mirror, checking her teeth.

– No, but I am so tired I wanna die.

Well I thought that was telling her! But she turned round and smiled at me with her head on one side like she was chewing me over how she chews me over like my mother used to do that to me. Where I didn't want no trouble but she wanted telling. So I repeated myself to rub it in.

– I am so tired I wanna die.

– Well, she said. – You're almost done now.

– Thank fuck for that, I said.

I rubbed the hand-dryer with my cloth.

– I'm all finished in here, I said, stuffing the cloth in my pocket.

– Excellent, said Linda.

– Well that's me done then, I said.

– Well no, said Linda, looking at her watch. – I don't think so.

– You could eat off of them fucking toilets, I shouted.
– What is beside the point, said Linda. – Where you gotta
do the canteen floor?

My aching knees hurt me when you ain't as young as
you was on all fours at my age kneeling at Linda's feet on
my folded bathmat what I brung from home to protect
my bones from the hard floor and my scrubbing brush
swollen and sunk in my bucket oh my fucking back. And
all the detergent and bleach what I work with over the
canteen and over home after the old man where he gobs
on the floor or caught short where he can't help his self
until my fingers peel and bleed. And that cut I done myself
what weren't deep but it went bad was just my luck and
they give me a jab over the surgery what fucking hurt me
the nurse missed the first time where she weren't all that.

But the canteen is almost empty now. Before the late
shift comes in. So I ain't got to crawl round feet and under
and all what is left over the other side of drivers playing
the machines by the gents like they ain't got no homes and
only a few of the girls round the edges on earlies finishing
up on their way home. What ain't no trouble out of my
way where them girls feel for me on my knees if I am old
enough to be your grandmother and Linda sat near me in
the middle now I am getting started but she don't give a
monkeys all the girls know I am her mum.

What they give her looks working her mum like a dog
but she don't care. She is pleased with herself on her face
how she holds her head up and smiles a secret thought
pleasing her where she reckons keeping her old mum on
when I am well past my sell-by date. She thinks she is
kind. Or I would be put out to grass.

Of what comes in and goes out. She keeps track in her
ledger in columns and opens a packet of Revels I seen she
took out of her new handbag and her mouth went soft

where she was looking forward to it. What they say hard work never killed no one the first slop of water out of my bucket I look at the floor all round me through table legs to the four walls and it don't seem how I gotta wash every inch of it but I can't. How it wears you down over the old man getting to me in the night the care if you ain't sleeping since I come out of Holloway and I don't think I can go on.

But I do. However long it takes where I don't spare myself and Linda breathing down my neck whether she watched me or she never watched if it's the death of me. Because I ain't one to cut corners when a job wants doing and ain't nobody gonna say I never made a good job of it. Just let me get on with it, Linda. What reckons it ain't so hard on the knees with a deck-brush and mop but I do what I do where my eyes ain't all that. Get your feet up out of the way, Linda. On my knees I can see what I'm getting all the crap round the table legs what you can't teach an old dog.

So she kicks her feet up and rests her heels on the edge of the table and she is popping chocolates in her mouth. I slosh water out of my bucket and then I'm scrubbing and she goes ooh she goes it's good to take the weight off.

I am scrubbing the floor under Linda's chair and above me her white legs. And then she slips her feet out of her shoes and lets them drop. What almost braining me as they fall off but I dodge and they hit the floor near my puddle and she's like pick me shoes up for me would you darling while you're down there mum please don't let me shoes get in the wet.

What is a fucking joke. I'm wiping the dirty water off of the floor and rinsing the cloth and ringing it out over my bucket and Linda sighs. And has to pick up her own shoes where I won't do that for her. Then she dangles the shoes in front of me and turns round and she's like do you like me shoes, Mum? Nice, ain't they? They're new.

And looks at my feet and she goes not like the crap they bang out down Hoxton. I mean, she says, two quid a pop telling everybody you ain't got fuck all? And they make your feet stink.
– Cheers, I says.
– Well, I mean, she says. – Ain't you got no pride?
– Eh? I says.
She puts her shoes on the table and pops another chocolate in her mouth.
– Here, she says, shaking the bag at me.
I sit back for a moment on my heels. Her feet look all soft and the skin of her legs is lard white and bald like she was still a young girl.
– Don't want no chocolate, I says.
– Suit yourself, love, she says. – Ain't no skin off of mine if you cut off yours to spite your.

Then shrugs out of her jacket and slings it over the back of her chair. The fancy watch flashes on her wrist nearly four o'clock what I got one more hour. She stretches and yawns and tells me to get a move on. Her hands are smooth and white like Mother's how the old girl smothered them in cream up to the elbows and slept in cotton gloves and couldn't even peel a potato without getting a rash off of the starch on her white skin she was so proud it was prone if she was hot and scratched herself to red wealds or blotches when she caught the sun or over the park the cut grass stinging at the back of her white knees where she got me or Dolly to do it once we was big enough to stand on a chair at the sink and use the sharp knife.
What she thought all that put her above others you keep in mind of years ago of your own mother when you ain't got a clue yesterday what you said you would pop round Gina's was it on the way home or Vic's jacket out of the cleaner's for him or a pound of mince the night before

to defrost. When you get indoors and settled in a chair with a coffee in front of the telly like you'll never get up no more and that sinking feeling when you remember what you didn't of done what you promised and you gotta get up off of your arse and get going again?

Then Linda is yawning. She raises her hands above her head how her sleeves billow and I see the plump whiteness of her bare arms. Fuck me. What's that writ all up her forearm?

How could I of forgot? She got such a clump off of Tommy up the side of her head I cried what she done to herself out of ink in the bedroom with a needle where she was courting I remember that Bosey from over Murray Grove with the black hair.

Where she was still my baby. His name up her arm. And I am scrubbing the floor on all fours how I remember my mum used to scrub like her mum showed her what learnt it off of her mum before what learnt off of hers and back to the first woman in her cave with an old bit of animal skin using the bristles with water collected from a stream while her old man was out and about what nothing changes all that much.

What Linda never wanted to learn none of that off of me. When the kids was kids and they all watched me and done what I done with their skirts tucked in their knickers and on their pink knees with a rag off of an old vest of the old man's all to holes and a basin of water and a chip of Sunlight Soap what we used to use before.

But not my Linda. Ain't no cunt been born what could drag her down on her knees with a bucket of suds. What ain't a bad thing if you start as you mean to go on where no one can't shit on you what just happens when you got a man in your life and kids to run after. Our Linda ain't never wanted none of that.

With her feet up and her mouth full of chocolate. And

a silky blouse tucked in her waist and pinstriped skirt and patent belt she means business and wants you to know it.
– And I ain't being funny or nothing love but that tattoo on your arm, I can't believe you never of got rid of it. And she stares at me.
– You what?

So I turn round and tell her she oughta of got it done when they cut that thing off of her chin. That ugly mole with the sprouting hairs. I ask her why she never of got the tattoo done while she was at it.

But she never says nothing. So I thought I never meant to hurt her but me and my big mouth what runs away with me sometimes might of cut her to the quick but I don't know if that was true or she never took no notice of me what was most likely because I am a silly old woman. Anyway Linda reckons she likes that tattoo.
– Yeah? I says.
– Yeah, she says.
I ask her why and she leans her head on one side and grins at me and says it reminds her what a moron she was falling for that arsehole.
– It's a warning, she says, and pops another chocolate in her mouth. – Men! she says. – You gonna scrub that floor Mum or ain't you?

I dip my brush in my bucket. Linda smiles and lowers her eyelids like it was fond memories laughing at herself when she was young. The tears she shed over that boy you'd of thought it was him what dumped her. How it was with our Maureen and Terry Harrison. What Maureen never really got over. And Pamela Bosey up our landing pleading how her boy had nothing but respect and affection for our Linda and she was breaking his heart. The look on Linda's face while his poor mum was pleading for him. On her high horse like she was nursing the truth about Bosey what even his own mother did not know him like she did. The woman was telling me how much she would welcome Linda into her family. How happy she would be if only Linda would change her mind. Then Linda glanced over the landing and clocked Bosey. Bosey was perched on the bonnet of his new car what Pamela bought him on the never because he was all she had and she done two jobs. Linda smiled at him. I thought she was giving in. He smiled back at her and waved. She flicked her dog-end in his face.

How his mum screamed and ran down the stairs! We listened to the roar of his car as he drove away. Linda was too clever for me by half, with all her ideas. She started to cry.
– Cup of tea, Linda? I said. – Forgive and forget if you love him. He loves you, Linda. He really loves you.
She looked up at me. Her eyes were red and wet where she couldn't stop crying.
– I'm not like you, Mum, she said.
– What is that supposed to mean?
– I don't know.
– I don't understand you, Linda. Do you love him or don't you?
She blew her nose.
– It's not that, she said. – I'm trying to resist him.
I looked at her.
– You what? I said.
– I'm giving him up, she said.
I don't know why that made me so angry.
– I'm giving him up, she repeated.

Where she needn't of bothered. She shouldn't of put herself out. Because the poor sod copped it six weeks later off of a ladder cleaning his mum's windows and landed on his head. I can't even remember his first name. I knew his old man. Linda sent a beautiful card and flowers cost her half her wages when she was working at Andersons with a beautiful message in it she just dictated to the florist what writ it down in her flowery writing right off of the top of Linda's head. Sleeping peacefully in a better place. And on the way home from the florist she turned round and said she did love him, with all her heart and soul.

– Well you should of thought of that earlier, I said. – It's too fucking late now.

But that was not what she meant. She said she never regretted what she had done.

– But we gotta go to the funeral, she said.

When they lowered the coffin into the hole I kept my head down. The fresh earth banked up at the feet of the mourners was black and full of worms and I never even thought what if it was one of mine under the ground getting feasted on until I looked up and saw Pamela standing there and it hit me what the burial meant for her and for all of us if we was trying not to feel nothing in case we went down where most of us weren't strong enough to remember or even believe that we all die sooner or later and some of us sooner than others. She never even noticed us. Tears was streaming down her face where she lost her son she was breaking her heart and I wept too over mine on the cards how they lived if I lost them too. What tears was not as plentiful nor as loud as Pamela's but too much for me and people was looking if I weren't even blood to him what was in his box nor neighbours because I hardly knew him where Linda kept him away from us when they was courting for her own reasons what you can guess why she done that if she was ashamed of her own family. And I was crying for myself. When the vicar was intoning a prayer for the deceased. Until Pamela dabbed her eyes and looked up and clocked us. She screamed at Linda over the grave.

– Sleeping peacefully in a better place my arse! She screamed. – You killed him!

Linda gasped.

– He was no good, she said.

Pamela glanced at the vicar like she wanted him to weigh in on her side.

– What did you say? she said. – What did you say?

The mourners was silent. Linda shouted at the sobbing woman.

– I said he was no good.

– Please, said the vicar.

Pamela blew her nose.

– You should of thought of that before you took his ring off of him, she said.

Linda pulled the ring off of her finger and flung it across the grave. The ring hit Pamela in the chest. She opened her mouth but no words come out. The ring rolled down the stiff front of her dress and dropped in the mud at her feet. We all looked at her feet. She was wearing black patent shoes and her ankles was swollen. She got down in the dirt and dug out the ring with her hands. When she stood up the knees of her tan tights was black and her hands was all muddy. She wiped the tears out of her eyes and left a stripe of mud across her white cheek. She was sobbing as she dropped the ring into the grave.

– Bless, she said. – God bless. God forgive.

Linda leant over the grave and cleared her throat and gobbed on the coffin. Pamela flew at her across the foot of the grave and tried to push her over. But Linda was too strong. She was only seventeen but she had a punch on her like all my kids can handle themselves when the time comes. Nobody takes the piss out of my kids. Pamela got a fat lip and Linda walked away, laughing and crying. Pamela looked down at her feet.

– My shoes. My new shoes, she sobbed.

My daughter strode across the cemetery towards the gates with her nose in the air. I pushed through the mourners to keep up, trying not to smile where Linda made a show of us like that but also she thought she was fucking magnificent and nobody could take that away from her. I thought she was magnificent. The mourners was tutting and muttering and enjoying the palaver was a relief after we was all getting the miseries thinking what if one of our own.

– Who does she think she is sitting in judgement and him only gone five minutes I mean it's not as if…

– It's not as if she was… I heard she…

– Never!

– When she was thirteen? Or was that the other one? The sister? People in glass houses…

Linda turned all of a sudden and raised her hand like she was going to make a speech and all the mourners went quiet to listen to her. You could hear big clods of earth thudding onto the coffin. All them people was agog, like they just could not wait to hear what would happen next, but Linda never said nothing. She couldn't think of nothing to say to them. She lowered her hand and called out to me across the graveyard.

– Let's get home, she shouted. – I'm famished. I could eat an horse.

An horse! I am scrubbing the canteen floor what I am good at and I hate it and who can blame me but I can't help myself how Linda strolled away from all them muttering women through the graveyard like she was leaving misery behind. Where she had made up her mind she never had no use for none of it.

And now she is lighting up and leaning back in her chair and puffing smoke-rings out of her mouth.

– What's so funny? she asks.

– You got a rule against smiling now?

– But when we was kids you used to kneel on an old towel

then, she says. – On the brown lino, before Vic put down
that nice bit of vinyl for you.

– What are you on about?

– Your knees used to go all red, she says. – You tucked
your skirt in your knickers to keep it out of the dirty water.
I hated the sight of the lumpy blue veins up the back of
your legs. I'm lucky, I've never suffered like that. I suppose
you never of got the chance to put your feet up when you
was carrying. I don't know why you didn't just…

– Just what?

Linda grins at me.

– You know what I mean, she says.

I scrub the wet floor so hard I make a hole in the lino
at the seam where it is wearing thin. I move the bucket to
cover the hole.

– You used to sing sometimes, didn't you, Mum, doing the
kitchen floor? she goes. – Or did I make that up?

Linda is laughing.

– Sing? I says.

– Yeah, she says. – And sometimes I used to ride on your
back.

I drop my brush and stand up and lean on the edge of a
table. I start to cough. Linda thumps me on the back.

– Ow! I says.

– What? says Linda.

– That hurts, I says.

– Sorry, says Linda. – You all right?

– I'm worried about the old man, I goes. – Dr Patel give
him some more of them pills.

Linda looks down at her polished nails.

– Yeah? she says.

– He's not well, Linda.

– I know that, Mum. He'll be all right. No good fretting
over it. He's an old man and he ain't never looked after
himself.

– We've been married fifty years come Christmas, I says.
– Fifty years! says Linda. – Well! We gotta have a knees-up.
I'll book the community hall. Get Victor to do the disco.
Karaoke. One of my special buffets.

I kneel again and dip my scrubbing brush in the
bucket. Linda points at the floor.
– You missed a bit, love, she says.
I slop water over the floor with my rag, scrub the wet
patch with my scrubbing brush, squeeze out the rag and
swab up the dirty water, rinse out the dirty cloth.
– Mum? What's that smell? Says Linda. – Bleach? How
much bleach you got in that bucket? You'll burn holes in
the fucking floor.
– Don't you tell me how to do my work, I says.
– Hard to get work off of the cards, says Linda. – Cash in
hand and that. I'm doing you a fucking favour at your age.
All the thanks I get.

Linda grins. She pays me two pound twenty five pence
an hour. Maureen gets two pounds where she is only her
sister there ain't no love lost between and I am her mum.
– Fucking slave driver, I says.
Linda raises her eyebrows.
– Well, she says. – If you don't like it you know what you
can do.

But I never said nothing because Maureen comes
across the canteen to tell me goodbye she has been on
since six and it's time for her to go home.
– We was just saying, says Linda. – Her and the old man's
been married fifty years this Christmas.
– I know, says Maureen.

So I stand up again and drop my scrubbing brush in
my bucket. My knees hurt and my back is killing me.
– What is the cat's mother, I says.

Then Linda starts telling Maureen all what she is
planning of cake and a finger buffet and crab sticks and

jellied eels and all that what she thinks is my favourite
but nobody never asked me what I wanted to eat or drink
on my big day. Nobody ever asks me. Not that I weren't
grateful to her but still. And Maureen puts her arm round
my shoulder like she can see what I am thinking and
then we are holding hands what sets Linda off where she
reckons our Maureen ain't never done nothing for me and
Linda is the one what I owes her. So I tell her to sssh but
she reckons I always liked Maureen more than I liked her.
She says I am off my rocker celebrating fifty years married
to my Tommy and nine kids where she is so glad she never
got married and asks me what the fuck that cunt ever did
for me.

Terry Harrison was still on the buses. Not down our way
but over Catford why no one ain't seen him for years until
he packed that in and moved over here. I thought some
driver walked in the canteen and got what was left of our
Linda's famous pie and chips and beans warmed over off of
Aggie a couple of minutes before we stopped serving what
was the spit of Terry with a bit of a gut on him and the
arse of his trousers all shiny where they spend all day in
the driving seat but he sat down right over the back by the
fruit machines and he smiled at me and it was that same
old smile.

What is so corny I know but it all come back. Not just
how I used to look at his face when he was sleeping and fill
up with love for him to overflowing so I had to wake him
up and show him how I felt about him or give him ideas
so he would show me but how he was so good to me. So
fucking good to me like no cunt from round our way was
ever like that even to his own mother.

So it was all porkies about Terry Harrison what Linda

said with his mad brother on the Costa del Sol. Terry Harrison pushed his knife and fork together on his plate and pushed his plate away. I noticed he left a great fat slab of Linda's shiny pastry how could he resist. He opened his newspaper and drank tea out of one of her white cups.

Terry Harrison was just the same old Terry Harrison sitting behind his newspaper in his bus driver's trousers like it was yesterday he told me he loved me. Like it was yesterday we walked side by side down Hoxton to the Queen's of an evening and by his side I knew everyone was looking at me he was so handsome and kind to me I felt loved.

We used to play darts together. Sometimes he beat me, sometimes I beat him. Why did he dump me? I thought he loved me. In the canteen I felt so stupid like it was yesterday he didn't want me no more. I could feel my face hot and red over the anger of it after all the years since I longed for him what everyone in Hoxton knew I was broken-hearted only shit-bags looked twice at me because I was second-hand goods now and every one knew. Why was he smiling at me?

Don't get me wrong I ain't one to complain but after our Maureen left I thought I was never gonna finish that fucking floor. With food up my nose all day and the gristle and that scraped off of the side of the plate where they spit out those bits in my Linda's lamb like the filters of Vic's roll-ups in his special wallet off of his boys in his scout troop scraped in the bucket where the sour cabbage and the old man coughing phlegm and germs and the bad smell off of his leg is more than enough to turn anyone what is worse of a night-time but I think I could eat something tonight where I am feeling a bit better not for

no reason but just because I am so fucking hungry all of a
sudden what has got to mean something.

Where Maureen says I got to keep my strength up. I
can't live off of fags and coffee and my sherbet lemons
what I do like a sherbet lemon and a sit down on the chair
after I seen to my Tommy and have a flick through my
book where I think I deserve a sit down after the day I've
had. It ain't the end of the world I let my place go where
you can't measure a person how clean is the carpet in your
front room of an evening what don't mean I don't give the
place a going-over in the morning and give Tom a wash
and his tablets and that before work where there's only so
much you can do and I don't care what nobody says any
different. And it ain't my fault as soon as my back's turned
where my Tommy is past caring.

Vic reckoned he was doing us a bit of liver and bacon
tonight was it what my Tom used to be partial before with
mash and the greasy bits out of the pan and button mush
if we was to push the boat out me working all hours like
a dog Vic said since I got out. After six weeks of that shit
they dish up in there what I done of my sentence I was
skin and bone even them off of the streets half-starved and
grateful for a bed and a bit of dinner gag trying to get it
down you. What with the worry of the old man on top of
everything else and poor Billy out there without me and
the thought of our Alan if he ain't careful I could go on the
turn against him. Where he never give two shits about me.
And never once come to visit what made me waste a V.O.

Or was it tomorrow Vic said he was in the kitchen. You
can say what you like but after he's been in there it is so
clean I don't remember my Tommy never even made his
self a sandwich where he only come in the kitchen in his
vest waiting for a clean shirt off of the ironing board and
likes to watch me ironing it for him all the years we been
together makes him feel how a man likes the smell of it

in his vest singing to me about the smoothing iron on a Monday morning she stole my heart away.

Let alone cook a dinner and dish it up all nice on a tray with a sheet of kitchen roll in front of the telly what we never had no roll before Victor moved in but he gets it his self out of the Co-op when it was on special where he said he couldn't live without kitchen roll. He puts a finish on the sink and drainer out of the showroom the Boy Scout in him like a new pin before he even sits his self down even if it do curl up a bit round the edges keeping warm in a low oven with the door open a little bit to stop it from. I could fancy a nice bit of liver and bacon. Or over the chippy if not or Chinese ain't too bad if you stick to what you know. Victor might treat us what I do for that man like a member of my family including his washing over the launderette if he don't take mine since way back when Susan done the off and I give him her room and nobody can't say we ain't fond of each-other.

Something flashing it were staircase lighting on the blink from the bus-stop after my shift or blue lights nee naw nee naw in the flats. It was a long day. I thought I'd never fucking finish. The old man's tins in a carrier bag out of the offy banging up my legs oh no where I'm trying to run so I can see what is going on. My feet my poor feet the ambulance parked in the grounds no and all them blue faces Aggie and Aggie's Mick over the landing in the light what the fuck. Is Vic creeping along the forecourt. Is it. Creeping under the overhang in his vest and those khaki shorts what his arms soft white arms pucker in the cold where he was too rushed to pull on his cardigan.
– Nonce.
What is my Tommy shouting. They got my old man.
– Nonce.
The old man is shouting at Victor. The old man is strapped down on a stretcher and they are trying to load him in

the back of the ambulance. I am running and Tommy is struggling and flailing his arms. How he has decided to try and sit up in the blue light spinning off of the top of the ambulance. Then Victor puts his hand on Tommy. Vic is trying to calm him.

– Nonce, Tom shouts.

I am elbowing my way through. The ambulance men shove Victor out of the way. My Tom is in the back of the ambulance. Vic is backing off towards the staircase. Our Susan is screaming somewhere out of the crowd what is my neighbours and friends all of them people what I am one of where they all know me and accept me for what I am. Looking at me now and looking away like I'm just some woman. I climb in the ambulance.

– Mum! Susan screams.

But I am sitting down in the ambulance next to my Tommy and holding his hand.

– Lie down, Tom, I says.

Aggie and Aggie's Mick and Alan's Sandra leaning over the landing having a good look what is happening to me and my Tommy. And her who lives up the end of my landing works in the dentist and twin sons watching me from the bottom steps of the staircase. Like we are something off of the telly. Her boys are crying. She slaps them up the back of the legs.

And our Alan peering out of his kitchen window into the back of the ambulance where my Tom is bellowing. I keep on telling myself if Tom got the strength to make all that racket he got the strength to live.

Then our Billy is moving forward out of the crowd on crutches.

– Mum. Mum.

Like I need any of that just now what with Tom like he is and Susan is hopping about on the cracked tarmac of the forecourt flashing her scabby legs in the blue light.

– Mum. Mum.

Do they not have no respect? Don't answer that question. I sigh and open my purse.

– How much? I ain't got much, I says.

– Ten? Five? Anything, Susan begs.

– And what about me? What was Billy making sure he never of got left out.

I fling some coins out of the back of the ambulance. The doors of the ambulance shut. I look at Tom. His face is purple. The bad meat smell off of his leg is choking.

– Help me, he shouts.

– Don't be frightened, stupid, I says.

Tom begins to cry.

– Mae'n flin da fi, he cries.

– Do me a favour, I says.

And looks away from my Tommy through the back window of the ambulance at the crowd outside the flats where Billy and Susan are scrabbling on hands and knees. With Billy's bad leg dragging behind racing each other to pick up my money where it has fallen. Alan leans out of his window and flicks a dog-end at them. What the sparks off of it scatter on the ground.

– Arseholes, Alan shouts.

The siren begins to wail.

– Hold my hand, says Tom.

– I am holding your hand, I says.

The ambulance man reckons my Tom needs something for the pain. I turn away as he slides a needle in his arm. I look at the bleeping monitor.

– Help me, Tom screams.

– What happened? I ask.

– My heart, says Tom. – Pain in me fucking heart.

The ambulance man fits a mask over Tom's face.

– That'll shut him up, I says.

Tom pulls the mask off of his face and slowly turns his

head towards me. I smile at him and squeeze his hand. He blinks and looks in my eyes.

– Where were you, you cunt? he says.

A HACKNEY CHILDHOOD

By Maggie Thomas

MY CHILDHOOD was so harsh it has taken me the best part of my adult life to get over it. My parents never showed me no affection – talk about poverty, talk about over-crowding. Kids today don't know they're born.

There were just too many of us, five girls and four boys in a three bedroom, it was always cold as I remember it and not enough of anything to go round. I'm not saying we went hungry, but because we were on the free school meals my mum reckoned we never needed another dinner of a night-time, it was help yourself to bread and marge even though she could of managed to scrape something together if she had put her mind to it. I got this empty feeling inside of me that has been with me as long as I can remember.

Friday nights after closing time my father came home and gave my mum a clump. All them brothers of mine and not one of them lifted a finger if he wanted to batter her. They just let him get on with it.

If one of us girls got in his way we got a clump too. But in the morning he was begging forgiveness in Welsh, his first language, and more or less his only one – it was hard to believe that he'd been living in Hackney since he was nineteen.

The scrubbing he gave himself Saturday mornings

was his penance where he used carbolic in the bath like he hoped the soap might wash away all what had gone on in the night of his drinking and violence. He made a right mess of shaving and his hands shook so bad he could not do up his shirt buttons. He wouldn't go out of a Saturday morning without a proper shirt she always found time to iron for him, and a dark blue blazer with brass buttons to look smart that she sponged and pressed under a cloth. I remember the smell off of his grey slacks drawn out by the heat of the iron while he stood in his underpants in the kitchen and waited before he took her out for a stroll down Hoxton, Saturday dinner-time, then back over the pub.

I used to be so angry she didn't sling him out on his ear or take us and run, but what she said she made her vows, nothing he did would change that. And anyway, where could we go?

Her mum and dad were dead. She said she got her wages off of him regular every Friday after work before he went in the pub if he was in work, even if she did have to stand on the pub doorstep and bar his way until he put his hand in his pocket. He never grudged her little bit of fun over the bingo and he never went with another woman, the whole of their married life, as husbands go she could of done worse.

My first night away from home I remember how much room there was in the bed. It was just the two of us, me and my new husband together not like at home with me and Maureen and Linda and Georgina top to tail in the double what I was used to and Susan in her little cot.

But my husband turned out to be no good like my father. Although with him it was drugs not drink. We had four kids before he died, the coroner ruled he poisoned himself with bad gear. He was only twenty-four. I found him in the front room with his thumb in his mouth where they blow and blow to get a vein up and the needle

still hanging out of his neck. Luckily the kids were still asleep. He was always just about to knock it on the head.

His death made me wake up and seek help to understand the feelings inside of me. I am now involved in a self-help group for the families of addicts and I have trained as a counsellor so I can give help to others, who have suffered like myself.

As a child I was afraid for my mum that one day my old man would go too far. Now after almost fifty years of marriage he is seriously ill. Day and night my mum sits by his hospital bed, holding his hand and talking to him, trying to keep him alive. Sometimes he can speak, other times he is unconscious.

My family is planning a big do for my parents' golden wedding at Christmas. Here's hoping for my mother's sake my father lasts that long.

I am telling my story not to hurt my parents, both of whom I forgive from the bottom of my heart, but to show others that it is possible to recover from a difficult childhood and break the cycle of neglect and abuse.

—And for the one hundred and fifty quid the magazine pays out each week for the star letter, says Linda.

– Not bad for a load of old crap scribbled on the back of an envelope, says Georgina.

My mum snatches the magazine off of Linda and flaps it at Maggie across the hospital bed.

– How could you, Maggie? she says. – How could you?

Maggie shrugs.

– Neglect and abuse? What do you know about neglect and abuse? says Georgina. – We was always loved.

– Did you have to read it out, Linda? I says. – Ain't the old woman got enough on her plate?

– It's her book, Maureen, says Maggie. – The one she gets every week. She would of seen it anyway. What's the difference?

– Look at the photo of me, says Gina. – I look a right state.

– And while you're at it washing our dirty linen in public what about poor Susan? I says. – Decided to keep that little story to yourself?

– I didn't want her to find out in a magazine, says Maggie.

– So fucking considerate, says Georgina.

– When were you planning to tell her? I says.

– When it's the right time.

– Don't tell her, says Mum. – She don't need all that.

– She ain't stupid, I says. – She ain't a kid no more.

Maggie turns and looks at me.

– Don't tell me you went and took it on yourself, she says.

– I ain't said nothing, Maggie, I says.

– So what are you on about? she says.

– I mean why she does what she does, I says. – How she lives. Ain't you never asked yourself?

Mum is peering at the magazine article.

– Whom I forgive from the bottom of my heart? she reads.

– Whom I forgive? Do you think our Susan will forgive you when she finds out?

– That weren't me what writ that, says Maggie. – They put that bit in for me. I don't forgive either of yous what happened to me. Not you nor the old man.

The old woman covers her mouth with her hand. Raymond stares at her. Maggie shrugs her shoulders and stands up.

– I don't know why I fucking bother, she says.

Mum takes off her glasses and wipes her eyes with her sleeve.

– At least I kept all my kids, she says.

The old man stirs in his bed. Mum stuffs the magazine in her bag.

– Do you think he heard all what we said about our Susan? she whispers.

– Nah, I says. – I don't think so.

The old man groans.

– Tom? Tommy?

But he don't open his eyes. His lips stretch and crumple over the hole of his mouth where no one ain't popped his teeth in for him.

– Can't hear you, Mum shouts. – You gotta speak up, love.

The old man lifts his hand slowly and points at his mouth.

– Where my hearing ain't all that no more Maureen, she says. – I can't make out a fucking word.

My dad's lips are the colour of liver.

– What is he trying to say?

I lean over the old man to listen and feel his faint breath in my ear.

– He's only asking for a fucking drink!

My mum pours some water into a plastic beaker from the lidded jug on the bedside cabinet. My dad opens one eye behind her back like he is winking at me. I don't know if he is smiling or what.

– Drop of water, Tom? she says.

He closes his eye as she turns towards him. She perches on the bed and cradles his head against her chest.

– There you go, she says, holding the beaker to his lips. The old man takes a sip and swallows.

– Well fuck me, says my mum. – He ain't never took a drop of water off of me before. Where he wakes in the night with a thirst on him he goes mad if I ain't got no more tins. You think that's a good sign?

Raymond laughs. Mother smiles at the old man and touches the beaker to his lips again. We've all been waiting seventeen days now since he was took bad. His chest weren't right even before all what he done in his life took its toll on him. Where he ain't never give a fuck how to look after his self nor no one else while I'm pointing the finger.

What is the upshot if a man drinks he ain't a good father whatever love he might hide from his kids deep in his heart where it ain't no use to no cunt. Whatever love bubbles up as tears what always caused me to lose touch of my own sorrow. After he set about me with a stick or that time he bit me. Like his tears was never gonna stop. So muggins ended up thinking it was all my fault. Where he was blubbering, the self-same carry-on with me what he done to my mum.

No, the old man don't look all that. His big dirty head pressed sideways against my mum's beige and black cardigan with a white pattern on it of zigzags and buttons out of brown wood. The balled tissues in her pocket by his ear showing through the loose knit, her ringed hand on his yellow cheek. Where she is helping him swallow another mouthful of water.

What he brung on himself. How his liver is only a fifth what it ought to function cleaning the blood the doctor reckoned what ain't clean no more. Why he is yellow. And red boils all the shit in his blood erupting the pump of his heart if one of the valves leaks and arteries what he choked up for his self and his kidney packed up and lungs rattling and bubbles of red foam and mucus out of the drain in his chest and out of his nose what slides down a see-through tube under the bed.

And the drip in the back of his hand dripping to fight the inflammation of his chest infection. With glucose and saline to keep him going and morphine for the pain management and something for the shakes now he ain't drinking no more what the doctor said we don't want him climbing the walls or screaming if he sees spiders on the ceiling he might frighten the horses. And it's too late now to cut off his leg.

– Tommy, says my mum. – Can you hear me?
My dad opens his mouth. Water dribbles down the front of her cardigan. She wipes him with a paper towel and lays his head back on his pillow.
– Can you hear me Tom?
– I think he's sleeping, I says.
She dabs at the front of her cardigan. My dad blinks and opens his eyes.
– Nora, he says.
– Oh Tommy. How you feeling?
My dad looks at me.
– What does she want? he barks.
– They've come up to see you, Tommy.
The old man heaves himself up in the bed.
– Get my Susan up here quick before I die, he says.

– Fuck sake, says Maggie.
– You ain't gonna die, Thomas.
– Hello Dad, says Raymond.
My dad closes his eyes and lets his self sink back down in
the bed.
– Dad? I says.
– Leave him, says Linda. – Let him rest.
– You better find Susan, says my mum.
– Me? says Raymond.
– You, she says. – There's a good boy.
– I don't know how, says Raymond. – Where she gets
about and all that these days.
– Ask Victor, says Linda.
– Please Susan, my dad whispers.

No I don't know why the old man was like that over her
more than he loved any of us. Since he was took bad she
was the only one what never bothered to pop up to him in
the hospital. Apart from Billy and my Tony but you know
what he's like. Even our Alan shifted his self.

Where Maggie never showed all that much when
she was carrying the old man never clocked. In a black
skirt of our Linda's unzipped and hitched up round her
middle and a big fluffy top over it so all what you saw was
a big kid with skinny legs swimming in those high white
wet-look sock-boots I would of given my eye-teeth with
a flower out of four petals on the toe she borrowed off of
Maxine Webster and never give back. Because the old man
never knocked no sense into her what a father says to his
daughter if he gives two shits. You can't go out dressed like
that. Your skirt is so short your arse is shining out of the
bottom of it.

So it was all down to our mum. What was the size of a
house where she was carrying Raymond at the same time.
But Maggie never took no notice of no one.

– Make me, she says. – Fucking make me. You and whose army?

We never had no idea who with or where she went or if there was more than one she never knew who to pin it on. She never brought a boy home. I heard my mum trying to winkle it out of her but she never let on. All she kept on saying leave off of me Mum I never enjoyed it.

– Hear that, Maureen? my mum says. – She reckons she never enjoyed it.

– Don't believe me then, says Maggie.

What I was thinking how could she of let herself get knocked up by some silly boy. Catch me letting anyone mess about with me like that. Some silly boy sticking his thing up you. And they was always after your tits, what I heard off of Julie. Leaving tooth-marks and that. I weren't never gonna let nobody do me.

Not that the old man wouldn't of belted it out of Maggie who she was going with if he had of clocked she was like it but he never clocked. And there was me thinking Maggie must of been with one of the boys from the flats. Or Christy McMahon what loved her since in the Juniors from the White Horse where his dad let him take crisp and nuts from behind the bar and all what he had away out of the cellar under his dad's nose when his dad was pissed remember that Strongbow in big brown glass bottles Maggie reckoned tastes like sick if you sicked up over it once then you gotta hold your nose next time to get it down you.

Or them what used to play out over the lock-ups at the back Maggie let them for sweets or fags or what she could get that Johnny Stevens or Petey Stevens when they went down to their uncle over the minicab Clapton to cream tips off of the drivers for cleaning the cabs what Maggie said a quick feel was worth two bob of anyone's money but reckoned she never once let none of them boys go no further.

Until my mum went down on her knees looking for a sock where our Georgina could only find one sock for school and dragged all baby things out from under and dumped them on the bed.

– What have we here? she said.

Them baby things was all new. In dirty packets of the fluff and dust what ended up. What Maggie made out like it was all a present off of her boss's other half over the pet-food stall down Chapel Street she worked of a Saturday where they never had no kids of their own so why wouldn't they spoil our Maggie rotten.

– You told the dog meat man? said my mum.

– Nah, said Maggie. – I never told him. She put two and two together. After my dinner over the pie shop Saturday I never fancied a pie but it was her treat where she told me something she didn't oughtn't of told me over a bellyful of steaming mash and liquor what all rose up inside of me and landed back in my plate. But I ain't worried. She won't say nothing. Because I know all what she gets up to when he is down his dad's to help his old man with his shopping and all that she can't contain herself when the stall ain't too busy creaming herself over that millet salesman from Loughton in my ear-hole what she says is hung like a horse I mean people in glass houses where the dog meat man ain't a nice person when riled she knows it would be more than her life's worth.

What shocked the old woman Maggie could talk like that. But six vests and six pairs of white leggings and a pixie bonnet out of red wool with white picot edging and six white nighties with ribbon ties what babies used to wear in them days and two matinee jackets with teddy-bear buttons and matching bootees and a pale fawn and orange and lime green pram blanket for a girl or a boy with soft fringes of twisted wool our Maggie let me twirl round my fingers more than my mum ever had for any of her babies. How we all knew it was not kids our Maggie was messing with.

– He must really care about you, Maggie, I said.

– Fuck off, said Maggie. – If he really cared about me he would of give me something for MYSELF!

Side by side on the chair in the front room my mum looked too old for all that and too knackered after seven kids already and our Maggie looked too young. My mum was resting her mug of tea on the hump of her belly. Maggie was lighting a fag. I thought it was disgusting they must of both been at it what made me wonder about my mum. Where I never heard much through the wall no more just the old man's cough and hawking stuff up out of his chest and flobbing it in the pot if I never give it much thought I would of sworn they was well past it. But that was where I was wrong wasn't I?

– I'm off out, said Maggie.

– No you ain't, said my mum. – You should stop in of an evening and rest yourself in your condition.

– I only done it the once, said Maggie. – And I'm paying for it now. I know I done wrong. No need to rub my nose in it.

– You need to rest, said my mum. – What ain't no punishment. Or none intended.

– Sod that, said Maggie.

– Where you going? I said.

– To play ping pong. Down the Feathers. I gotta get out and enjoy myself while I still got the chance.

– Can I come?

– Nah, said Maggie. – I don't think so Maureen.

Across the back of her thighs when she reached up to do her lipstick in the mirror I saw the red weald where the edge of the chair had dug in.

– I worry about you, that's all, said my mum. – Getting into trouble and that.

– Trouble? said Maggie.

Her pale lipstick made her face look dirty.

– Yes, said my mum. – Trouble. You know?

– Yes, I do know, said Maggie. – But that's one thing you ain't got nothing to worry about on that score no more ain't it. Where I am in the club already? I mean it's too late now.

Then she managed to screw a tanner out of my mum for her subs over the Feathers what she reckoned she was in arrears with the youth club and my mum just opened her purse. Billy and Alan must of been playing out what they got up to in the flats and that as they was boys and big enough to look after their selves if they never come back until after it got dark and my mum hollered for them.

Linda and Georgina was melting white fat to fry chips in the kitchen where I had done us a plate of bread and jam for our tea but they was both late in from school so I ate it on the floor by the fire, roasting my legs and reading Titbits with a gut-ache all that mouthfuls of soft bread with a thick scrape of marge and red jam out of a tin what was a shame to let it go to waste. In the haze of hot fat melting through the open hatch I sifted through the dog-ends in the ashtray by my mum's feet but she had smoked every fag to death. And all that was left of the old man's roll-ups was ashes and little screws of sodden paper where he sucked and sucked until he burnt his fingers.

So Linda and Georgina was eating chips in the kitchen and the old man was dozing on the chair with my mum's head lolled on his shoulder. Then I heard Maggie's boots stomping along the landing on her way home. She come in and leant against the wall just inside the front room door. I thought she was lucky they was both asleep.

– That was quick, I said.

She never said nothing. She was looking at the telly.

– Don't wake them up, I said.

– I ain't fucking stupid, she said. – Whatever you lot might think.

– Because you got all shit on your face, I said.

– Yeah?

– Yeah. And your legs is all dirty.

Maggie tugged at her top.

– Twos up on your gum, I said.

Maggie pulled a lump off of her gum and flung it at me.

– Ta, love, I said.

She chewed. I chewed. She sparked up a fag.

– Twos up on your fag, I said.

– It's me last one.

She stretched her gum out of her mouth and snapped it back in. She poked her tongue into it and blew.

– You frightened? I said.

Maggie's bubble popped. She peeled the gum off of her cheeks and chin and put it back in her mouth.

– What?

– When the baby comes out?

– Shut up, said Maggie.

– Hope it ain't a big baby, I said. – Big ones is supposed to hurt more.

– Like you're the fucking expert.

– I'd be shitting myself if it was me. Any minute now, ain't it?

– Four weeks.

– Was he nice? I asked.

– Who? said Maggie.

– Why did you let him?

– Leave it out, Maureen.

– I'll help you, I said.

She laughed.

– What? I said.

– How you gonna help me?
– You gonna breast-feed it?
– Fuck off, Maureen.

Maggie squelched her gum round her mouth and blew. My piece of gum was too small. The pink smell coming off of it. Her bubble popped and woke up my mum.
– Get upstairs, Maggie, said the old woman. – Before the old man sees you like that.
– Make me.
– I could swing for you sometimes.

I heard the hot fat swell when Linda dropped more chips in the pan. Maggie stood right in front of the old man and stuck her hand up her jumper and scratched herself. Her jumper rose up and I got a good look at the blue veins of her belly where the white skin was stretched tight over the baby. A brown line cut her in half long-ways from her belly button into her knickers where her skirt was unzipped and gaping underneath.
– What do you want? I asked. – A girl or a boy?
– Fuck off, Maureen.

The old man snorted in his sleep and opened his eyes. Maggie pulled down her jumper. The old man closed his eyes again.
– I hope it's a girl, said my mum. – For your sake. And I hope she never brings no trouble to our door. What would be a fucking miracle under the circumstances.

Maggie raised her shoulder to wipe her nose.
– I am itching all over, she said.
– That's what happens, said my mum. – Bet you ain't had nothing to eat neither.
– I had chips on the way back from the Feathers if you don't mind, said Maggie, sniffing. – What is my business and ain't none of yourn.
– No need to be like that.

– I'm just saying.

My mum lit another cigarette.

– And you got dirty knees, she said.

– It's raining out, said Maggie. – The puddle mud got splashed all up the back of my legs. Where I was walking home across that strip of grass. And I tripped up. I fell over. It was dark on the grass and I never saw that little fence.

– You wanna be more careful, said the old woman, and picked up her magazine.

The old man was muttering. The palms of Maggie's hands was grass green like when we was little kids she used to make out she was a gee-gee playing giddy-up over the park with me on her back.

– Don't he never give you no peace, Maggie? said Linda, coming in from the kitchen with a plate of chips.

– Do you have to, Linda? said my mum, looking up from her book.

– What? I said.

– Still trying to pretend it was the immaculate fucking conception? said Linda.

– The fucking what? I said.

My mum swiped me over the side of my head.

– If you never of buried your head in the sand this might never of happened, said Linda.

– You what?

– Well, said Linda, looking at my mum with her head on one side.

– So it's all my fault now is it? Don't you dare try and put this on me, Linda. It ain't my fault she's like she is.

– Don't talk about me like I ain't here, said Maggie.

– Well, said my mum.

– Give us a chip, Linda, I said.

My mum lit a new fag off of the butt of the old one.

– But you never warned us, Mother, said Linda. – You

never learnt us nothing.
– What?
– We ain't kids no more.
Mum laughed.
– In my day you used to get a slap if you talked dirty, she said. – All that fucking talk. It ain't nice.
– I'm going to bed, said Linda.
– Me an all, said Georgina.

Mum rested her fag on the edge of the ashtray and hugged herself. I took a couple of quick drags.
– Tell Aggie to phone the ambulance, Maureen, she said.
I stubbed out her cigarette.
– What? I said.
– The pains, she said. – It's started.
I stood up.
– Get yourself cleaned up, Maggie, said Mum. – You'd better come up the hospital with me.
– I wanna go to bed, said Maggie.
    I popped next door to Aggie. She let me dial 999 on her red telephone. I could hear my mum shouting at Maggie through the wall. Afterwards Aggie's Mick give me a warm sweet out of his pocket. Mick asked me if I was courting.
– Leave her alone, Mick, said Aggie. – She's only a kid.
    When I got back indoors the old woman was still shouting.
– Maureen is too young, Maggie, she said. – Just do what you're fucking told for once in your life. I can't go up the hospital on my own. Linda and Georgina are in bed. Fetch me bag down off of the top of my wardrobe. Wash your fucking legs.
– I wanna go to bed, said Maggie.
    Mum bent over with the pain. Maggie sighed and stomped up the stairs to get the bag.
– I'll come up the hospital with you, I said.

– Nah, said my mum, pushing me away. – Just leave me alone.

I sat down on the chair next to my dad. I could hear Maggie's angry footsteps thump in my mum's bedroom, then she must of turned on the tap in the bathroom to wash her face and wipe down her legs.

– Will you move it? Mum shouted.

– Why pick on me? said Maggie, coming down the stairs.

– Why me?

– Because you might fucking learn something, said Mum.

But Maggie never learned nothing. It all went too quick. She was sulking on the way to the hospital then it was like my mum set her off. They was both at it, heaving and groaning in the back of the ambulance. By the time they got to the maternity ward Maggie was wheeled screaming out of the lift into the delivery room.

Lucky for Maggie she had Susan almost the same time my mum had Raymond. So my mum come back from hospital to the old man with both babies. Making out like she had had twins. A boy and a girl. Wonderful. One small and fair and the other huge and bald as a fucking egg.

But no one was trying to make out like the twins was identical. In real life Raymond and Susan weren't even born on the same day. Maggie had hers first so tiny what they had to incubate while Mum was having our Raymond what got stuck. My mum's contractions just stopped. Maggie never even needed no stitches. After they took Susan away she got down off of the delivery bed, had a wash, and popped in to see the old woman.

– Ain't yourn out yet? she asked. – I dropped mine already. What was you gonna learn me?

And she went to school the morning after like nothing had happened. But Raymond wouldn't come out. In the end they give my mum a general anaesthetic and took the forceps to the baby's head. By which time she got over it the other baby was ready to come home.

Poor Maggie was only thirteen. She never wanted a baby. She give up Susan to our mum to be brought up as a sister until Maggie was old enough what was not uncommon in them days not like now they have special schools and all that for school-girl mums to help them keep their babies what is reckoned to be for the best all round. And Maggie give my mum a cut off of her wages towards Susan's milk and that what the dog meat man raised her Saturday money where his wife tried to take Maggie under her wing on a hiding to nowhere and backing the wrong horse if she thought she would get back any respect.

Not that Maggie never wanted our Susan but she never wanted no baby. The baby was taken off of her and put in an incubator before she even got a chance to give it a cuddle. Maggie never found out whether Susan was lovable or not lovable. It was nothing to do with the baby, what the baby was like.

How Susan cried in front of all them people in that clinic that time the social paid for her to go in rehab she asked me to go down there and sit in on a family meeting and every single person in that group was chain-smoking including me.

Susan cried and said she had always felt unlovable. Although she had no idea her sister was her mother and her mother was her nan. So I said I can't speak for nobody else but I always loved you Susan from the first moment I held you in my arms. Some babies make you feel like that. You was in my head and my heart all day long at school what was a joke anyway over Shoreditch where I sat at the back and waited for home-time. And as soon as the bell went I was over the road and up the landing and played with you and give you your bottle and changed you like you was mine and I used to curl up in your cot with you when you couldn't settle.

But Susan couldn't hear me what I was saying. She sat in the group and she was crying across the circle from me nobody loves me sob nobody loves me sob sob until I wanted to slap her all them people thinking we didn't love one of our own.

Even though the old man always favoured her. He never played with any of us when we was small but he used to throw Susan up in the air and catch her and laugh and laugh and nuzzle in her neck until she almost wet herself and ran screaming to the toilet. What was hard for poor Raymond. What was a bit slow where the cord got caught round his neck restricting the blood to his brain at birth and my mum was no spring chicken neither when she fell what probably never helped. Looking up at the old man playing with little Susan on his knee you could see it on Raymond's puzzled face he was waiting and waiting and waiting for his turn.

Where Maggie was out every night my mum let her go like she had any say in the matter because Maggie got too moody if she stayed in and we was all glad to see the back of her. Maggie wanted to enjoy herself and my mum was hoping that giving birth must of learnt her not to fall again what was a laugh really seeing as my mum kept on falling. Where we all thought Maggie would take Susan when she got married and left home. My mum was going to find a way to tell the old man. Then I kept on thinking Maggie would come for Susan once she got settled. It weren't Maggie's fault. She knew Susan was happy at home with the old man doting on her where he never give a toss about any of his own kids.

So Maggie left Susan behind when she went like she believed the story my mum told the old man the baby was his little daughter. What called my mum Mummy and called the old man Daddy. Sitting on his knee and reaching up with her little hands to pat his big red face. With the gold baby rings on her dimpled fingers he bought down Bethnal Green for his little princess where he never bought us nothing.

What Maggie thought she done for the best. Not to unsettle the poor kid. And I looked out for her as much as I could look out for her where I tried to watch her back but she was so headstrong and hell-bent on going her own way. But I done my best to take care of her. And I never wanted Maggie to take her because I loved her and Maggie never had all that much to offer. What ain't to say nothing against that Peter Lucas Maggie shacked up with what was a gentle person and done his best in spite of his bad situation. And he was always polite to me when I used to pop up to Maggie sometimes with Susan in her pram where Lucas played peep-o with her even if he had no idea Maggie was her real mum. He was a quiet and tidy person. And he never once wanted no money off of me. Not that I had fuck all if he had of asked me. What was probably why he never of bothered.

The monitor is bleeping. Raymond wants to know why is the old man so yellow.
– Because he ain't well, says my mum.
– Why? says Raymond.
– Don't upset yourself, she says.
Raymond sniffs and raises his wet face.
– I thought you was never gonna let nothing bad happen, he sobs.
– I thought you was gonna go and find our Susan, she says.
– You said you was never gonna let nothing bad happen, he says.
– Fuck sake it ain't my fault the old man's been took bad, she says.

– But you promised me, Mum, he says.
– You are as thick as shit sometimes, she says.

Raymond rocks in his chair. I put my hand on his shoulder to comfort him. Mother closes her eyes and her head nods forward.

– Cup of tea, Ray? I says.
– Nah.

I pat him on the shoulder. My mum is fast asleep in her chair. Georgina has gone home to get Dennis's tea. Linda and Maggie are at the window, their heads together. Raymond's mouth is open and all the stumps of his teeth is jumbled together in the front of his jaw what nobody ain't never bothered to have it seen to what makes me feel sad and guilty and angry on his behalf and on my own for my own troubles.

– Cunt's gonna die, Raymond says, standing up. – I don't care what she says.
– Happens to us all in the end, I says.
– But I was waiting for something off of him, Raymond says.
– Yeah? I says. – Like what?
– I ain't never had nothing off of him, says Raymond.
– Don't hold your breath, I says.

– You look like shit, says Linda.
– What, says my mum, opening her eyes.
– You, says Linda. – You better get home and get some kip.
– You still here, Raymond? says my mum.
– No, says Raymond.
– Ain't no point knocking yourself out, Mum, says Linda. – I'll come and fetch you if he wakes up.
– I'm all right, says my mum.
– You need to rest, says Linda.
– I wanna be here when he wakes up.
– If he wakes up, says Linda.

– Do what? says my mum.

We sit in silence. We are listening to the old man trying to breathe. Mum is crying. I put my arm round her shoulders but she shrugs me off. I thought I had years and years left of my dad's life to go on hating him. He is going to die before I have finished.

Linda stands up.

– There ain't no point in us all just sitting here, she says. – I can stay here with the old woman if you want to go in to work Maureen.

– Nah, I says. – You're all right.

– I can't pay you for any days you don't work you know that don't you? she says, picking up her bag. – To make ends meet or break even if I don't want to go under. Where I'm paying out extra on Aggie's cousin as it is?

– I know, I says.

– What nobody can't blame me for trying to make a fucking living, she says. – What ain't easy let me tell you when you are starting out and people just want to drag you back down. The canteen won't run itself. I never said I was running a fucking charity.

– Ain't it, I says.

The ward is quiet. I lean back in my chair and try to fight my eyes closing how the weight of them pulls my head forward and my chin rests on my chest.

– Maureen! says my mum. – He's waking up. Thomas? Thomas?

– Dad? I says.

The old man opens his eyes.

– Help me, he croaks. – I can't breathe.

My mum shouts for the nurse. The nurse's shoes squeal on the lino.

– Help me, my dad shouts.

The nurse gives him oxygen.

– I'll fetch the doctor, she says.

My mum is standing over my dad, trying to calm him. I am holding her hand.

– I'm fucking dying. I can't breathe, he says. – Help me. Where's Susan?

– Sssh, says my mum. – Raymond's gone to fetch her.

The nurse comes back.

– So where's the doctor? I says.

– He'll be with us as soon as, says the nurse.

– Cunt, says Thomas.

– Sorry, says my mum, to the nurse.

– No worries, says the nurse. – The drugs administered to ease pain release the inhibitions. The drugs release anger. It's a common side-effect of his medication. I should have warned you.

– You what? I says.

– No, says the old woman. – He's always like that.

The ward phone is ringing. The nurse goes to answer it. I am holding my mum's hand and she is holding my dad's hand. My dad is trying to lift his head up off of the pillow but the strength is all gone out of him.

– Thomas, says my mum. – Tommy.

My dad's eyes close.

– I can't handle this, says my mum.

– I'm here, I says.

– I'm losing him, she says.

– I'm here, I says.

My dad's eyes open.

– I'm not ready, he shouts.

My mum squeezes his hand.

– What's happening? he shouts. – Where am I going?

– You ain't going nowhere, she says.

My dad tries to sit up. My mum puts her hand on his chest and pushes him back down in his bed.

– You gotta rest, Thomas, she says. – The nurse said you gotta rest.
– Fuck that, says the old man, and raises his hand to her.
– Fuck you.
My mum flinches and ducks. My dad tries to hit her again. She dodges out of his way. He makes a fist and swings for her. He misses and rips the cannula out of the back of his hand.
– Now look what you've gone and done, I says.
  My mum goes to fetch the nurse. My dad starts to cry.
– Stop fucking crying, I says. – You're upsetting the old woman. What's the matter with you?
My dad sniffs and shows me his bleeding hand.
– I'm dying, Maureen, he says.
– Well hurry up and get on with it, I says.

The nurse pulls on rubber gloves.
– I'm sorry, sister, says the old man.
– Never mind, says the nurse, snapping the ends of her rubber fingers. – Now let me see.
  My dad lifts his swollen hand and offers it up to the nurse. The skin is bruised and torn and bloodied round the site of the cannula and his horny nails are yellow, full of dirt. She takes his hand between her rubber fingers like she don't want to catch nothing off of it.
– Who's been a naughty boy then, she says.
My mum looks away.
– Gotcha, says the nurse, stabbing the old man with the needle.
– Oww!
– Oops missed. Sorry about that. Let's try again shall we?
– Oww!
– Oh dear. Make a fist now for me, Mr. Thomas. There's a good boy. I can't do it if you keep on moving.
– Oww!

– You great big baby. Hold still now for me will you?
– Oww!
– There! says the nurse. – That wasn't too bad now was it?

My dad rests his head on his pillow. My mum is stroking his arm.
– I don't want to die, he says.
– Nobody wants to die, says the nurse, connecting the drip to the new cannula.
– I don't want to die, my dad shouts.
– Now now, says the nurse, preparing a syringe. – This'll knock him out.
– I don't want to die, my dad sobs.
The nurse dabs his arm with surgical spirit.
– Hang on a minute, I says. – I need to talk to him. Just let me…
The nurse sticks him with the syringe.
– Dad? Can you hear me?
His head jerks backwards.
– Uh, he says, and he is spark out.
– That's better, says the nurse. – He'll be under now for a few hours. You all go home now and get some rest. I will call you if anything happens.
– But I wanted to talk to him, I says. – What if he don't never wake up?
– Come on Maureen, says my mum.

———————

Where I meet my Victor every day over the corner cafe he makes me eat whether I wanted the hot special or anything like that off of the menu with two slices or just a sandwich for my own good before he lets me have afters with custard to play by his rules and prove he still cares about me what is more than you can say for my own family.

151

– Morning Susan, says Ahmed.

– Morning darling.

– Tea, Susan?

But Victor was late today or was I too early. Ahmed let me wait. And give me a cup of tea where he knew Victor was good for it and put in extra milk for me over and above what he puts in for all them other people.

– Susan, says Ahmed. – Have a cup of tea love. While you are waiting for your friend. The sugar is free.

Then Victor come in with our Raymond and it was egg and chips all round and made me eat it. But Raymond said the old man was on his way out and was asking for me. I never believed the old man would of been like that about me but that's what Raymond said. I never even knew he was took bad. Or he was in the Royal London if Victor told me I remember it went in one ear and out the. Where I was all right in myself before they come in the cafe but not for long how it goes with me now if I am all right for a bit but it don't last. So Victor finished my chips for me. But he give me something after I had my afters and I went in the toilet. And when I come out our Raymond was gone.

I just wanted to go home and have a lie-down what my Victor says is me all over. But he took me in his car. And dropped me outside by the main door how he never wanted to go up with me to the ward where he said he weren't family what was. But he made me promise. So I am on my own and I ain't feeling too clever in spite of all what Victor give me a ten pound bag. But Raymond did warn me. The old man is all wired up.

– Daddy. Wake up. It's me. Susan.

– Uh.

He is moving his fingers. I was gonna touch him but I don't know if his hands is all blown up like mine of puncture wounds what they done to him or would he hit me. What weren't a surprise last time he battered me in the flats what I was doing was his way of showing me. If he was pleased to see me or Raymond might of made a mistake. Where he don't look too pleased.

– Raymond told me to come up, I says. – He reckons you wanted me. But if he was joking me?

– Susan, he says.

– Hello, I says.

I don't know how our two hands must of come together if he took mine or was it me he is squeezing without paining me where he can't hurt me no more. But is trying to tell me something I don't want to know.

– Uh uh stupid.

– What?

He opens his eyes. I don't like the look of him.

– Nobody don't think nothing, I says.

Where he is almost barking at me. I don't want to listen.

– They think I don't know, he says.

– I swear I don't never no more, I says. – Not since that last time I ended up where I ended up. What taught me a lesson. Where I am under the doctor now he put me on medicine?

– Uh.

– I been really trying, Dad. What they been saying?

– Susan, he says.

He is trying to lift up his head. I shove his pillow down the back to prop him up.

– You are worth more than the rest of them all put together, he says.

– You what?

– But you ain't mine, he says.

– What?

– You ain't mine, Susan. I love you. But. They think I don't know.

– You mean Mummy done a dirty on you?

– Don't be disgusting, Susan.

– What then?

– She ain't…

– Do what?

The old man's eyes are closing.

– Dad? Tell me. What are you saying?

He snores loudly. A bell rings on the ward. A nurse parks her trolley beside his bed.

– Dad? Can you hear me?

– He's tired, says the nurse. – Visiting time is over. Let him rest.

– Was it Maureen? I says. – Nurse? Can he hear me?

– Time to go, says the nurse.

– Can he hear me?

– Time to go.

– But I've had a nasty shock, I says, and look up into her eyes. – Can't you just let me sit here for five minutes? Please darling?

– Five minutes, says the nurse, looking at her watch.

But I knew it weren't Maureen because Maureen never would of abandoned me. So I am staring out of the window and whistling like I never clocked the nurse is dispensing some tablets off of the medicine trolley into a plastic beaker like something caught my eye over the grey roofs. But I am watching her turn her back out of the corner of my eye to feed pills to the patient in the next bed what gives me a chance to scan the rows of bottles and packets. Where she leans over the patient with a beaker of water to swallow the pills and I open my bag and help myself. What tablets weren't controlled or nothing like that but beggars can't be. So when she turns round I am legging it off of the ward.

– Come back you thieving little cow, she shouts.

But none of all what I lifted for myself off of the trolley was soluble. So in the toilets I am crushing tablets with my spoon in a disposable cup with water out of the tap and trying to press out the lumps with my finger. I got new works on the cistern I nicked off of the trolley but the pills won't dissolve. I ate some but I got works and I want to use it. I wanted to lock myself in the cubicle but the lock was gone where they took off all the locks in the bogs on the ground floor of the hospital to discourage people from.

So I am sat on the bog trying to dissolve the tablets in the plastic cup. A security guard kicks the door open. The door slams into my legs. The plastic cup flies out of my hand and spills on the floor.

I reach for my bag but the guard is too quick. I topple off of the bog and fall on my hands and knees. The security guard catches me by the hair. I try to yank my head away but the guard will not let go. I jerk my head down and try to lick the crushed pills off of the wet floor.

The guard is like no you don't you junkie scum and I am begging him give us me bag darling have a heart I need to take me medication for me diabetes. I need me insulin.

But he reckons the other one's got bells on so I offer to suck his cock and all that what I would of done it to set me free but he never wanted nothing like that off of me where he said I was scum and he never wanted to catch nothing. He held me until the old bill come and took me down the nick. What I was thanking my lucky stars in my cell I had eaten a handful of temazepam and tramadol and all that in the hospital what took the edge off until the doctor done his rounds and give me some more. What I had to beg him but still.

Where I told the doctor I had just discovered that I was not who I thought I was. What he agreed with me must of been very destabilising. I told him I was trying to top myself in the toilets doctor where I had just found out my mum and dad was not my mum and dad and him what I always believed was my dad was on his death-bed. That's why I stole the drugs. I told him that the security guard rescued me. I said I didn't know what I might of done to myself if he hadn't of saved me. Can't you give me something, darling? Because I feel so sad over my family circumstances.

What weren't really lies because if I started to rattle I knew I would feel it. The one phone call they allowed me of course I called Victor. He had to stand bail in case I never turned up at court but he weren't worried about that. He would make sure I turned up. He said he would take me to court his self and bring me back home again after. Unless they put me away what was mitigating circumstances in my defence how I wanted to top myself and he reckoned I might get away with it.

And don't think I weren't grateful all what he done for me because I was grateful and I told him so. But he wanted to take me over home where he was sure the old woman was at work and we would not be disturbed. He opened the car door for me and I got in.

– But I'm ill, darling, I said.

– You're always ill, said Vic.

– Don't be like that, I said. – Ain't you got anything for me?

– What do you think? he said.

I was so grateful he got on my nerves how I had to be nice to him to make him like me. But he liked me less the harder I tried and I couldn't stop trying. So he weren't all that nice to me. And sent me up to his room over my mum's what used to be mine. With another bag out of his sock and a spoon because I was a pain in the arse and he wanted his money's worth of peace and quiet off of me. What weren't my fault if he wanted to spend all his money on me.

Then he come up with a mug of tea and custard creams what he said was for me but he ate it. I was sat up in his bed, still trying to find a vein. The pink candlewick bedspread was on the bed in my day before I never wanted

to go back home no more and my mum knew she would benefit off of it if she let the room.
– I can't never go up the hospital no more, I said. – I can't never go and see the old man no more.
And I was crying how I had been stupid again and made my life worse what nobody never stopped telling me how I made my life worse by my actions.
– The old man will be coming home soon though, said Victor. What we both knew was a lie.
– Yeah, I said.
– Want me to help you? he said.
– Yeah, I said.
– There you go, he said.
And I was like uh uh and never wanted him to say nothing to me if he was planning to spoil my moment what would be over soon enough anyway.
– That nice? Feel better now?
– Uh.
– There's a good girl.
– Uh.
– There's a lovely girl.
– Uh.

Until he got the hint and shut the fuck up trying to reach me when I never wanted nobody to reach me. But I was smiling and he tidied up. I felt love towards him where he backed off and let me.

If I slept or what.
– What self-same bedspread used to be on this bed in my day, I said. – When I was a kid.
– I know, he said. – I remember. And it's bald now like me!

– And the cracks on the ceiling where I was on my back looking at the rabbit and there's the duck. Can you see him?
– I can see him.
– When I was a kid I used to think the duck and the rabbit

was looking down on me.

– Don't upset yourself, he said, and laughed.

What I never understood. He was sat in a chair by the bed and laughing when I was trying to talk.

– Something me dad said over the hospital, I said. – He was trying to tell me something.

– You don't want to take none of that to heart, he said.

– He said me mum weren't me mum and that.

– People lash out when they ain't well.

– You think me mum is me mum?

– The day she brought you and Raymond back from the hospital I popped in with flowers, he said. – And you was blessed with a mouth like a pink rosebud. I used to let you suck on my finger to keep you quiet when your dummy went AWOL.

– But what if me mum weren't me real mum?

– You don't want to go down that road. Your mum is your mum. You know that.

– I know it weren't Maureen, I said.

– You are who you are, he said. – What is the history of the human race and you can't get away from it. What makes us who we are today.

– But you love me, I said.

– For my sins, said Victor.

– Will you hug me?

I was reaching out my arms.

– Please Victor?

But he sat in his chair and never moved. He never even looked at me. What made me feel bad. Where it should of been him begging me.

– You need to rest, he said. – After all what you been through. You must be exhausted. And I'm tired too.

– Oh Maureen, said my mum. – I want you to sit with our Billy for me. Where his leg was paining him so bad in the night Lorraine called the ambulance and they admitted him?

– But I don't want to sit with our Billy, I said.

What is not some judgement thing on my high horse like if you take drugs I don't want to know you but I got my own life to lead. And unless Billy is knocking on heaven's door I can't be arsed all the whining and moaning he begs me like I ain't got better ways to spend my time and I got to draw the line somewhere.

Until my mum told me Lorraine said poor Billy was kicking and screaming he never wanted to go in no fucking ambulance but never had no choice. Where I couldn't help myself feeling the pain he was suffering over his bad leg and my eyes filled with tears. Because he is my brother and nothing can change that.

And not long after they sedated him on his trolley the doctor took one sniff of his leg and decided he had contracted that flesh-eating disease by the time they fetch the undertaker there ain't much of you left. What my mum said was handy they transferred him to the London on the next floor to my dad on intravenous antibiotics where she reckons it ain't right letting poor Billy fester on his own like he ain't got no cunt to take care of him so we gotta take turns.

– Oh Maureen, she says. – Will you sit with him? Please Maureen? While I sit with the old man?

– But what about Lorraine, Mum? I says. – Where is Lorraine? Why can't Lorraine sit with Billy?

– Because Lorraine got nicked for possession with intent. The day after Billy ended up in hospital. And their kids was took off of them in temporary foster care over the other side of the Lee Valley.

Where I never intended to hurt nobody. What they don't realise when they are like it they think they should be free to choose to do what they want but if you choose not to see them because the self-pity and blame and regret and all that shit of how they feel and his skinny body full of holes and burns and sores what he keeps on scratching and picking with his dirty fingers makes me sick to my stomach and my heart where I love my brother how he can live like that perpetrating double any pain what my dad did to him onto his own kids I know that our Billy is outraged like I have no right.

And the old man never went as fast as I thought he was going. My Tony and Craig have to get their own tea because I am up the hospital every night after work sitting at his bedside trying to think what it is I have something to say to the old man before he kicks the bucket before it's too late. Not that I get even one word of complaint off of the pair of them where our Craig just helps himself to some Pot Noodle and my Tony goes up his mum's.

How it makes you feel on the ward under the smeary yellow light and grey curtains hiding the windows what drains all the life out of me where I never went to work the first few days after it happened and lost all sense of what time is it and got so glued to my seat by his bed I never got to the toilet just in time and almost wet myself.

Where me and my mum never even take our fag-breaks together in the stairwell like if we leave him on his own for a minute he would go and die on us as soon as our back is turned. So all the waiting and watching of him would of been wasted.

I don't want him to go behind my back. Linda would phone me over at work to the payphone in the canteen to tell me he's passed, Maureen, painlessly, it's for the best, he never suffered, he's gone now, I was holding his hand.

What would wind me up no end. But after the first few

days I just couldn't keep it up. I never wanted to leave the old man but there weren't no way round it where I was skint and Linda reckoned she never had the cash flow to sub me no more so it was dribs and drabs over the garage for a week or two if I wanted to eat until Linda was on my back coercing me to work six shifts or could I do more if I wanted some of my mum's shifts back to back with my own what would help all of us to keep ticking over. Or she would give my job to Julie's mate. What was bad enough Linda reckoned the old woman was up the hospital all the hours talking to the old man like he give a fuck what news of the family like Raymond caught a fish or Susan's brief said unless luck was on her side what with her previous and that she was looking at two years. Did I want my job or didn't I? And that Terry Harrison's been asking after you Maureen. What is it with yous two? Because if you don't want your job Maureen you've only got to say. I'll find myself someone more reliable. What wouldn't be hard.

So it's me and the old woman watching over my dad night after night after work or me on my own with the old man while my mum pops upstairs to our Billy. What is so bored and so lonely my mum says not even his kids come up to him to cheer him up where they are fostered over the other side of the Lee Valley the woman what took them in said it was too far and she didn't want no upset where they was settling in to a new school and got the social worker to back her up against us.

Where my mum is tormenting herself over them kids getting took out of the family on top of all the worry over Billy's leg what ain't never happened to any of our own before she is so ashamed and upset to tears them poor souls with strangers where they do not belong. But with the old man took bad Maureen and our Billy might lose his leg and me and you up the hospital day and night well what choice is it?

Not that nobody asked me. I thought the kids was over Lorraine's mum's. Them kids is good kids. It's not their fault Billy and Lorraine live the way they live. Still, the social worker said they only went under a temporary care order what she regarded it as an incentive for Billy and Lorraine to clean up. Then they can apply to the court to get them back. My mum just let them kids go.

When I could of made up beds for them in Dawn's old room and I would of helped them get off of the glue and that if Dawn and Craig pulled together we would of got through it. I would of made sure they got to school and that. Even if I had to take them myself.

What is hard in the canteen working my own job and half of my mum's job so I can get half of my mum's money off of Linda to tide my mum over and keep my own money coming in what I cream off a few quid off of it for my mum and all. Although it does my head in she buys Billy fags and sweets and that out of it. I don't know the rights and wrongs of it out of my money I earn for her so she can buy food and that to keep herself going but I keep quiet for her sake because how she is over our Billy makes me sick. She is so eager to make him take advantage she never once thinks about me.

And my Tony is on the sick his self with his back playing up although he is handy with the hoover and that making sure most of my work is done for me by the time I come home. And no one to look after Craig driving his fork-lift on ten hour shifts and his money what keeps me and Tony in fags even though Craig don't smoke and never did smoke however my Tony took him over the pub and bought him his first pint and twenty B and H he never even felt tempted. Whatever got said. He never took no notice. What is our Craig all over.

Even though he is courting some girl he met over Julie's caravan Clacton when he went down there for his holidays last year with a couple of his mates. She was in the next caravan with her baby and her mum. So Craig and his mates give them a hand with their bags and the sterilizer for the baby's bottles and that out of the boot of her mum's sister's car when she was dropping them off. And in the photos after Craig got home it was Craig and this girl Lisa and her baby Chelsea playing happy families on the beach and over the fair. And how it turned out this Lisa lives over the road from Georgina in them flats by Haggerston Park like our Craig felt comfortable she was from our manor and must of picked up on it. And never had to break no ice where there weren't none. It was the baby's dad what was a big Chelsea fan.

And now every Saturday Craig takes Lisa out if I borrow him my car to buy bits for the baby and of a night-time her mum has the baby and Craig takes her to the pictures or a pizza just the two of them at Pizza Hut or she likes that Harvester what I've never been but I've seen it on the telly.

And you are probably wondering like I am when the two of them are going to get a place together but Lisa don't want to leave her mum on her own and Craig says he is happy at home with me. Lisa's mum don't mind Craig staying over of a Saturday night I've talked to her on the phone about all that she says Craig is such a nice boy as long as they're careful. So I ask Craig if it ain't about time you started to make a life for yourself away from me and your dad and he reckons I was making him feel like he ain't wanted no more so I give him a hug and tell him he is wanted more than anything and we leave it at that.

What is nice to hold him however big they get ain't never too big for a cuddle to let them know if it gets too hard they always got me to come home to. It ain't easy out there when you ain't got nobody behind you. How a mum feels. Where I been watching Craig how did you get so tall

I am frightened sometimes when I look at you if you ain't never gonna catch up with yourself.

And that green apple smell off of Dawn's hair and fags and frying underneath I breathe the same fabric conditioner as me. I hold her and close my eyes. Dr Patel reckons that my daughter must make two eggs for one of mine she gets knocked up so easy. Where I only fell twice and a good thing I only split myself down the middle. Mine both know how much they are loved. Not chipped in little bits how it must of been for my mum. Not that Dawn is like that with hers.

The same as any kid wants. Because my dad couldn't hold me or pat my head or kiss me goodnight like there was something wrong with me or holding his self back what was even worse if he wanted to touch me. If something bad might happen between us. How I come downstairs after my bath with my hair twisted up in a towel and the heat coming off of my skin in my mum's bathrobe what Dolly give her one Christmas with the spidery black flowers all up the back of it he wouldn't let me sit on his knee. Or touch his face after my long bath with my washerwoman's fingers.

Where my mum still has the scribble up her front room wall I got a hiding for using one of the pens she brung me home from the bingo. The marks on the wallpaper look like scribble but I was trying to write something. I held the pen in my hand and waited for words to flow out of the end of it. I made shapes like writing and felt something turn over inside me.

I knew the old man couldn't see me behind the chair. He was supposed to be watching me. Mum was over Auntie Dolly's with Alan and Billy but she left me indoors. I called to the old man to read to me off of the wall. He heaved himself up out of his chair and stretched his self and yawned and rubbed his eyes. I saw inside his mouth and the armholes of his vest gaped to show me the dripping beards in his white armpits and where he caught the sun his shoulders was burnt brick red on the roads working casual for Murphy over the summer when he felt like working. The ripple of the blue tail of his mermaid I thought was the spit of my mum when the old man flexed his muscles like Popeye to make Julie laugh that time she popped up when my mum was over the bingo. My dad took off his vest because Julie said it was all dirty. He made her sit on his knee. She was stuck on his knee because she never wanted to fight him and make herself look stupid where my dad was acting like everything was just jokes to make Julie laugh.

– Look, I said. – I writ you a story, Daddy.

– Cachau bant, he says, and give me a clump.

– Ow, I said.

He give me another clump.

– Will you read it to me, I said.

He hauled me out from behind the chair and took off his belt.

– Read it to me, I said.

I thought his trousers was going to fall down. He belted me until I pissed myself. I slid down the wall and watched him threading his belt back through his belt loops. From the floor I watched him bend backwards at the knees like Elvis in front of the mirror to comb back his hair. My legs was stinging.

– My little Maureen, he said.

He was fumbling with the buttons of his new shirt. He couldn't do up his own buttons.

– Help me, Reen, he said.

I squelched across the wet carpet and he knelt down by the door, away from the wet patch. I was glad he asked me to help him but my fingers hurt where I was grappling

with his shirt. The slits of the button-holes was tight in
the stiff placket and my knuckles grazed the threadbare
cloth of his vest what set my teeth on edge. My face felt
hot in the glow coming off of him like we was burning up
together after he belted me. Through his vest the hair on
his chest was springy under my fingers and he breathed on
me out of his open mouth how a dog breathes, panting to
cool his self, until all his buttons was done up.
– See, he said, and cuffed me gently round the ear-hole.
– What? I said, but he went out.
   I could hear him and my mum having words on the
landing.
– Cont, he shouted, and then she come in with the kids.
– The old man is blubbing on the landing, she said.
– I writ a story, I said. – I asked him to read it to me. Sorry
I writ on the wall.
– Silly sod can't read, she said.

What he is up to now with his eyes closed gurgling
whether he can hear us or maybe he can't hear no more.
I wouldn't put it past him to make out like he is dead to
the world not because he wants to spy on us what we
are saying but he can't stand my mum's grief. Where she
is crying over him in the hospital, breaking her heart
because she don't want to lose him. The monitor is still
bleeping. We better be careful what we say.
   Not that I don't have nothing to take my mind off of
watching him die. You should see me. I ain't let myself go
even working all them hours straight through my dinner
on coffee and fags I wash my hair and blow-dry it before
work and put on mascara and blusher and a bit of lippy
in sheer plum what ain't too bold but enough where I am
trying to make the best of myself I think you know why.
Not that I am planning a dirty on my Tony. I just can't help
myself thinking about Terry Harrison.

As long as my Tony never sees me if he gets up to use
the toilet in the early morning or a drink of water out of
the kitchen I flee from him quick out of the front door and
along the landing or hide myself in the bathroom if I ain't
ready until I hear him pull the chain and go back to bed.
All I need my Tony starting on me where he's bound to
think my hair is shining and a nice top under my overall
where he ain't as thick as all that. In my jeans with a good
shape from the back he used to say my arse like a peach he
would love to take a bite out of it.

Not that nothing is going on with me and Terry
Harrison. But I know he is going to say something. He
only went and said something to Linda. He asked Linda
if I was happy with my Tony. He must be waiting for the
right moment to say something to me.

But the monitor bleeps and my legs ache like I used to
get growing pains when I was a kid what is lack of sleep
and overwork and worry over my dad where I still ain't
said nothing to him. My mum is asleep now. I slump in the
plastic chair and close my eyes. And I am thinking about
Terry where I come over the hospital on his bus. I watched
him haul his self up and into the driver's seat in the garage
and clocked the shiny arse of his busman's trousers. He
turned on the engine and my seat began to vibrate. I was
in the front but I couldn't see him behind the concertina
blind. But I enjoyed it was Terry Harrison joking with
one of the other drivers out of the open window when
he pulled away because he was well-liked over the garage
where he was more easy-going than my Tony and he never
lost it on the road what was a hazard in his line of work
if you was one of them people. So what I got riled on his
behalf when a Range Rover overtook us on the inside?
And gunned up the bus-lane like he owned the road I
admit it and I ain't proud what is my personality if I would
of rammed the cunt up the arse. Terry's patience made me

smile. Even though my dad is dying.

Then my mum takes off her glasses and rubs her eyes.

– What's so funny? She says. – Penny for them?

– I was daydreaming.

– It's all right for some. Some of us ain't got much to smile about.

– Cup of tea?

– Twist my arm, she says.

When I get back from the machine she is sleeping again. I touch her gently on the shoulder.

– Thanks for the tea, Maureen, she says.

– I got some chocolate and all. You want some?

My mum holds out her hand.

– But what am I going to do when he cops it? she says.

– You can come and live with me, I says. – I ain't using Dawn's room no more.

– I got Victor, says my mum. – What time is it?

– Seven.

– I gotta see Billy. Thanks for the chocolate. All right I give it to him? I'll tell him you got it for him special. What might cheer him up a bit to think you was thinking of him.

I sigh.

– Why don't you pop in to him? she says.

– Nah, I says. – You're all right. I'll sit here with the old man until they sling me out on my ear.

– Billy ain't finding it easy, she says. – What shall I tell him from you Maureen?

– Tell him get well soon, I says.

My dad opens his eyes as soon as my mum disappears through the swing doors.

– Maureen, he says.

– Dad.

– Look at me, he says.

I lift my head and look at him.

– Put your teeth in, Dad, I says.

– Ma'en flin da fi, he says, trying to smile.

– You don't have to be sorry, I says.

My dad starts to cough. The tears are running out of him. How to tell him the clumps and beltings and shouting and tears all what he has subjected me to and ignoring me and pushing me away ever since I was born and crying over me how he sobbed and blubbered after he lost it with me it was too fucking late.

– I am sorry though, Maureen, he says. – I never meant it.

– I know, I says.

– Rydw in caruti, he says.

– Do what?

– I love you, he says.

I don't say nothing.

– I love you, Maureen, he says.

– Yeah, I says.

– I do, he says.

– What do you want me to say? I says.

He closes his eyes. I get out of my chair and pick up my bag.

– Where you fucking going? He asks.

– To the toilet. All right?

– Come back to me after.

– Yeah yeah, I says.

I spark up a fag in the corridor and sit down on the edge of a parked trolley and read a poster how all members of hospital staff have the right to carry out their duties without the fear of verbal or physical assault. The poster makes me cry remembering the old man and my Tony what loves me and I love him if you can call it love that binds you to another person whether you like it or you don't like it your life is mixed up with another life and it feels like how do you separate when you can't take no more. Where my lot all reckon it's too late now to change my mind even if they ain't got no time for my Tony. I made my bed. Except for Maggie what is forever on at me to bin the cunt.

I ain't got no tissues so I'm wiping my nose on the back of my hand. You know when you have a good cry sometimes you feel a bit better afterwards well this ain't like that. I wipe my eyes on my sleeve and my shoulders stop shaking. I take a deep breath and I'm thinking I got the crying all over and done with but I don't feel no better and then the tears start coming out again like they ain't never gonna stop.

– Hello Maureen.

I don't uncover my face but I recognise the voice. I feel his hand warm and steady on my shoulder.

– Maureen?

– What you doing here?

– You're crying, Maureen.

– So fucking what? I got a right to cry.

Terry Harrison holds me and lets me cry all over him until his shirt is soaked. He gives me his hankie and I trumpet snot in it then give it back to him. He fetches me a cup of tea and holds my hand. I sip my tea and sniff.

– You stalking me, Tel? I ask.

– Me mum's done her back in, he says. – I come straight from work. I heard your dad was taken bad.

– Tell your mum hello from me.

– I still love you, Maureen, he says.

– You broke my fucking heart, I says.

– I'm sorry, says Terry Harrison.

– You're sorry? You never even told me to my face. That fucking hurt, mate.

– I'm sorry, he says. – I weren't well.

– You weren't well?

– I thought I might hurt you. Physically, I mean, when I come out of the nick. I sort of lost control over myself when I was in there I was so angry over the injustice I wanted to hunt down my brother and kill him. They put me in solitary so I never hurt no one. I was under the doctor. They give me pills to keep me quiet.
I sniff again.
– I saw you on your bus after you come out, I says.
– I know, he says.
– You looked depressed, I says.
– I never told nobody how I felt, he says. – Even my mum never knew.
– You should of told me. We could of got through it.
– You was unfaithful to me in my dreams when I was inside, he says. – With my brother.
– I am sorry about that, I says.
And Terry smiles.
– It all seemed so real at the time, he says.
– Hmm, I says.
– Gotta laugh, he says.
– Yeah, I says, crying.
– Have a good cry, says Terry.
– All them fucking years wondering, I says. – Wondering why. Asking myself why you never wanted me no more. You could of trusted me.
– Yeah, says Terry. – I was stupid. I was young. I thought I was dangerous. I couldn't trust myself.
– Yeah well, I says. -You ain't young no more.
– No, says Terry.
– Fuck, I says.
– Come for a drink with me one night? says Terry.
– My Tony would kill me.
– Just a drink, Maureen. Where's the harm?
– You know where, I says.
– Is that a no, then?

– No, I says.

Over Terry's shoulder his mum is shuffling towards us along the corridor in a hairy brown dressing gown.

– Terry! she shouts.

– What you doing out of bed, Mum? says Terry.

– Who's that? asks his mum. – What does she want?

– Remember Maureen?

– Maureen Thomas? What do you want with her? After all what she done to you?

– It's all right, Mum, says Terry. – She never done nothing.

– Don't you let her reel you back in, she says. – They're all the same in that family. You're too soft, that's your trouble. You know that don't you? Too fucking soft.

– Don't upset yourself, Mum, says Terry. – Let's get you back to bed. I'll see you later, Maureen.

– Yeah, I says. – See ya.

Terry Harrison's mum begins to shuffle back down the corridor.

– She's losing her marbles, he says.

– Yeah, I says. – Take care, Tel.

– Take care Reen.

– See ya.

– Bye.

– Tel? I says.

– What?

– You married?

– What's it to you?

– Don't fuck about. You married or what?

– Was, says Terry. – Not no more. We just sort of fell apart.

– Kids?

– We couldn't have no kids. Anything else you wanna know?

– Not right now, I says.

– Can I go now? he says.

– You can do what you fucking like, mate, I says.

Where I am so tired of my dad on the way home the cunt waiting for me to come back on the ward would serve me right if you copped it in the night not knowing whether your Maureen loves you or forgives you for everything how you was towards me what you need me to say so you can rest in peace. And I never said goodbye to you what you wanted off of me whether I love you is just words but it wouldn't of killed me to put you out of your misery. If you do care. You poor sod what did your best under the circumstances you reckon? Where you said it to me what must of costed you and it was the first time you ever said it to me my whole life. Rydw in caruti. Do I feel loved?

But not enough to go back up the hospital. I am too tired to go back up there in case you cop it in the night and tell you what it is where if you was really dead now and it was too late how would I?

And Terry said it. Them three words when we was kids my Terry made up for everything what weren't bandied about over home what don't mean to say I doubt they would if they could but they didn't know how. Whatever warmth they must of had in their heart when my dad wasn't down the pub and my mum over the bingo what she reckoned took her mind off of her troubles.

It took me a while to say it back but I said it. And meant it. I love you Terry Harrison. What weren't easy for me in them days how my lot put the mockers on me mooning over that soppy cunt. The calm and quiet off of my Terry where he was so gentle you might not notice you was happy just talking and going out for a walk. He said he wanted to marry me. He never drunk more than two pints. I weren't used to nothing like that. He walked away from trouble. Nothing ever happened.

Unless I made something happen when I was with him if I lashed out like I just needed to slap some tart over the pub was looking at my Terry or to have a pop at him if he was getting on my tits.

But it was myself I wanted to hurt after he dumped me. Nobody would look twice at me no more where they all knew. I felt ugly. All the shit-bags round our way come after me in the street like I was up for it with anyone now I never had no choice. My mum dragged me over the Queen's with her and the girls to cheer myself up but the old man come in and took one look at me and told me to get home. He said I weren't welcome in the corner of the snug mooning over that soppy cunt with my long face in his boozer.

When I needed my dad. What I was crying over on my way home why he couldn't of put his arm round my shoulders and told me something I wanted to hear. You are a lovely girl, Maureen. Whatever man gets you will be the luckiest man in the world. I just want you to be happy, Maureen. Don't be rushing into nothing.

If I had of got the feeling inside of me my dad was behind me even after the shock what happened with me and Terry Harrison I might of took one look at my Tony and told him where to stick it. But my dad weren't behind me.

When I was over the White Horse with Julie. One of the girls at her work was getting married and they was all up for a bit of a laugh. My mum told Dolly I was too quiet and I weren't eating since Terry dumped me. So Dolly told Julie why not take Maureen out with the girls to cheer her up after all what she got let down bad by that Terry Harrison. It's no good sitting indoors moping. Come and have a bit of a giggle, Maureen. Them girls is all a good laugh when you get to know them. Maybe a night out will bring you out of yourself.

So Julie done my hair for me and I lent a nice lemon jumper off of our Linda and I drank a few lager tops. But I felt left out all them stories I never knew what they was on

about. Them cheerful birds laughing over the boy in the
post-room I never knew from Adam what Julie said was
only funny if you was there.

Linda's top was itching me. I went to the toilet and I
saw in the mirror where I had scratched my neck my skin
was streaked with red how it gets when I don't feel right.
I never wanted to come out of the toilet. I never felt right
about myself. All them silly little girls laughing over some
boy I felt like a woman all the pain I suffered until Julie
come in the toilet and fetched me back to our table.

I took a sip off of the top of my lager. Julie nudged me.
– Don't look now but them two on the high stools by the
gents the tall beardy one keeps on looking at you. – The
one with the big dog. His mate is talking to that girl
behind the bar what used to go with your Frankie before
he got married.
– Yeah? I said.
– Yeah, she said. – And your one's at a loose end, Maureen.
Where his mate is all over that girl he can't keep his eyes
off of you. They ain't from round here. His dog ain't half
big. And yellow like a fucking wolf. He's on his way over,
Maureen. Don't turn round.

I turned round. The dog put his paws in my lap. The
dog licked me.
– He likes you, said Tony.
– Yeah? I said.
– He's got good taste, said Julie.

The dog settled at my feet. Tony bought me and Julie a
drink. He reckoned he was flush after a big win so I went
for a short. He sat down next to me. Julie said without so
much as a please or a thank-you. Didn't your mother never
learn you no manners?

But I wasn't bothered about none of that. I was sick
of listening to them girls giggling over the boy in the
post-room.

– You courting? he asked me.

– Nah, she ain't, said Julie.

– I was, I said. – But I ain't no more.

– Shut up, Maureen, said Julie.

– Who was he? he said.

– Some bloke, said Julie. – From round here. You won't know him.

– Terry Harrison, I said.

I wanted to say his name. Julie kicked me under the table.

– Terry Harrison, he said. – Terry Harrison.

– Do you know him? I said.

– I ain't had the pleasure, he said, smiling.

  I took a mouthful of my vodka and orange squash.

– Drink up, he said.

I took another mouthful and pushed my glass away.

– Where you going? said Julie.

– For a breath of fresh air, he said. – Come on, Maureen.

  He kissed me up against the wall round the side so hard I got the taste of blood in my mouth. His beard was scratching up all my cheeks and chin. His hands went all over me where I wanted him to touch me and where I never wanted it out in the street he was going too fast. What if my mum passed on her way back from the bingo?

– Don't do that, I said.

– Shut your eyes, said Tony.

– Do what?

– Shut your eyes.

I shut my eyes. He cradled my face in his hands and kissed me gently. I pushed him off of me and opened my eyes.

– So what happened with you and Terry Harrison? You give him the elbow?

– What's it to you?

– I don't want no secrets between us, said Tony.

– He give me the elbow.

– Yeah?

– Yeah.

– Why?

– I dunno. He must of just went off of me.
  Tony looked at me.

– You must of give him a reason. What did you do?

– Nothing, I said. – I swear. I never done nothing.

– Well, said Tony. – Never mind. You learnt your lesson.
I don't care what you done to him. You're mine now
Maureen.

– You what?

– I'm gonna give all my love to you, he said.

– Yeah? I said.

– Yeah, he said. – All of it. All what you deserve.

But he made me feel like a piece of shit. So I walked out
on him. I made up a couple of bottles for our Craig and
strapped him in the pram with a few bits in a carrier bag
and Dawn on the way and he never even tried to stop me.

– He won't take you back, Maureen, he called after me.

– What are you on about?

– Terry Harrison.

– I'm going up my mum's, I said.

– You looked in the mirror lately, Maureen? Ain't nobody
gonna look twice at you now you fat cunt.

I pushed the pram over home. I threw a penny up my
mum's window and dragged the pram up the stairs. My
mum come down and told me to bed down on the chair
in the front room. She said the old man was over the pub
where Mick and Maggie done a lock-in. The baby was
sleeping in his pram. She said I could stop over home until
I was ready to go back to my Tony. She made me a cup of
tea and flung a pink blanket over me. She lit a couple of
fags and give one to me. She sat in the old man's chair and
asked me if I wanted a biscuit to dunk in my tea. She said
nothing don't never look so bad in the morning.

But when she heard the old man's key in the lock she flew up the stairs. The old man woke the baby.
– Cunt slung you out? he said, swaying over me. – Caught you at it?
The baby was crying in his pram.
– It's all right, Craig, Mummy's here, I said.
The old man bent over me. The fumes coming off of him if you lit a match he would of gone up.
– Go home, Maureen, he said, pulling the blanket off of me.

I put my shoes back on. The old man wrapped his self in my blanket and sat down in his chair. I popped a dummy in the baby's mouth.
– Mum said to stop over home until it blows over, I said.
– I don't give a fuck what she says, said the old man. – You go home now.
– The baby needs feeding, I said. – I got a bottle in my bag.
– I said go home, Maureen.

I called up the stairs but she never answered. The old man laughed.
– Go on, he said. – Go home you fat cunt or I'll give you a clump.

I pushed the pram through the quiet streets. I was cold. The baby was crying. I cuddled him on my doorstep to settle him before I went back indoors. Tony was asleep in the chair. I heated the bottle and crept up the passage and took the baby in bed with me to keep me warm.

I get off of the bus after the hospital and I am hoping and hoping my Tony is out. I put my key in the lock and I swear if he is indoors I will bung him a couple of quid just to get rid of him. Like when the kids was kids in the summer we used to give them two bob to go out and get some crisp and sweets to eat over the park.

When we was love-birds. Of an afternoon with the curtains closed in the front room or wherever he wanted me panting hard and thumping behind me before the sulphate took its toll. What was good news for me. Where he had killed off all what I felt for him. If he was rough with me and I felt sick with myself afterwards because I liked it. Or the tenderness of his mouth in my ear-hole grunting and slumped over me until he heaved himself off.

But there weren't nobody home. So that's a fiver off of me the bookie will have to go short until next time. I'm gonna put my feet up. Some rubbish on the telly where I don't like it too quiet. After I make myself a cup of tea. I'm gonna put my feet up and spark up a fag and think about me and Terry Harrison. What I still love and he loves me. I know that.

Not just the sex but his kindness I want so much to hold me now the old man is on his way out. However long it takes. Where my Tony is frightened of hospitals he can't even pop up to the ward for a minute to pay his respects.

I squash the tea bag in a spoon. Out the kitchen window I can see my mum upstairs in her back bedroom lit up behind white nets how she forgets if you turn on the light she can't see out but I can see in what she is doing. She takes off her glasses and puts them on top of her brown cupboard and rubs her eyes in front of the mirror like she has just woken up to the mystery of old age what nobody thinks won't never catch up with them. She looks bony and frail. Where she can't remember what she done with her glasses my tears well up how sad for me watching her patting the bed and running her hands over the top of the dressing table.

She must of popped home for some bits for the old man or for Billy. My phone is ringing. Terry must of got my number off of Linda. If he wants to take me out for that drink or what. That nice top I bought myself still in the

wrapping with batwing sleeves I can wash my hair quick to get the fried smell off of it.
– Mrs. George?
– Who is this?
– Mrs. George? It's about your boy? Craig? I'm so sorry.
I close my eyes.
– Mrs George? Can you hear me?
– What's happened?
– He's in the ambulance now. There's been an accident.
   I light up. I forgot Craig was on lates.
– It's his leg, says the caller. – He brought down a stack of pallets on himself off of his forklift. I'm so sorry.
– Is it bad?
– I dunno. Maybe crushed? she says.
– Who is this?
– Only Sheila on reception what they told me to find the number in Craig's file and give you a ring. I'm so sorry Mrs. George. We all are.
– Sorry? I says. – It ain't your fucking fault.
– Thank you, says Sheila.
– Thank you, I says.
   I dial my mum's number.
– I need you, Mum, I says. – It's our Craig. Come up the hospital with me. He's had an accident at work. I'm scared, Mum. I think it's bad.
– Where's your Tony?
– Fuck knows, I says.
– I'm sorry, Maureen, says my mum. – You know I would of done it but I can't. I've got to go to our Billy.
– Billy can wait, I says.
– He needs me, says my mum. – His leg is on the mend and they have put him in detox. In that place down by the canal where our Susan went before? I can't let him go through that on his own.
– I need you, I says.

– You'll be fine, says my mum.

I had forgot our Craig like I lumped him in with my Tony and just let the two of them get on with it. What with my Dad how he is and thinking about you know who whether the grass is always greener or he was the one I was meant to be with if you believe all that crap destiny and all that like we was made for each-other. What you can only tell by hindsight I reckon even when there is a perfect fit at the beginning if one person grows more as the years pass by you can bet the other one just stays the same or he gets so you hate him with all your heart and soul what I ain't saying is how I am over my Tony but I ain't far off sometimes. I just forgot Craig. Because I was too angry and sorry for myself over my dad and my Tony. And mooning over Terry Harrison what broke my heart the first time round and I don't never want to go through that again.

– Mum? I says.

– Not now, Maureen, says my mum.

– Not now? I says.

I can hear her sucking on a fag down the end of the line.

– You listen to me, I says. – I ain't got time now to tell you all what I think but before I go to Craig just to let you know you have let me down and the feeling puts me in mind of all the other times in my life you never looked out for me when I needed you.

– You better get yourself over the hospital, she says.

– Listen to me, I says. – I could reel off a list as long as your fucking arm the times you should of protected me and not let things happen but you couldn't because how you are with my dad and with our Billy and Alan you just sort of forgot me.

– You'll cope, Maureen, she says.

I am shaking so much I can hardly get my key in the car door. The shaking is fear over Craig's leg and anger with my mum where she can't hear me what I am saying and guilt me dreaming about Terry Harrison when Craig is hurt as if my dreams made them pallets fall off of the fork-lift.

Half way to the hospital at a red light I am thinking I wish I had phoned Dawn to come with me or even our Linda. Some-one to hold my hand. But then the light changes and I just keep on. The shit in my head if they save Craig's leg I will stay with my Tony forever. Please god look after Craig. Although it feels like there ain't no one up there what gives a fuck about the likes of us.

I get that gut-ache in the car on the way to the hospital and up in the lift past the third floor where my Dad is dying and the fourth where they cured Billy's leg and on up to surgical on fifth where they took our Craig. Craig is in surgery. A nurse gives me a cup of tea.

– The surgeon is expecting a probable favourable outcome, she says.

I think about ringing Lisa or Dawn but I can't make myself get up from the chair in the little room where the nurse parked me in front of the telly. The telly is not switched on. I can't reach across the coffee table and press the button. What is the shock making me so tired I can't move. I am waiting for the probable favourable outcome. I glance at a magazine. I read a recipe for spicy mince with red and green peppers. I start to cry thinking how Craig ain't had no dinners off of me since my dad was took bad. Where I left him to fend for his self.

And the top he bought me for my last birthday I turned forty six I don't mean he give me the money and told me to get myself something or took me down Hoxton. Craig went up West to Debenhams and bought me a white crochet top what you wear over a white camisole with spaghetti straps in a gift box. I thought Lisa must of gone with him to pick it out but she couldn't find no one to stay with the baby so Craig went up there all on his own. He said he thought I would like it.

And it fitted me perfect over the Macbeth for a couple with my Tony and my mum and Linda and Georgina who said the top looked nice and I felt proud of my kids where neither of them ain't on the gear or nothing like that what marks them out from the rest of the kids round here if I say so myself what don't take away from the truth of it.

And I am trying not to think about the chipped bone splintering and mixed with clots of blood and strings of muscle and leg meat our Craig never done nothing to bring it on his self but work a sixty-hour week take home one sixty and the marrow dark red-brown out of the crushed bone. What he give me thirty out of it towards my home and is an innocent person doing his best to pay his way.

The nurse had to shout.
– Nora Thomas? Nora?
Where they had tied back the curtains out of the way and stripped Billy's bed.
– Mrs Thomas?
What the shock of the marbled vinyl I never knew was zipped over the foam mattress under the bottom sheet come in my head first and I put my hand on it to steady myself. The vinyl was damp what they give it a sponge down between patients. I never knew it was like that. To kill all known germs when all the covers was balled up on the house-keeping trolley and ready to be boiled in the hospital laundry if all that never went private or out-sourced what the lowest bidder would pay slave wages to the likes of me if I never got work off our Linda. They sprayed it and give it a once-over. And the litter was all swept underneath to the skirting of used swabs and sweet

papers and the frame was sprung like nobody ain't got no
hope of freedom out of the jaws of that man-trap what was
all in my head but still. Where I was frightened. Because
people ain't got no idea what it was like. Over the hospital
when I went on the ward and my son weren't there no
more.

– Mrs Thomas?

But I stared at the bare mattress. I looked in Billy's bedside
cabinet. His boots was gone and I thought he was dead.

– Mrs Thomas!

The nurse had to shout at me. She told me Billy was on
his way to the detox like I would be overjoyed by the news
my son was on his way to the detox what nobody even
thought to consult me if I wanted him to go there or not.
But she said he was a grown man and able to make his
own decisions where she never knew him like I did. She
told me to go home and get some rest.

Where I was up the hospital the day before he never
looked all that bad. Because he had been resting in bed
for ten days off the streets and his leg was saved for what I
am so relieved they never took it off like they said it would
come to if he never fought. They said he must of been a
fighter all along to keep going like that what surprised me
I thought he was too weak. And never had much about
him is harsh to say of one of your own kids I know but he
was like that since he was a kid and never grew out of it.
The surgeon said he was tenacious what I never bothered
to argue how I was his mother and knew better.

I was glad he was alive. But the detox they made Billy I
never been in one of them places before. Although Susan
had done it last year by order of court what never done her
no good.

– Mum, he said. – What the fuck.

– Hello Billy.

– You doing up here? We ain't allowed no visitors. How

did you get in?
– I just walked in off of the street. There ain't nobody on reception.
– I don't wanna see no one right now, Mum.
– Come home, son, I said. – Come home, Billy.
He looked at me. His face was pale and clean like I never remembered he could look like that. His eyes was full of pain what I will never forget.
– Leave me out, Mum. I wanna get my kids back, he said.
– But I got a plan, I said.
– You got a plan?
– We'll talk to the social workers, I said. – All we gotta do is tell them you're at home with me now. They'll give you your kids back if you tell them that. I wanna help you.
– I gotta get off of the gear first, he said. – The doctor's gonna assess me in a minute. You better go now.
– But Victor's out most nights with our Raymond.
What was me trying to make him think about what I am suffering. What I never should of said. Not that nothing like that made no difference to him.
– Or they watch telly upstairs, I said. – I ain't got no one to talk to when I get in from the hospital.
– I gotta do this, Mum, Billy said. – Go home. Leave me alone.
– But we're family, Billy.
– I'm sorry, Mum.
– You're my son, Billy. I need you at home with me.
– They said they was gonna warn you don't come up here to me where I don't need all this. I got enough shit in my head of my own shit. They've give me six months to live unless I get off of the gear. Me kids need me.
– I'll look after you over home. What is the best place for you. And the kids. Look at the state of this place.
– Leave me out, Mum. I'm ill. Don't you want me to get better? What is an illness I need help to overcome. And

they said they can help me.
– I got money, Billy.
– Don't you want me to get off of the gear?
– I had a big win on the bingo before the old man was
took bad. I put it in the post-office for emergencies. I can
take it out again.
– Don't Mum.
– I ain't talking peanuts, Billy.
– How much?
– Five hundred quid.
– Five hundred? Show me the book.
I opened my bag and showed him my savings book. He
took the book off of me and put it in his back pocket.
– Come on then, he said.

I can't see no point in spinning this out. It gives me a bad
feeling milking the suspense out of Craig's misfortune,
what it was like for me, waiting for him to come back on
the ward. The surgeon saved Craig's leg. You can see all
the metal pins and braces poking out of his calf and thigh.
One of the few doctors ever in my whole life talked to us
like we was equal to him what looked after our Craig like
he was his own son. I wanted to get something for the
doctor where I was so grateful. I thought and thought if
he smoked you could of give him a couple of hundred fags
or a box of chocolates if he had a sweet tooth or whisky or
anything like that if it was against his religion but I never
knew nothing about him. So I chose an ornamental plate
of a hunting scene with real gold what come with its own
hanging bracket out of that gift shop out by Gant's Hill on
the A12 where they do all that fancy lamps and carriage
clocks when I should of been at work killing myself for our
Linda what cost me an arm and a leg. What was Terry's

idea I got the doctor something like that. And took me up there after his shift where he used to deliver round there when he was moon-lighting on the vans and knew where to come off of the A12 and where to park and all that. What weren't nothing but a harmless outing in Terry's old motor where he kept his eyes on the road and I never said much and he waited in the car when I went in the shop and dropped me at the hospital after what weren't even on his way home out of consideration what I was going through and respect for my situation not because he never wanted to get his leg over if that was on offer. You should of seen the doctor's face when he unwrapped it. His eyes lit up.

Lisa was a bit funny with my Craig at first. I thought she was going to puke the first time she was on the ward. She couldn't look at him. She only stopped for five minutes then made out like Chelsea needed a clean nappy and it was time to go home.

– It's not her fault, Craig, I said. – She'll get used to it. It's the shock.

– She won't come back, said Craig. – I love her, Mum.

– I know you do, I said. – She's a nice girl. She loves you too.

– I love her, Mum, said Craig.

– I know, I said, stroking his damp forehead.

– Where's my dad?

– What?

– I want my dad.

– You know what he's like about hospitals, I said.

Let my mum work her own shifts if she wants to buy drugs for our Billy. I ain't working half her shifts for her no more and I ain't gonna give her none of my money. I am fucking angry with her for springing Billy out of the detox before he even started his treatment but not half as angry as our

Maggie. What found out what my mum done and went over home and give her a clump. I could hear her shouting and hollering where she left my mum's door open.

– Why are you trying to kill him? Why don't you want him to give up? You don't want him to give up because you're frightened if he gives up he won't want to know you no more. He'll look back over the years and blame you for buying him drugs. You know he will. He'll blame you because you never looked after him properly. You never once put your foot down with him. You never once acted like a proper parent to him. You just let him shit on you what makes you weak so you are no good to no cunt. Do you hear me? All he wants off of you is some strength to feel like you are capable of being a mother to him. You are not like a mother to him. A good mother does not let her kids shit all over her. You let him do what he wants to you. How do you think that makes him feel?

I am smiling. It ain't just me listening to our Maggie. Her voice carries all over the flats. I imagine all the women on our estate what have sons and daughters and husbands like it all sitting up and listening to her what she says you just let him shit on you makes you so weak you ain't no good to no cunt. I think about myself and my Tony. I picture all the women down our way what suffer and turn a blind eye listening to our Maggie and finding the strength to sling their loved ones out on the street and slamming the door and getting on with their life. How women can stand up for ourselves and say no what I don't think is a lot to ask.

I take another week off of work to sit with our Craig. I pop in to the old man now and again but most of the time I just let my mum get on with it. She is working seven shifts a week over the garage and sitting with my Dad half the night then over home with the rest of her money after she buys her fags and that to give what is left to our Billy.

She gets herself a few bits off of Victor's wages what he gives her every Friday of bread and milk and coffee and biscuits and sweets what they all like when they are on the stuff because she wants to feed him because he is her son and he needs her.

But she won't buy him no proper food. Only cheap bits of bent tins off of that stall down Hoxton what she can run to after she buys his fags and all those tenners and fivers she bungs him but it don't make no sense to me. How she lets him fleece all her wages off of her for his heroin and crack and fags and that but she won't get him nothing nourishment like eggs or cheese or meat what anyone would think was a false economy if she was hell-bent. Although she do pay her telly stamp and charges her electric key if they don't want to sit in the cold and the darkness with nothing to take her mind off I'll say that for her even if she has to ask me to charge it for her sometimes if she thinks she has got me to fall back on. And she ain't never signed off of her book where she works off of the cards for our Linda like over the school what was cash in hand no questions or how would she ever of paid her rent?

So I am up the hospital to Craig about two after Sunday dinner round Dawn's what I cooked a nice bit of pork shoulder with Paxo in a tin on the side and roast potatoes and gravy and cabbage and carrots and ice-cream for afters and Barry did the washing up. I look through the glass panel of the ward door and there is Lisa and Chelsea over by Craig's bed. Chelsea is holding Craig's hand and smiling and he is all pink in the face Lisa has come back to him. Chelsea looks round and sees me peering through the ward door. She toddles towards me and waves at me through the glass. I open the door and she runs into my arms.

– Nan, she says. – Nan nan.

Craig looks over at us.

– I'll take Chelsea over the family room, I says. – Let yous two get a bit of peace.

– Don't take her, says Lisa. – I want her here with me and Craig.

Craig looks across at Lisa and looks up at me. I lift Chelsea and swing her on to Lisa's knee.

– Is that all right, Mum? he asks me. – We just want to be… I smile.

– I'll see yous all later, I says. – Enjoy yourselves. I'll go and see the old man.

I know my mum won't be on the ward with my dad where Linda has got her doing Sundays over the garage now she needs all the work she can get. My dad's eyes are shut. He looks like shit. I say hello but he don't open his eyes. Where no one could be arsed to button his pyjama jacket the thick skin of his belly hangs off of his body in yellow folds. What is fucking dirty. And no one ain't put themselves out to shave him where my mum is so tired once she gets up the hospital after work she ain't got the strength left to clean him no more.

And yellow sunshine pouring through the ward windows gleams off of his tilted head. I am on my own with my dad. What damage he has done to his self. His fist dangling over the edge of the bed what everything is different between us now he is too weak to hit me. I ain't frightened of him no more.

– Nurse, I says. – Can I wash him?

She gives me a kidney bowl. She gives me a disposable cloth and some cotton wool. I fill the bowl with warm water.

– Dad, I whisper.

I dip the cotton wool in the water and loosen the dried snot and blood round his nose and mouth. I wipe the shit off of him with the cloth. I wash his eyes, his black neck.

All the happiness of being a mum and love and hope and work that comes of being a mum or a dad when you put your kids first and do your best for your kids and listen to your kids don't cost nothing even if you are skint you reap what you sow. The poor sod missed out on all that. Where your kids grow up and you grow older like they are slowly shunting you on towards death and over the edge to live on without you what don't seem so bad when you think by then if you have done your job they will be big enough to look after their own selves.

I wash his hands and try to dig up one good memory of me and him over the park or in the grounds like you see men over the flats teaching their kids to ride a bike but my dad weren't never like that. And all I can say of mitigating circumstances I bet no one never taught him nothing. He never once told me nothing where he come from of his own family.

– Can you hear me, Dad? I says.

– Maureen?

He opens his yellow eyes.

– Hello mate, I says.

– You don't think a lot of me, he says.

– Yeah well, I says.

– I ain't worth much, he says.

I button up his pyjama jacket.

– What ain't where I never of loved you, he says. – It were the drink what undid me.

My dad reaches out his washed hand and cuffs me gently over the side of my head.

– Maureen, he says. – Maureen.

His other hand is uncurling by me on the pale blue bedspread. He is offering me his hand. I take it but I don't say nothing.

– Cheers, Maureen, he says, and closes his eyes.

I must of fell asleep over him. Where Mum has come up after her shift with our Linda.

– How is he? she says.

– Sleeping, I says, wiping my eyes.

– We saw the nurse when we come in, says my mum. – She reckons the doctor will be round soon.

– Good, I says.

I get up and let my mum sit down on the chair.

– The doctor will see you now, says the nurse.

My mum stands up.

– Your husband is a strong man, Mrs Thomas, says the doctor. – He has a reasonable chance of pulling through.

– Fuck off, says Linda.

– Believe me, Madam, we are doing our best for him, we are doing all we can.

– Thank you, says my mum.

– Excuse me a moment, says the doctor.

He moves away, examining some notes on a clip-board. The old woman raises her eyes to the pale green ceiling.

– Thank god for that, she says.

– You been crying, Maureen, says Linda.

– No, I says.

– I don't know why you would even bother crying over that old cunt, she says. – He won't never shed no tears over you.

The doctor glances over at us. My mum is laughing. He looks away, sticks the clip-board under his arm, and trots off out of the ward.

– Fucking Paki, says Linda.

– So what about my party then? says Mum.

– I've baked one of my famous fruit cakes, says Linda.

– Some of the old man's lot are coming up from Wales, says my mum.

– So it is still on then? I says.

– Of course, says my mum. – Give us all something to look

forward to. A proper knees-up. You heard what the doctor said. The old man will be out of here before you can fart.

LOCAL WOMAN HITS LOTTERY
JACKPOT

Mrs. Nora Thomas, matriarch of the locally renowned Thomas family of Chaucer Court, Haggerston, was the winner of seventy thousand pounds on the National Lottery last Wednesday when all her numbers came up.

Unfortunately for Mrs. Thomas there were two hundred and twenty-eight other winners with the same combination of numbers, so the jackpot had to be shared.

The winner, who has nine children, twenty-one grandchildren, and eight great grandchildren, says she has not yet decided how she will spend her winnings.

Linda Thomas, the eldest of the winner's five daughters, said Mr. Thomas is at present unwell in hospital, but that he should be strong enough to attend the big family knees-up she is organising to celebrate her parents' Golden Wedding next Saturday.

"I hope this news will give them a boost," she said. *"My mother deserves a bit of luck. We are all hoping that they will treat themselves to a luxury holiday once my father has regained his health."*

What was a turn-up! Where I never won nothing crossing my fingers and toes every Saturday night and the Wednesday I held my breath watching them balls out of the machine except two or three tenners over the years and fifty quid once that week I splashed out on a few extra tickets off of my system what you could say was lowering the odds and nothing ventured after I won fifteen quid over the bingo what was all I had to show since it first started when we was all hoping against hope and very quick to believe we stood a fair chance of changing our lives forever.

But still I persevered you could say was foolish dreams or I was just stuck in the habit where it give me a buzz if I won or if I never won nothing I still got to go through it what was a waste of money if it was worth it or not but I got that feeling one way or the other on the edge of my seat and I must of liked it. Else I wouldn't of kept on with all them small losses week after week. What sadness stayed with me even after I won if that was the whole point. To feel sad even before I knew I had to share it with all them other people. Like you can't believe one after the other the balls bubbling out of the machine making me laugh and laugh how you feel in a dream when you know it ain't real but you still feel the same pain and humiliation.

And don't think I never checked. Knowing my luck I checked and checked again. Nine, twenty-one, eight, fifty five, twenty-seven, two. No mistake! I'm a millionaire!

What was lucky for me Victor was over the T.A. with Raymond along for the ride where Raymond will go anywhere with him of an evening just for something to do with his self if he is doing a disco over the Scout Hut or Manor Boys our Raymond carries his record boxes for him or the community hall because Raymond gets a bit bored playing pool by his self on the little table they all clubbed together for him in his room where he's never been one for the pub or any of that what his mates if he had mates what he never did have no mates when you come to think of it.

So when my numbers come up I was on my own. Not that if Raymond was indoors he would of been sat with me. No. Where he spends hours and hours in his room playing pool against his own self trying to come out on top what can't be very satisfying for him.

But even if Raymond had of popped in to me in the front room on his way up the stairs. How he was a bit slow on the uptake even the shrieks of laughter parked on my arse in front of the telly waving my ticket what ain't his fault he would never of put two and two together the old man always says he was dropped on his head I thought weren't a nice thing to say to me like I never kept our Raymond from harm when he was a baby.

Or was he born like it. If he is deep all what Raymond takes in or what is the matter with him when he cries in his room. If I should go up to him or what. But I don't never go up to him.

Not that Victor would of took nothing off of me neither. What ain't his way where he is all give and no take if he don't never like to find his self on the receiving end so he ain't obligated to feel grateful to no cunt or beholden how you feel if you ain't careful? He won't take nothing in return even thanks what he don't want no thanks how he is with people when he helps people. Where I always end up feeling all what I owe him if he was totting it up in his head until you ain't got no chance ever getting straight.

Before I got used to it. If he is a mug or what but that's
how it is. And he reckons what I extend my friendship
over and above all he helps me out is worth every penny
and his choice if he wants to be like that towards me
for his own reasons and ain't for me to argue with him
because he likes it like that.

Not that I don't share my home with him but he knows
it ain't out of the kindness or goodness. He puts his hand
in his pocket every Friday and always a bit extra for myself
in the week to tide me over whether I need it or even if I
ain't you couldn't say no if he was flinging it at me could I?
And he is never skint.

But he do have a gob on him where he likes to talk
over the pub so I was glad he weren't with me when my
numbers come up. But he means well taking our Raymond
out from under my feet even if Raymond ain't under my
feet where he keeps his self to his self on the pool table
in his room and ain't much company for nobody but
Victor lets his mouth run away with him. And I don't like
the click of the balls over my head and the thud on the
cushion when Raymond comes home and cries upstairs
under the covers or his face buried in his hands muffled or
his low noise he makes when he pots the black. How it is
with them people all snippits in your bosom Victor can't
help his self over the pub leaning in to show he belongs
and to draw people in what is only Alan and Sandra or
Gina if she gets out or Linda deigns to sit at my table or
Aggie and her cousin and Aggie's Mick what is the limit
of pegging out my dirty washing but still. He pokes fun or
jokes if he is cunning getting the drinks in and smiling at
all them people to be pleasant and if they like him at my
expense sometimes it feels like what ain't no law against it.
Because he is my friend and winks at me to show me how
he feels about me and he don't mean nothing by it. Where
he wouldn't want to take nothing off of me. But never

bothers even to try with our Maureen what won't give him the time of day. So what if he talks about our Susan. As long as he don't know I won nothing.

And Billy weren't indoors neither. Where I work and work only to come home for him to take my money off of me and out the door I suppose somewhere inside him he must be grateful but you could of fooled me. But he weren't in.

Where I don't have to buy no tins for the old man no more. What is a big saving I can tell you. So Billy is at my door all the hours when he's blown all what I give him the first time of asking where he knows I ain't done all my money after my fags and that if I ain't been over the bingo still in my purse or the Co-op to get a few bits or spuds and that down Hoxton what ain't worth it now just for myself of an evening if I want chips and that and pie if there is pie left over for nothing off of work? And Raymond pops something in the microwave before he goes out of a night-time with Victor. Unless we all stay indoors and Victor cooks us one of his dinners some warehouseman over the meat wholesalers what Vic done him a favour years ago he ain't never forgot of chops or a piece of brisket he knows how to pot-roast what is more than you can say for most people. Otherwise he tells me not to bother. He'll treat our Raymond to a doner on the way home.

The same day poor Susan got eighteen months and Maureen's Craig come out of hospital on crutches what was a miracle he could walk at all. I really thought I was in the money. If it was happiness or what would you call it. Sort of dazed and crying and smiling how I was rolling in it like a pig in shit.

I was sure my old life was over. I will never forget that feeling I treated myself to a few nice bits with all what I had in my purse scraped together for the electric key what

was off of the bone what I never normally ran to that ham
they do over the Co-op with white fat and crumbs. While
you wait the girl sliced it for me with the knife sharpened
over the years until the blade is worn away almost to a
skewer and you can see her mouth watering.

And a fresh soft cut loaf and a bottle of salad cream
and a soft round lettuce and a box of After Eight mints
for afters what I am rather partial and forty fags and a big
jar of coffee and a tub of peeled prawns. The electric will
have to wait. I put a Gazette over my bits in my basket so
anyone what knew me what was every-one round here
I never wanted no one to peep in my basket and ask no
questions if you're luck has changed Nora or what.

What with me thinking I'm a millionaire. Nora Thomas
in the money! And you would of thought the same if all
of your numbers come up my old life was over. Millions
I had coming to me! What I don't think was daft or just
wishful thinking under the circumstances.

But not like some corny berk on the telly with six new
motors lined up outside his mansion where the big winners
all want the same things what is making a show of yourself
and all what you got out of it. How could that be happy
when all your friends think you don't want to know them
no more. Or are they all after you for what they can get.

Or a villa in Spain by my Dolly the sunshine and sea
and Sangria now I got the choice I can do what I like.
What gives me a headache when the sun shines and
shines and all them flavours I just want to go indoors
and lie down in the dark and get some peace and quiet.
Or jack in my job what I hate and a nice house out at
Hainault we could live out the rest of what we got left. Yes.
And enough over to give my kids a lump each of cash if
they would all forsake the place they was born and bred
and live a decent life for their selves and their kids what
was a new start at least. Except for Alan what can fend for

his self the game he's got his self into. He don't deserve nothing. I swear I won't give him a penny.

Without scrimping and scraping how I have scrimped and scraped all my life just to eat and get our fags and pay the rent and put clothes on the kids' back. Where you walk in a shop and buy what you want without checking what is on special or own brand beans and sauce and that what ain't the same and cutting coupons to save twenty pence. You can eat what you want and do what your fancy takes you without no cunt telling me to move my arse that floor needs scrubbing.

And enough left over after all that to help Billy so he won't never have to suffer no more. Where I ain't never got enough money after I fork out for my fags and the electric and the telly and phone and all what I got to pay out on the catalogue I ain't never got enough over to give him for what he needs. Yes I know I should of left him in that place.

So he gets up to all sorts since Lorraine got done where she used to look after him. What can't add up to much more than a couple of hundred a week I reckon if I could come to some arrangement with our Alan wholesale or that.

Swindled out of my millions how I felt when I made my claim. Seventy grand? You sure? How could of all them other punters chosen the same numbers as me what was my system of my kids, grandkids, great-grandkids, door number, birth date, and the number two for me and my Tommy together side by side all them years and loved each-other ever since we was young and stupid.

Seventy grand. I was shouting down the phone. Is that all? What was more than I ever had in my life before or since and more than I'll ever get again knowing my luck. And all my dreams out the window.

Seventy grand. A nice little chalet by Camber Sands or Canvey Island a caravan like Julie's when the old man gets his strength back we could go down there weekends and holidays off of work and enjoy ourselves eating whelks on the beach and fish suppers and over the bingo.

Or a two-bedroom Linda was saying Walthamstow Marshes was it or Canning Town ex-council she was looking at rental investments what I thought was no better than round here but no one would swap with you if this block was the last block on earth even their one bedroom for my three bedroom if you think I ain't tried. But over Canning Town nobody knows you from Adam. Nobody knows all your business how it feels when your kids rob and ponce and sell the stuff to your neighbours' kids and grandkids what is all the fucking misery I have to live with every day of my fucking life. What is the more shame I endured the other morning before work where Alan shut up shop and took Sandra to Hastings for her birthday surprise. When I cried on my way through the flats to the bus stop because I witnessed a queue of hunched and scabby kids rattling outside his door, waiting for him to come home? Where he never thought to get one of his boys to look after his customers for him if he wanted a day out but he never give the poor sods a second thought. And must of been out of pocket on account of it what was his problem where you can't trust nobody the game he has got his self into.

Or jack in work until the money's all spent where Billy would start on me as soon as he found out. Day and night until it's all gone Billy milking me where I know I should stand up to him but I can't. He'll have it all off of me. Whether he robs me or I give it to him of my own accord what don't make no odds. And all the rest of them on my back it ain't fair Mum you should of give some of it to me. You didn't oughta let Billy bleed you like he does bleed me what they reckon ain't fair on the rest of them. My Stephen's boy needs shoes, Mum. My big end's gone, Mum. Help me, Mum.

Seventy grand! I wonder how much them rehab places
what can get you off of the drugs and that for good and all.
Can't be all that dear otherwise why would people bother
if they was that flush they wouldn't have no problem
buying drugs in the first place. Maggie was telling me the
place where she goes sometimes as a volunteer. Just to talk
to people. If they ain't got no wages to pay out to them
people. They can't charge the earth for that.

Because I never wanted to raise no false hopes I am on
the bus up the hospital with the cheque in my bag where
I decided to wait before I told my Tommy of my good
fortune until the letter arrived off of the postman first
thing this morning in case even my seventy grand turned
out to be a mistake. What I never thought would take all
week. So I zipped it in the zip pocket of my bag and took it
in work and never said nothing what was tempting to see
the look on Linda's face if I waved it at her but I managed
to restrain myself. But now I can't wait to show it to my
Tommy. Where we are grid-locked all them people going
where they go and none of them don't look very happy
on their journey I am impatient to get up the hospital and
full of hope the money might raise Tommy's spirits and
give us a new topic of conversation how to spend it what
is like hen's teeth every day if he wants distracting from
his situation but I can't think of nothing to say to him no
more. Where he has wore me out what ain't lack of love for
him if anyone would get tired like that having to hold all
that new tenderness for him inside me now he ain't well
and I know that. Where he ain't been so easy to love.
    But Terry Harrison is one of the best on this route
not like some of the new ones what think it's dodgems
out there and don't give a toss people flying up the aisle
if they jerk forward or slam on the brakes because he is a
natural or how does he push on and they give way what

works for him when he is insistent. I don't think he saw me. He would of said hello. Because he knows I clocked him sniffing round our Maureen after his shift like he ain't got no home to go to and I ain't as slow as all that what Victor told me Terry's wife pissed off to Spain years ago now with some of the girls from work ten days full board and never come back. Where they never had no kids to tie her down and she must of wanted a bit of fun before it was too late how some girls ain't afraid to let go of what they know and start again where I ain't got the bottle. But what a agony to die knowing you missed out on all what is life about meaning kids of your own why she never of come home maybe if they was a bad combination. How poor Terry must of felt. Was she guilty all the pain she put him through or maybe she just walked away and never looked over her shoulder how he must of needed her or if he never of needed her no more why she done the off in the first place if she couldn't live like that. Not that I ain't got no regrets of my own life and I know it's too late now for all that but sometimes you can't help thinking what if you never done what you done. When the kids was kids and I was stuck indoors I never even got dressed no more and I never wanted to feel all them feelings what I wanted to end all that. Until I was just sobbing in bed and couldn't sleep and my kids was downstairs in the front room how I knew they was better off without me I was so bad I told the big ones to keep an eye on the little ones for me and I would come down when I felt a bit better. I was howling into my pillow. However hard I tried but no one weren't listening to me.

Not that Maureen gives him the time of day. She blanks him over the garage and all that old game like she don't know him. If she is giving him a dose of his own medicine and serve him right how he broke her heart and she never of deserved it. Until he offers his self to her to take her away from all the shit in her life. If he don't turn her head where he is still a bit of a looker and she has her memories of him what she ain't never forgot. And he takes care of his mum what I heard not like my lot what wouldn't piss on me if I was on fire. I am frightened for her. We don't want no trouble.

But I had to wait so long for the cheque we was sat in the dark with no telly and I had to pop out on the landing to boil the kettle on the lead Aggie let me plug in her hall socket until Victor took my electric key over the showroom for me to charge it and the lights come back on. Not that I know what to do with the cheque now they sent it. Aggie said to sign on the back and she wanted to put it in her bank but that don't seem right. I gotta give it some thought. Not that I don't trust Aggie but seventy grand is seventy grand. I keep on looking in my bag to make sure the cheque's still there and just this once to celebrate out of the offy what a little drop won't kill him for my Tommy chinking in my bag where they had them miniatures a drop of what you fancy three for the price of two what a little something to cheer him up won't do him no harm just this once.

And I'm smiling on the bus how only last week Vic had to borrow me a few quid for Billy because my purse was empty. After I paid out all what I had to pay out and bought my fags and done the rest of my wages over the bingo and Vic had to charge up my key. He took out his wallet. I don't know why he is so pleased if I have to lend off of him. But I took ten quid for Billy. Vic was smiling. He loves all that. Billy done the off. Victor took my Raymond out. I put the telly on. And look at me now!

A go in one of them rehab places for our Billy would set me back what was a small price to pay if you ask me the end of Billy round me day and night for what he can get. I never knew how bad it was until Lorraine got put away.

Where before he was feeding off of her now it's all down to me. Even if I never saw him again. If he turns against me like Maggie and her kids what don't want to know me. I am ready to let it. I am so sick of it.

And maybe they'll sort out our Susan in Holloway. You never know some of them do come out better than what they went in. And one of them motorised cripple carts for Maureen's Craig a bit like driving a fork-lift if he wants to get about and that. What would be a big thank you to Maureen what has been good to me over the old man and that where he ain't been well and if Maggie would forgive me the stunt I pulled bringing Billy home out of that other place where I swear it weren't even clean. I know I've only got myself to blame after what I lured him with my bingo money where I missed him and now he's at me day and night however much I give him he still wants some more.

I know I done wrong. And the boys in care he got even more reasons to feel bad. And the worse he feels the more money he takes off of me to make his self feel better. And the worse I feel the more I can't say no. So the harder I got to work is killing me just keeping myself going where I go up the hospital every night to sit by my Tommy and every night I fall asleep in the chair so I can't even look after him properly I am such a prat although I say it myself I can't go on like this no more.

And some nice bits for Dawn's girls four matching fur coats in navy fully lined with hoods and muffs to match out of that trendy shop in Chapel Street what I know Dawn would give her eye teeth or the Dalmatian ones with ear-muffs and something for Linda new shoes or she likes a silky blouse what ain't nothing to her with all her rental investment and all that but it's the thought what counts. And Georgina needs a washing machine. Where her Dennis is on the sick it's hard to manage over the launderette with six kids and a new car for our Frank out at Beckton what is a long way and after that a holiday for me and Tommy if I could persuade him to go on holiday with me what no amount of money can make somebody go away if they want to stay at home and feel sorry for themselves. Not gallivanting where you don't belong. Even if we did get ourselves a caravan Canvey Island or Clacton what is only a few quid on the coach he wouldn't never fancy it where he reckons the coach makes him puke and a pint is a pint whatever pub you sup it by the sea-side they skin you alive.

So what about me. After Billy's clinic and Frankie's car and Dawn's kids and Linda and a washing machine for Georgina and something for Susan when she sends me a V.O. Alan ain't getting fuck all off of me. And I forgot Raymond if he would give his right arm for a fishing rod where he told me one night he would love to fish in the cut again and over the River Lee like he says he used to go fishing when he was a little kid of what I ain't got no recollection if Vic took him up there where Raymond can get quite wistful sometimes over anything like that.

What about me? The more I think the less if I'm stuck with my old life a new coat or a set of teak units for the front room or a bedroom suite or a leather settee or a nice bit of carpet up my stairs and passage or a new fridge freezer or this or that I mean what's the fucking point. All I want is Billy off of the stuff so he can get his kids back and my Tommy home with me where he belongs to me.

They want to give them stairs up to the ward a good sweep. My feet are killing me. No I don't like lifts. Not even after the day I have had over the canteen to drain the deep-fat fryer and clean it where I was already knackered after I done the toilets what our Linda pushes me so hard I don't know if I am coming or going.

Not that she never appreciated all what I done extra for

her or never give me an extra four quid on top of my money because she did give me an extra four quid for my extra work but I don't need it no more what I got in my pocket where I was in half a mind to tell her where to stick it.

But I ain't decided what to do yet. If my Tommy was indoors in his chair gobbing all over my carpet and pissing his self and all that would I feel how I feel so tied to him since he has been up the hospital? No. What I forget how I wanted to fuck him over sometimes before when he was bringing me down and down where you can't go no lower but now where am I? If I ever would of done it. When he was indoors in his chair if I could of binned him.

No. I don't want to get stuck in no lift. If you was with people to talk to but on my own would be even worse with all the shit in my head what no one don't never want to be stuck on your own with all that. I'd rather struggle up the stairs. My poor feet! The litter on the yellow treads how can people? I finish my fag on the landing outside the ward where I'm trying to get my breath back after my climb and stick it in the sand bucket.

And in through the double doors. I want to see my Tommy. Where he's doing a bit better I want to show him the cheque and make plans for us. We hold hands and talk now like we never really got the chance before. How I can't never go nowhere without him. Even if I got the millions what I thought I was entitled. Unless he was coming with me to finish what we started after all these years I ain't giving up on what we got. What is all my life I got left.

Past the nurses station where you'd think they'd of knowed me by now. But most of them girls off of the agency you never see a face twice. I open the curtain round my Tommy's bed but his bed is empty. The mattress is stripped bare. They must of moved him to a different ward. The monitor by the bed is switched off.

What have they done with my Tommy. Where the

cleaner has mopped the floor round his bed the streaks of the mop is still wet. All his bits off of the bedside cabinet. His bed socks where his feet used to get cold and sweets and his baccy tin they used to wheel him out in the corridor in his bed for a smoke of a night-time with all his drips and wires and that when he was desperate after I went home.

– Mrs Thomas, says the nurse. – I'm so sorry.

She hands me a brown paper bag. I open the bag and smell Tommy's smell coming off of his socks and his baccy tin. I close the bag.

– You what, I says.

– I'm so sorry, Mrs Thomas, says the nurse. – We tried to call you at home but there was no answer.

– I was at work, I says.

– He passed painlessly, in his sleep, says the nurse. – He never suffered. I'm so sorry. Would you like a cup of tea?

– He done what? I says.

– About an hour ago. We did all we could for him.

– Where is he? I says.

– We just took him down, says the nurse.

I stare at her.

– To the morgue, she says. – Would you like to see him?

– The morgue? I says. – The doctor reckoned he was getting better.

– I could take you down, she says. – To say good-bye? Sometimes it helps.

– I thought you said he passed, I says.

– Yes, says the nurse. – Painlessly, in his sleep. Would you like to say goodbye?

– It's too late now, I says.

On my way home it ain't no different every night coming back from the hospital on the bus leaving my Tommy behind. I read the evening paper on the bus and forget

my husband is dead. I let myself into my home and Billy
is sitting in the old man's chair. Victor must of let him in
earlier.

– Get your arse out of that chair, I shout.
– Do what? says Billy. – You got my money? I ain't feeling
too clever.
– Your father's dead, I says.
– Do what?
– He's dead, I says.

Billy rises slowly out of the chair and shuffles over to
the window. He begins to cry how he's never been a good
father to his boys.
– You do all right, I says. – Under the circumstances.

Billy pulls back the nets. In the grounds Alan's Sandra's
kids is mucking about with a ball by the wheelie bins. An
overflow pipe is splashing water on the roof of the sheds.
Billy howls how he wants to get his kids back off of the
care order.
– Yeah yeah, I says.
– No Mum, he says. – I'm gonna knock the gear on the
head.
– Yeah yeah, I says.
– No Mum, says Billy. – I've gotta get my boys back. I can't
live like this no more.
– Heard it all before, I says.

Billy flops back in the old man's chair.
– Don't believe me then, he says.
– I don't, I says.
– I'm on a waiting list for funding, says Billy.
– What you mean go in one of them rehab places? I says.
– I'm on a waiting list, says Billy.
– How long?
– Six months, a year, says Billy.
– A year? Your kids won't know you no more. I'm gonna
phone Maggie over.

– What for?
– About that place she goes down there sometimes to talk to people? Where they rehab people and all that.
– What's the point? says Billy. – I ain't got the funding.
– No harm in asking, I says.
– I ain't feeling too good, says Bill.
– Hold your horses, I says.
    So Maggie gives me the number of the rehab place. I ring up and a lady answers the phone.
– My son is a drug addict, I says.
– Yes? says the lady.
– I want to pay to get him a cure, I says.
– Does he want rehabilitation? says the lady.
– Yes, I says.
– Can I speak to him? says the lady.
– She wants to speak to you, Bill, I says.
Billy pulls a face.
– She won't bite, I says.
    Billy cries down the phone then hands it back to me.
– Good, says the lady. – We have a place here for him. We can help him.
– How much? I says.
– That's difficult, says the lady.
– Yeah? I says.
– Seventy, says the lady. – Give or take.
– You what? I says.
– Seventy thousand, says the lady. – For the twelve weeks.
– You having a laugh, I says.
– No, says the lady.
– Seventy thousand? I says.
– Yes, says the lady.
– Fuck off, I says, and put the phone down.
– You should of left me in that detox place, says Billy.
– I know that, I says. – I am sorry I done that to you.
He looks at me.

– I am sorry too, he says.

What must of been a first. But I weren't thinking nothing like that at the time because I knew he was in pain over his kids where he couldn't get no comfort no more off of them. I thought he was going to come to me for a cuddle instead but he can't. He buries his face in his hands and sobs.

– Would you go in rehab though? I mean if you had the funding?

– Too right, says Bill.

– Ok, I says. – You're on.

– I ain't got the funding, says Bill.

– I got it, I says.

– Fuck off, says Bill.

– All of my numbers come up, Billy, I says. – On the lottery?

– If all your numbers come up you would of got more than seventy grand, says Billy. – Seventy grand ain't fuck all if all your numbers come up.

– I got seventy grand, I says. – Shared jackpot. I'm serious.

– You got seventy grand off of the lottery?

– Yeah, I says.

– Where is it? says Bill.

I take the cheque out of my bag and wave it at him. He tries to snatch it off of me. I stuff it back in my bag.

– Will you go in the clinic? I says.

– Yeah, says Bill. – I will.

– This is serious, Bill, I says. – Don't muck me about.

– I know, he says.

– Ring them and tell them then, I says.

– You ring them for me, he says. – I ain't feeling too clever. I need the toilet. You got some money for me?

I slip out when Billy is in the toilet and double lock the front door from the outside so he can't escape. I shout up the landing for Alan but Sandra says he's gone over the

White Horse. And left her indoors to wait in for the gas
man. I find Alan in the snug with a pint of lager.
– Mum, he says.
– It's the old man, I says.
– What, says Alan, making little biro marks up and down
the columns of numbers in his notebook.
– He's dead, I says.
– Yeah? says Alan. – I'm sorry.
– Yeah, I says.
– Did he suffer?
– Painlessly, in his sleep, the nurse said.
– They always say that, says Alan.
    I pick up Alan's pint and take a big slurp out of it.
– I told Billy, I says.
– Yeah? says Alan.
– I got him locked up indoors, I says.
Alan looks up from his sums.
– He wants to go on a cure. I won something on the
lottery. Maggie give me the number of a clinic. It's all
booked. Can you take him down there?
– What's brought this on? says Alan. – Because the old man
kicked the bucket like Billy wants to get his kids back?
– Something like that, I says.
    Alan chuckles. I sign the lottery cheque on the back
and he takes it off of me.
– Come on then, I says.
– Now? he says. – Right now?
– Yeah, I says. – Before he changes his mind.
    Over home Billy is trying to climb out of the toilet
window. Alan gives him something to tide him over.
– I can't sit in a tail-back on the M3 with Billy rattling in
the back of the car, he says.
    While Billy is sorting his self out and Alan is guarding
him I go over the Co-op and buy a bar of soap and a
toothbrush for Billy to take with him to the rehab. When I

get back he is nodding out in front of the telly. His few bits
of clothes he brought round for me to wash are drying by
the fire. I stuff the damp clothes in a carrier bag.

– Come on Billy, says Alan. – Let's be having you.

– Look after him for me, I says. – Make sure you ring me
when you get there. Promise me to give the cheque to the
lady.

– What do you take me for? says Alan.

I wave good-bye to my sons and go back indoors. I put
the kettle on and spark up another fag. I look in the fridge
to see if there is anything to put in a sandwich. I make a
coffee and open a box of cake and go in the front room
and switch on the telly.

I like that Pet Rescue where the vet is so nice it soothes
me to see how he helps all them sick animals. He is
holding a guinea pig with pus in its eye. He has a nice
voice. He has nice hands. All right so I am mad. But you
gotta trust people sometimes. What use is seventy grand
to me anyway if Billy would of had most of it off of me one
way or the other. I might as well take a gamble on him at
least this way he's got a chance. Billy wants to get his boys
back off of the care order. He has got feelings. He cried real
tears over them kids didn't he?

Even if my Alan did a U-turn at the end of the road
and sold my lottery cheque on to one of his mates. No one
wouldn't give him no more than thirty grand. That's what
they're like them people.

Poor Billy is nodding in the back of the car and Alan
has thirty grand in his pocket. Then what? Alan dumps
Billy at the side of the road. Billy finds his way home.
Then Alan has Billy round his neck for the rest of his life
begging off of him for what he needs where he's got every
right to beg off of his brother after what his brother went
and done.

Or the two of them together into the sunset on a
bender until the money is all gone. Where Alan has been
saying he could fancy a break from Sandra gets on his
nerves how she clings like a limpet and is all over him
like flies round shit even on the tablets off of the doctor
what she reckons just ain't strong enough. But Alan would
be nothing without her. Because she irons his socks and
is more of a mother to him than I am. Even if he did
come home to keep me company how lonely I am where
Raymond won't come out of his room no more and Billy
gone I ain't never ironing no socks for no cunt. And Alan
won't even have a drink with Billy where the arse out of
Billy's jeans and his dirty boots and that Alan says makes
us all look bad over the pub and nobody wants to look bad
if we got the choice to make something of ourselves.

Or bang bang you're dead like when they was kids.
Alan ain't backward at coming forward when the need
arises if Billy starts to get on his nerves. Bang! That'll shut
you up, Bill. How he whines and whines we all feel like it
sometimes but you gotta be patient, Alan. Giving it all the
bollocks family ties and all that but you don't give a shit.

Dragging your own brother out the back of your car
no problem off of the road into the forest and digging a
hole where Alan knows Epping like the back of his hand.
Where he was running errands on his bike for some big
man when he was a kid what I had no idea in them days
what went on how our Alan got started where you got to
start somewhere. You read in the papers an old man out
walking his dog barking over a dead body in the bushes
or joggers or kids making a camp in the undergrowth
something pale in the dead leaves what has worked its way
to the surface where the villains is too idle to dig a proper
grave. What used to be human beings like you and me.

But what a mess in Alan's car. He'd have to set the
car alight like on the telly they burn the car to hide the

evidence and report the car stolen. Joy riders. What a waste that nice car what he ain't even taken the plastic off of the seats yet and promised me an outing to Canvey to blow off the cobwebs as soon as the old man was out of danger.

Or one last big bag on the house before you knock it on the head, Bill. I can see Alan smiling. He does the spoon business and all that for Billy while Billy unbuckles his belt. He hands Billy the needle. And Billy takes it off of Alan and sticks it in his groin. The only place left what he uses to inject his self now the rest of him ain't no good no more what Lorraine told me he ain't got no more veins.

Thank-you, Alan. Billy's last words and then the needle slides in for the last time where Alan put in double or treble to make sure. What is the side of it sickens me the most not the begging and grovelling and all the bollocks what they say and the scabs and blaming me and the poverty what they bring on their own children what is bad enough but nothing turns me over to my stomach like the look on his face when the needle slides in.

Then my Alan's got to cover his self to make it look like an accident. Staggering into casualty crying my poor brother the addict has taken too much drugs in Alan's arms and a few tears mustered even Alan done it on purpose he's gonna feel a bit sad. What wouldn't be the first time Alan stepped over the line. If you ask me there ain't all that much difference selling the stuff or a bullet in the back of the head. Bang!

The kid on Pet Rescue looks the spit of our Gina's Stephen's boy. The vet gives the guinea pig an injection. The kid starts to cry. What starts me off crying because I remember my Tommy is dead and fuck knows what Alan has gone and done to our Billy. Where I asked Alan to do me a favour and never thought if he said yes to please me what weren't very likely or if he was bored in the pub and was happy to go for a spin in his new motor or to make amends for his offending behaviour. Because I am a stupid old woman.

Boo hoo. Tommy's chair is empty. Tommy is gone. What it's been like night after night when I get back from the hospital only up till now I've had Billy knocking on my door bumming money or fags or something to eat or anything what he can get out of me until he cleans me out. It is so quiet. And even after he cleans me out just to shout at me in the night what a cunt I am up my windows when I won't open the door because I need my sleep and sometimes I have to protect myself. And now my Tommy ain't never coming back. What am I supposed to do with myself of an evening?

The kid holds the guinea pig in his arms after the eye operation. The vet has extracted a piece of straw or seed of grass that had gone and lodged itself in the pet's eyeball. The kid's face is so happy when the guinea pig wakes up. I put my hands together what I ain't done since my mum died and pray that our Billy is still alive. I ain't praying to god but give me strength Tommy to go on without you not that you was much use when you was with me. But until you went in hospital we never spent one night apart. Not in fifty years. Now you ain't here no more. I can't believe I ain't never gonna see you no more but I will not let myself pretend you are still over the hospital. Please keep Billy safe. I know I'm dreaming but you maybe got some sort of power now you are dead over all what happens in this family to keep my kids safe where you never bothered when you was alive. You just never bothered.

And I got to ring the bus garage. So I ring the bus garage.
– Linda? I says. – Is Maureen still there?
– What's happened, Mum? What's the matter?
– Has Maureen gone up the hospital?

– She's still here, Mum. She's cleaning out the ovens for me.
– Tell her to come up to me after work, I says. – And you Linda. Both of you. I'm gonna ring Maggie and Georgina. And Frank.
– Is it the old man? she says.
– Yeah, I says.
– Is he worse?
– He's dead, I says.
– You what? says Linda.
– He's dead, I says.
– Dead? says Linda. – What about the party? What about my fucking cake?

The kid takes the guinea pig home and is holding hands with his mum in their back garden. The kid's dad is carrying a baby on his shoulders. Clean washing flaps on the line and sunshine and a bike and a doll's pram and the guinea pig eating dandelions and that where no one ain't mowed the lawn and the grass is long and green and full of flowers.

What starts me off again boo hoo where I never made it nice like that for my kids boo hoo until the phone rings and I blow my nose and spark up another fag.

I'm praying it's Billy on the phone. I'm trying to send my longing wishes for Billy down the phone to make it Billy on the other end of the line.
– Hello? I says.
– Mum! says Billy. – The cheque ain't no good.
I sit down.
– Billy! I whisper. – Thank god.
– What's the matter with you? he says.
– Where are you? I ask.
– At the treatment centre.
– You got there then?
– You ain't got no faith in me, Mum.
– It ain't that, I says. – I'm a silly old woman.

– What, you thought Alan was gonna do me on the way
down.

– It crossed me mind, I says. – I wouldn't of put it past
him. For the money, I mean, Billy, not nothing against
you.

– He never laid a finger on me, says Billy. – He reckoned
you must of really loved me to spend all that money on
me.

– Well, I says.

– But the cheque ain't no good, Mum, he says.

– What?

– They took the cheque off of our Alan and told him to go
but they're sending the cheque back to you.

– What's wrong with my cheque?

– You pay monthly when they send you the bills. You gotta
get a cheque book and that. Put the cheque in a bank.

– Right, I says. – Maureen can help me sort it out. What's
it like down there?

– Blinding.

I heard him take a deep breath.

– Mum? he says.

– I have got faith in you, I says.

Dear Maureen,

what nobody won't tell me, you gotta tell me,
what I know you know, who is my real MUM and
my real DAD. I know it ain't you because you
wouldn't never of done this to no kid of yourn.
Where the old woman never treated me no different
my whole life like I was one of her kids I will
always be grateful and think of her as my mum
whatever happens but please tell me Maureen.

But I hope and pray it ain't Maggie. Because she
ain't got a ounce of kindness for me and despises

the bones of me the way I am and her kids hate
me.

I see Lorraine at assoc but she said she don't
know nothing. I can't tell you what she gets up
to but it ain't nice how she treats people in
here and the things she tries to get me involved
you don't want to know even me what is supposed
to be her sister-in-law she ain't got no mercy
and thinks she is doing me a favour getting me
involved in all that. And is so tight it's untrue
what she gets hold of in here ain't nobody's
business.

You will never believe what Victor turned round
and said to me. He was like "maybe the old man
was trying to disown me because of the way I am."
Like everything is my fault. How can I Maureen
where no-one ain't never looked out for me I
never felt loved except by you what I thought was
my big sister and still do if you ain't the one
what give birth to me. I wish it was you Maureen.
Because you are the best of them all what ain't
saying a lot but I mean it. I know I shit on you
all. I cried after what Vic said. I know you hate
him. But he ain't as bad as you think.

What brings me to tell you something bad what has
happened to me. I am five months gone. When the
baby is born where I have been doing what I have
been doing it will have to be weaned off of the
stuff. Like that girl next door to our Gina her
baby was born like it and she turned out OK. They
wean the baby off of it bit by bit.

But the nurse weren't all that nice. So I
complained to the doctor. I told the doctor the
nurse said all sorts to me "how could I do that
to my own baby where the drugs go right through
the placenta in its little body and its brain"
what I never knew that and ain't no joke. Even
though I told the nurse none of it weren't my

fault where I had no idea I was pregnant if I
ain't had a period now for years and you know
there ain't nothing of me. What was a surprise
where I thought somebody might of cared about
me if I was pregnant. They might of felt sorry
for me and treated me with respect. Not even the
doctor weren't on my side. What was upsetting for
me.

But then the doctor reckoned it weren't safe
to make me rattle in my condition so they are
keeping me on the methadone and reducing it
slowly. So by the time the baby is born I should
be almost clean if all goes well. And out of this
shit-hole soon after.

What was good news for me, where one of the
screws in reception told me they lock you in a
cell and leave you to rattle whether you are
pregnant or not. Probably just to frighten me
what weren't nice Maureen.

It ain't easy thinking what damage I have done
but I try not to think about it, how I been
living and that, how could I of been so stupid.
I just eat up my dinners now for the sake of the
baby what needs food to grow. What is muck what
they give you although Victor come in last week
and give me some tobacco and sweets and that
although I never told him my news. What keeps me
going, Maureen. Otherwise I would top myself if
they give me the chance.

You don't know how it feels, when everyone hates
you for what you are. Nobody understands. Where I
can't help myself

Not that I was planning a baby but maybe a baby
of my own will help me keep it together what do
you reckon? The social worker says I'll get a
flat out of it, what will be better than going
back to the old woman because they won't let me
take the baby back to where I was living before.

```
Whatever the old woman says I ain't never going
back over home. Anyway some of them people don't
like kids in that squat. Not that there ain't
nothing wrong with staying over home if the old
woman slung Victor out. And give me back my old
room. But she won't never do that. I need my own
place, to give the baby a safe home. I won't be
on my own. Where the baby will keep me company?

Please tell me, "who is my real mum and dad." I
don't feel right being a mum if you don't know
who you are.

Luv Susan.
```

What hurt me how I was on my knees with my head in the big oven scrubbing out the burnt grease off of the floor at the back when Linda poked me right up the arse with the toe of her shoe.
– Maureen, she says. – The old man's dead.
  I stood up in my overall and took off my rubber gloves. I wanted to punch her on the nose.
– You what? I says.
I wanted to make her say it again.
– It ain't my fucking fault, Maureen, says Linda.
  I marched round the serving counter into the canteen.
– Where you going? Linda says.
– Looking for Terry Harrison, I says.
– Oh, says Linda. – Terry Harrison.
  The canteen was quiet. Terry was in his corner by the fruit machine. Where he sat every night after his shift over a cup of tea and his paper and his fags just to be near me.
– Maureen, he says, knocking over his chair as he got up. – What's happened? Is it your dad?
He held me and I cried.
– I love you, he whispered.
– You what? I says.

He wiped my tears off of my face with a serviette and unbuttoned my overall. I looked down at his big dirty hands fumbling with my buttons.
– Get your coat, he says. – You need a drink.

We never knew no one in the pub where he took me. The saloon bar was orange. Loops of red tinsel was draped off of the low ceiling and we sat side by side in the snug near the fire and I blinked at the fairy lights twinkling round the curly shelf brackets. Two men was playing darts. Terry was holding my hand. I poured brandy into myself out of a big glass. I melted holes in the red vinyl fabric of the bench seat with my fag. I picked at the holes until they shed crumbs of yellow sponge.
– Drink up, says Terry Harrison.

The brandy helped, but I was worrying about my mum. However hard the life he lead her what was all over now that hardship whether you like it or lump it and keep on smiling and having a few of a Saturday night with your kids and their kids over the Queen's Head or even the White Horse if they drag their selves away from their lives where family is all you ever had of your own and all you got left.

The brandy takes the edge off of the pain in my chest. My Craig is waiting indoors for me to change the dressing on his leg. Terry Harrison is touching my leg with his leg. And the busman smell of the road and oil coming off of him. If he still has his own special smell of his clean skin when we was kids how he used to fuck me over and over if I bury my nose in him. My Dawn would go mental.

Craig is waiting indoors for his tea. Sausage out of the freezer in the microwave or what else is there burgers from frozen or a couple of them cheese pizzas with chips and that where the doctor said he must eat after what he's been through with some peas and carrot on the side. And tablets to help him to sleep after the accident where you

lose your appetite over the traumatic shock but at least he's
alive and they never had his leg off.

– Penny for them, says Terry.

– I gotta tell my kids, I says.

– About us? says Terry Harrison.

– I meant about the old man.

– Right, says Terry. – Sorry. You gotta tell them now?

– Later, I says.

– Right, he says.

– What do you mean, us? I says.

– Us, he says. – You and me.

– Tel, I says.

– Yeah?

– Take me home with you.

– I thought you'd never ask.

   In the back of the cab he never kissed me. Like he
was saving it up until he got me home. Or what else was
happening? He never said nothing. He put his arm round
my shoulders and squeezed me to him but he never kissed
me. He was breathing in my hair and maybe giving me
time where he thought it was only grief making me want
him to kiss me. So what if it was grief. But I knew Terry
Harrison. He knew I wanted him to kiss me but he would
not be happy if the thought crossed his mind he might be
taking advantage of me after I just lost my dad.

   His place is a bit neat. Not like he spends hours tidying
but like he never makes much mess. The draining board in
the kitchen is dry and bare and a clean white mug hangs
off of every branch on his mug tree. The top of his stove is
scoured white and there ain't no strings of melted cheese
or puddles of fat in his grill-pan. The plastic washing-up
bowl is dry and empty.

   We never flung off our clothes and did it on the
stairs up to his bedroom what we should of done I
suppose. Terry Harrison makes two cups of tea first and

opens a packet of Hobnobs.

We sit side by side on the settee in his front room and smoke and hold hands. Terry unfolds his hand out of mine and dunks a biscuit in his tea. What makes me feel old. We are old. The bottom crumbles off of Terry's sodden biscuit and sinks to the bottom of his mug. My Dad is dead. No wonder I feel old.

– Biscuit? says Terry.

– Nah, I says. – But you go ahead, Tel.

Terry helps himself to another biscuit. Craig must be getting hungry. Still, maybe he could phone over to Lisa and she'd bring the baby up to him. He'd play with the baby while she warms up some soup for him. Or could he hobble on his crutches to the kitchen and make his self a sandwich. What wouldn't kill him just this once.

Because I want to be with Terry Harrison. I am looking at him all the love and concern and kindness in him and his big dirty hands. I want his hands over me. Where Tony fucks me without touching me no more. Tony can't be arsed to touch me.

– How's your Mum, I says.

– Better, he says. – She's moved in with my sister.

– Nice, I says.

– Wanna look at the telly? he says.

– Nah, I says.

– Drink?

– Nah, I'm all right as it goes.

– How you feeling? he says.

– I'm all right, I says. – I know what I'm doing. Whatever you think.

– What d'you mean?

– You think I'm in a state, I says. – But I ain't.

– I don't wanna get hurt, says Terry, smiling at me.

I put down my mug and stub out my fag.

– Let's go upstairs, I says.

The bedroom is cold. Terry switches on the electric
fire and closes the curtains. The fire whirrs and gives off
a smell of singed hair and dust. The doors of the brown
wardrobe are shut. A blue shirt on a wire coat hanger
dangles off of the back of the door. The brown bed is high
and lumpy, covered by an Indian bedspread with a red and
green pattern of flowers and leaves. I sit down on the edge
of the bed and take off my shoes. I place my shoes side by
side on the bed-side mat.

– All right? he says.

– Not too bad, I says.

The bedspread must of looked festive once, when it
was new. I watch Terry empty his pockets on the top of
the chest of drawers. On the dressing table a portable telly
is balanced on a stack of phone books. Terry takes off his
jumper and his shirt. The hands of the clock on the chest
of drawers by the bed glow in the dark. Terry turns his
back on me. I watch him unzip his busman's trousers and
let them drop.

– Taters, he says.

– Ever-so, I says.

Terry gets in bed in his underpants and lights a fag.

– You gonna join me? he says.

I take off my jeans and fold them up and put them
on the floor. The lump in the back pocket of my jeans is
my letter from Susan. What feels to me like one in and
one out, meaning my dad is dead but Susan is bringing a
new life into the world, what is false hope and nothing to
rejoice over. She never even asked after the old man.

– Don't watch me, Terry, I says.

– You're beautiful, Maureen, he says.

I take off my top. I take off my socks.

– Look at you, he says.

– Don't, I says.

But he did make me feel proud of myself. How it is after

a couple of kids I ain't a young girl no more where your tits flop when you take off your bra and my big soft bum stripped naked in front of him but I never had one bad thought about my self. How he looks at me. He makes me look at my self through his eyes. I don't mind my self, how I am made. I am just me. I am still here. My dad ain't here no more. What it ain't easy to understand.

I take off my wedding ring.

– You're shivering, Maureen, he says.

I get in his bed.

– I love you, says Terry Harrison. – Come here.

– You pig, I says.

– What?

– Take off your socks.

– Sorry, says Terry.

We are laughing. I wish we'd flung off our clothes and done it on the stairs when I was in the mood. Terry is kissing me and messing about with my tits. I am thinking about the Indian bedspread. Where did he get it? His wife must of left it behind when she done the off.

Still, at least it's clean. I hate that smell of a dirty bed. A man's warm oily head smell and stale scented soap however much you love someone. What it was like in my Tony's room over his mum's when I was first going with him. Where he was a grown man his mum refused to change his bed for him.

– Tel, I says.

Terry lets go of me and sits up.

– You ain't in the mood, he says.

– Nah, I says, curling up in the bed.

– Never mind, he says.

– Sorry, I says. – Don't get pissed off with me.

– You just lost your father, he says.

I uncurl myself and sit up next to him in the bed. Terry takes my hand.

– Remember all them poems what you writ to me when I was inside? he says.

– What you sent back to me? I says. – I wonder where they ended up.

– They're in here, says Terry, pressing the palm of his hand to his heart.

– What you on about, I says, trying not to smile.

– Off by heart, says Terry. – Every one of them.

– You never! I says.

– Fuck all else to do in that shit-hole, says Terry. – You want me to prove it?

– Nah, I says. – You're all right.

Terry slides back down under the covers and lies on his back. He is staring at the ceiling. I slide down beside him.

– Well? he says.

– Well what?

– What's going on? he says.

– Nothing, I says.

He reaches over and takes another fag out of his packet.

– Twos up, I says.

– What do you want, Maureen, he says, handing me the lit cigarette.

– Me? I says. – What do I want?

– Yeah.

– Dunno, I says.

– I want you, says Terry.

– I know that, I says.

I pass him the fag and prop myself up on my elbow so I can see his face.

– Your kids is grown up, he says.

– I love Tony, I says.

– What are you doing here with me then? he says.

I roll away from him.

– I'm sorry, he says.

– Well, I says. – I don't know what I'm doing. Do I?

– I'm stupid, says Terry. – I never meant to take advantage.

– I know, I says. – You're a good man, Tel.

– I love you, he says.

– I can't think straight, I says.

– It's the shock, says Terry.

– Shock?

– Losing your father, he says.

– Oh, I says. – Nah. It ain't that. I ain't shocked. I can't believe he hung on for as long as he did.

– You'll miss him, says Terry.

– Hmm, I says.

– Was there things, says Terry. – What you and him never said?

– Nah, I says. – We done all that when he was up the hospital. We done all that. Waiting for him to die. I got my head round it then.

– Oh, says Terry. – Good.

Terry is rubbing the back of my hand with his thumb.

– It's me, I says.

– What about you?

– All them years with my Tony trying to make it come right. It's wore me out, Tel.

Terry is rubbing the back of my hand with his thumb. I feel like he's making a hole in me.

– What do you mean? he says.

– He ain't happy, I says, pulling my hand away. – Nearly thirty years trying to make him happy. What is hard work. And I ain't getting nowhere.

– You're wonderful, Maureen, says Terry.

– Yeah yeah, I says.

– No, says Terry. – I mean it.

– What a life he's led me, I says.

– But you stood by him, says Terry.

– What does that make me? I says. – A mug?

– No, Maureen, says Terry. – You're a good woman.

– So if I leave him?
– Do you want to leave him?
– What about my kids?
– It's down to you. Your life. Your happiness.
– Happiness? I says.
– You could be happy with me, he says.

I roll back towards Terry in the bed. He doesn't move. I can hear him breathing slow and calm in the dark, waiting for my answer.
– I am happy with you, I says.
Terry turns towards me.
– Don't wind me up, Maureen, he says. – You know what I mean.
– I mean right now I'm happy, I says.
– Where does that leave me? says Terry.
– You'll have to wait, mate, I says.

Terry reaches for another fag. I can hear his lips on the filter, dry and papery.
– Twos up, I says.
– Here, says Tel.
– Cheers.

I take a long drag on the fag and blow smoke-rings up to the ceiling. The ceiling is yellow. A dusty bulb is hanging inside a thonged shade of dimpled yellow paper.
– I got a hard-on so bad me balls ache, says Terry.

I reach across and take his cock in my hand. He groans and rolls over towards me and folds his hand over mine. His cock is hot. I take another drag on the cigarette before he takes it off of me and stubs it out. He holds my hand tight in his and moves his arse backwards and forwards so his cock strokes in and out of my hand. I look in his face. His eyes are closed and his mouth is open. He looks boyish, like when we was kids he used to wank over me if we never had no rubbers. But we ain't kids no more.
– I'm gonna come, he says. – I ain't had it in a while.

– Got any rubbers? I says.
– You sure? he says. – I picked up a packet just in case.
– You got me in the mood, I says.

LOCAL BOY SCOUT leader and long-term member of the Territorial Army Victor Maplin was killed on Saturday night when he fell from the balcony of a flat belonging to a family friend.

* * *

TRAGIC ACCIDENT KILLS SCOUT LEADER

* * *

Mrs. Nora Thomas, with whom he had lived as a lodger for many years, was with the victim when he fell. The victim had escorted Mrs. Thomas home after the funeral of her husband, who is known to have passed away last week after a long illness.

Mrs. Thomas was too shocked and upset to talk about the incident, but it is understood that the deceased was sitting on the balcony rail outside the home he shared with Mrs. Thomas and other family members, drinking a cup of tea with Mrs. Thomas after the funeral, when he lost his balance and fell backwards, hitting his head on a bollard just before he reached the ground.

Detective Inspector Whitman, in charge of inquiries following the accident, said that Mrs. Thomas was the only witness to the tragic fall. The police expect the inquest to produce a verdict of accidental death. Mr. Maplin had no family.

Miss Linda Thomas, 50, daughter of Mrs. Thomas, said that her mother was devastated after her double loss. *"Instead of celebrating fifty years of married life on the 9th December,"* said Miss Thomas, *"my mother buried her husband and lost her best friend."*

The horse she insisted she could run to out of the insurance what she had a couple of grand coming to her once the agent done his paper-work and a groom in top hat and black gloves if we all chipped in for the cars to follow the coffin to the graveyard and black ribbons plaited in its mane gleaming the black leather harness and all that flared nostrils and flubbery mouthful of clanking metal and teeth jangling and steaming on the tarmac outside St. Anne's or even three grand at best the agent reckoned minus deductions what weren't a lot after a life-time how my mum insisted she don't want it said she never give the old man a good send off.

In the fancy carriage with the cut glass panels they slid him with the flowers what was his last journey. Where they all come out of the flats and watched it prancing down Hoxton you couldn't help yourself not to think where his life went now it was all gone. And it hit me then, he weren't never coming back. His greasy old chair over home and a few empties rolled under it my mum must of missed when she tidied up the front room and his baccy tin and his slippers all what was left. Where a part of me understood how the old woman decided to bury him in his blazer with the brass buttons and slacks she got cleaned special for the occasion and a new white shirt and black tie if it meant something to her to look his best in the coffin and the other part of me reckoned what a waste of good money. What happiness with my mum and drink and work and nine kids I thought was the saddest thing where he was too angry or what else was it. Too angry.

But I had forgot if you lose somebody how it pains me

in my chest and throat. I had forgot all that. But once it started I had to bury my face. Even my face hurt. My dad is dead. Not that he ain't never gonna be happy or any of that but just he went and that's what happens.

But his flowers! All dragons out of carnations off of his Welsh cousins in red and white and green what come out of the woodwork and Husband and Dad and Thomas and Pop and Grandad and roses off of the Macbeth and all what the neighbours laid out in the flats of sprays of pinks and yellow chrysanthemums and gyp on the pavement under my mum's balcony and ferns propped against the wall of the outside stair-case in them little wicker baskets with that green sodden stuff what do you call it to keep them alive so plentiful even our Alan got choked up looking for the bouquet he ordered off of the florist he reckoned set him back two hundred quid. What got lost in all the floral tributes off of our neighbours if they weren't thin on the ground like the old man was somebody or out of respect for my mum where people knew her life and never blamed her for nothing what made her feel better if she sniffed in a hollow voice how we was well liked round here in spite of everything.

And there was one from Terry Harrison not flash or nothing for my sake but just enough and a nice card filled in what he must of gone over the florists and writ it his self where I recognised his writing with sympathy at this hard time with best wishes from Terry over the garage to make out like we was hardly even friends and made me blush how we was at it since my dad died.

I am smiling. I don't know what to do with my feelings for Terry Harrison at my dad's funeral like all the hurt of Terry all my life since he dumped me where I was used to feeling all them bad things about myself confirmed by him how I was dragged up to feel shit he is taking off of me at last and I don't know myself unburdened of all that like I ain't the same person.

Where I come into the damp darkness of St Anne's and Billy is sat at the back with Maggie and a minder from the clinic or nurse what used to be on the stuff by the look of him but he must of knocked it on the head now and wants to share his experience like our Maggie wants to share hers.

I stand behind Billy and he turns round. He winks at me. I smile at him. Music is coming over the tannoy what would of made anyone feel depressed where them clinic people know what is what sending a minder with Billy to bury his father that dreary music and the mouldy church smell and candles and all the family giving him the once-over to check if the treatment was working where he is sobbing and moaning over the old man you could see in his face how he would give anything to take away that pain.

What the clinic rules even on a day out whether it is a wedding or whatever you are not allowed nothing to oil the wheels even a bottle of that lager afterwards over the community hall off of Aggie's Mick what went over to France in his van like piss them clinic people class as a drug. Like you wouldn't believe Billy says the pain wracking him once all the methadone and crack and heroin and temazepam and that was clearing out of your system he got boils on his arse like fag burns that the gunk out of it stinks on your fingers and it hurts so much you can't hardly sit down. Not even something off of the doctor to get you through the day however bad you feel like crying and crying over your dead father you just gotta talk and let it out what they do in them places stirring up all the memories what is supposed to do you good in the long run. Only two paracetamol four times a day what Billy says is like pissing in the ocean and one ibuprofen every six hours don't even make a dent in it.

– Thank fuck they let you smoke in there, he says.
– Even the ones what never smoked before where there ain't nothing else to do. I am on forty or sixty a day now what Mum sends me cartons off of the fag man to keep me going. And she sends chocolate and sweets we are allowed in the meeting room in a circle on hard chairs with all them people smoking and munching sweets and crying and telling about all the bad things what was done to you when you was a kid. Like you wouldn't believe the stories what some of them poor sods suffered how they was messed about with. Where we took the odd clump off of the old man what never knew no better but we never suffered nothing like that when we was kids. Where we was always loved ain't it Maureen? Some of them people ain't never felt nothing like that. I reckon we was the lucky ones.
– Yeah, I says.
– Yeah, says Billy. – We done all right.
    And Maggie next to him in the pew holding his hand how she is there for him now he is clean she reckons it is a time to rejoice.
– Don't forget I lost my Pete, she says. – Don't forget I been there.
– Like you would let us forget, I says.
– What's that supposed to mean?
– Well, I says.
– I just want to help Billy, she says. – I know how hard it is to make changes. I been there, remember? I just want to give him support.
– You got the T-shirt, I says.
– Don't be hostile, Maureen, she says, over her shoulder.

I look up at the ceiling of the church. Billy's minder slides along the pew to give us some space.
– Well, Maggie says. – You are hostile, Maureen. Because

of who you are and how you live.

– Do what?

– Because you're still with that cunt.

– You mean my husband? I says.

– How can you do it to yourself, she says.

– Leave me out, I says.

– Why? she says. – Why don't you bin him?

– I love him, I says.

– You love him, says Maggie.

– He ain't all bad, I says.

– He ain't all bad, she says. – He ain't all bad.

– This pain, says Bill.

– Listen to yourself, says Maggie. – I love him. He ain't all bad.

– It ain't my fault how he is towards me, I says.

– No? she says.

– Ain't you never loved nobody? I says.

– Jesus, says Billy, hugging himself. – Like when your dad dies? Whether you loved him or maybe you did love him. Whatever. You need somebody. And Lorraine ain't even writ to me once since she was banged up. That fucking hurts.

– I know, I says, reaching out to put my hand on his shoulder. – I ain't no stranger to all that, Billy. You ain't alone with them feelings.

– Tell me about it, says Maggie.

Billy wipes his eyes on his sleeve.

– I always thought you lot was doing all right, he says. – I thought it was only me what couldn't…

– We all suffer, I says. – We all give ourselves a hard time over it.

Maggie turns round and smirks at me over the back of the pew.

– Here, she says.

– What? I says, sniffing.

– Take my hankie, Maureen, she says. – I don't think I'm
gonna need it.

I blow my nose and set Billy off crying again in the church
all the bad things he's done and laughing all the good
things he is gonna put everything right with his kids and
the old woman and that while he still has the chance not
like our dad he says what has totally blown it big-time.

The minder from the clinic slides back along the pew
and puts his arm round Billy. I give my brother a kiss
on the cheek and go and sit down next to my Tony. My
mum is sat right in front of us in the first pew with Victor
and Raymond and my brother Frank in his bus driver's
uniform with the bus smell coming off of him and the
knitted top what they wear on the buses under their bus
driver's jacket in the winter to keep their selves warm.

We stand up and sing the hymn my mum chose and I
feel sad for her the singing is so thin in the church. Where
none of us knows the words past the first couple of lines
except my mum and Tony's mum. On the hymn sheet the
mauve ink is all blurred since school assembly you forget
don't you? Where he makes us lie down and all that. Still
waters where it goes so high keeping up makes your throat
ache. What is a long time ago now for most of us and the
singing is so weak it never covers up the sound of my
mum crying.

She looks shrunk in her old black coat and where
Linda told her she weren't to let herself go no more now
the old man has passed and it was her chance to make
the best of herself if she had time on her hands she got
her hair coloured and permed in tight curls what looks
like a poodle from the back and don't do her no favours.
She keeps reaching up to fiddle with the new black scarf I
bought to drape over her shoulders for the extra warmth
and to look a bit more smart if none of us was able or

willing to fork out on a new coat for her. Victor pats her on the forearm to offer her comfort. If I glance at his dimpled hand on the back of the pew where the gold band pinching his fat pinkie my mum told me was his mum's wedding ring he kept for his self where nobody would have him. Or he never wanted a family of his own if he was happy in ours so why should he bother? Because I am thinking where have his hands been. What ain't something I want to think about if I can't help myself sometimes.

So I am trying to sing he leadeth me for my mum's sake and the bus smell coming off of our Frankie with my eyes closed I don't want to let myself. And the dirty musky smell in my nose from last night. Where I told my Tony I was over Dawn's to help her with the kids what was the truth if he never found out I dropped in at Terry's on the way home. His skin smell how he lowered his weight into me so hard gasping his flavour I don't want to remember in the church. What was only an hour stolen for myself between my husband and my daughter but it was long enough. Of love to sustain me through all what I had to get through of my own troubles.

Because of my dad in his box on trestles at the front with the lid screwed down and all them lilies like wax shedding pollen on the varnished pine what my mum thought looked more shiny than the stained oak and was not as dear although she protested that weren't never a consideration and was lined with lead all the same what offered more protection. The lilies are lifeless and the coffin looks too short and narrower than I think of my dad where you forget how they shrink when they get old. I am crying now. If I should of told him I love you whether I did or how do I feel now he has copped it and it is all over. I know I should of told him. Where he done his best what was crap. But like Billy says no one never messed about with us.

I look at my Tony staring into space over the top of
my mum's head and his lips moving what ain't the words
of the hymn or prayer but calculating odds minus tax
where he put a tenner what must of been his last tenner
on Fat Chance five hundred to one in the three o'clock he
never told me but he left the ticket in his coat pocket and I
clocked it where I was looking for tobacco when I was out
of fags and too tired to go out. What was a stupid name for
an horse.
– Tone, I whisper.
– Ssh, he says.

Frank puts his arm round my mum. Victor has hold
of Raymond to stop him from hurting his self. Raymond
pushes Vic away and bangs his head off of the back of the
pew. What he gets like if you upset him.
– Come on son, says Vic. – Come on son.

Raymond bangs his head off of the back of the pew
and roars the noise he makes when he loses it and puts the
wind up my mum.
– I can't handle this, she says.

Victor looks at her as if for permission what he has
to do to stop Raymond hurting his self. My mum shrugs
meaning help yourself, Victor, do what you like to him.
Vic sits on Raymond's back and folds him up. Raymond
coughs and farts all the air pushed out of him under the
weight of Vic grinning like Hitler in his uniform he wears
on special occasions with his hair oiled and the smell of
stale biscuits. Until Raymond submits and Vic gets off of
him. Raymond is sobbing and heaving with his face in
Vic's lap.

My mum is crying in Frank's armpit. What my brother
got out as soon as he was earning over Canning Town in
a warehouse he was took on as a packer at fourteen and
my mum couldn't wait to see the back of him. Where
the old girl in the office took a shine to him from the off

and offered him a room in her home for a pound a week because her own son went to Australia she couldn't help taking it personal if he wanted to emigrate and weren't never coming back. And she was just round the corner from the warehouse what Frank saved on time and bus fares and done him a cooked breakfast and his washing and a dinner after work what she was going backwards all what she paid out but Frank told my mum the old girl thought it was money well spent for the company what made her feel young again. And my mum was glad to see the back of him. Until Frank got her going if that was intentional on his part or he was just tactless telling her how the old girl looked after him like he was her own son. Then my mum cried over Frank after he went where she never thought she would of missed him at all. What just goes to prove that absence makes the heart grow fonder at least in my mum's case if she is a contrary old cow when she wants or maybe it's like that for everybody.

And I got my own kids to be proud of. I smile at my Dawn. She blows me a kiss. Her girls is on their best behaviour over the mystery of losing their great granddad where it is the first time they'd lost one of their own and they are in awe of the body in the box.

– Why did he die though? whispers Bella.

– He weren't well, whispers Dawn. – We all gotta go in the end.

– Go where?

– To heaven.

– Even you, Mum?

– Ssh.

– Even me?

– Yeah, in the end, says Dawn.

– Even Natalie? says Bella.

Tony's mum tut-tuts at the end of our pew where she never did make no bones reckoning her son was lowering his self getting mixed up with the likes of us. I mean to say

Tony's dad had his own shop what we never heard the end of they built up the business from scratch like they was the only ones what understood the meaning of hard work over Bethnal Green called George's Fine Meats Family Butcher. And neither of them wanted to take on board how it weren't easy for the rest of us to try and get somewhere in life if you ain't never been brought up to nothing like that. Or even if you was. Where Tony's mum sat out the back by the fire at a little table with a nice white cloth and drank tea and done the books while his dad worked with the saw and the cleavers. And she never got her hands dirty what the girl was for, she said, to wrap mince and belly strips where it made no sense to keep a dog and bark yourself. To pop out at dinner-time with her gloves on to fetch a few bits then had the girl wrap a nice steak or a couple of chops to take home the perks of the trade I mean if a butcher can't eat well then who?

And she knows all the words of them dreary hymns. Trembling under her hat and matching coat and dress she sponged and hung up after their last outing ready and waiting for the next time in the wardrobe with mothballs by the smell coming off of it. Where all the old bags from her lunch club and who she played cards with over the cold autumn and winter was dropping like flies. To sing and shed a few tears over her dead husband no matter whose funeral and offer up a prayer and feel lucky to be alive. Where Tony's dad passed on so soon after his early retirement what she warned him against when he sold the shop and put the money in the savings bank to draw on it if she was in need of a bit extra on top of her pension. Or to treat my Tony what she made it clear to one and all was always her favourite out of all her three sons what don't say a lot for the rest of them. And made them all turn against their own brother.

And our Craig is doing his best. His voice creaks in

pastures green over the other end of my pew holding hands with Lisa and little Chelsea what don't know no different, her sweet voice da da da da skipping along the pew in her new shoes.

But Craig ain't standing up to sing on account of his bad leg. Lisa's baby bag is open next to him. The inside of the flap is printed with ducks and rabbits frolicking in grass with pink and yellow flowers in it. Craig lifts his big hand and lays it across the bulk of the bag like he is claiming it, all what you need to look after a baby, the wipes and a stack of clean nappies and bum cream and powder and a bottle of weak tea with cow's milk for Chelsea with two sugars how she likes it if she gets thirsty or a bit fractious. And the elephant made of pink fleece what I got her for her birthday and some board books chewed all round the edges when she was teething and a packet of biscuits and orange mush in a plastic pot what Lisa makes out of carrots and Chelsea's baby spoon and fork in a pouch Dawn got her out of Argos. And spare clothes in case Chelsea messes herself and Ribena and all that tissues and cotton wool and bibs and all you have to cart around with you when you're a new mum. Or stuck indoors all day climbing the walls or tearing your hair out where you get so tired sometimes just getting yourself dressed is too much effort. Don't think I don't understand. How Lisa gets black smudges under her eyes and Craig takes the baby off of her never mind he ain't her real dad and over the park or Britannia where he was learning her to swim Sunday mornings before he done his leg in. And he tells Lisa to get herself back to bed what makes me proud he ain't an arsehole like his old man. What he must of got off of me. He ain't nothing like my Tony. It makes me want to cry.

I wish a choir of heavenly angels would pipe up and drown out my mum's singing where the second hymn ain't

a tune I ever heard before and I can't make out nothing of
the words on the hymn sheet because I ain't got my glasses.
I get a sinking feeling of despair for my mum's hopes on
top of all what I am feeling over the funeral where she
wanted her kids and all family raising their voice with
her for my dad in the church what nobody ain't singing
along to the groaning organ over the tannoy and I can't
even make myself try. Only my mum and Tony's mum and
a few of the other old women making a tinny noise and
warbling where they ain't got enough breath between them
to make no odds and my mum keeps on coughing.

Bella yawns and bangs the toes of her new boots off of
the back of the pew in front. My mum takes no notice and
Victor don't dare say nothing because he is wary of me and
for good reason.

– Told you not to bring them fucking kids, Dawn, says my
Tony.

– Ssh, I goes.

– Ssh, hisses Tony's mum.

Dawn leans over and gives Bella a kiss. The baby stirs.
Barry sticks a dummy in her mouth. Jessica and Natalie
are fidgeting. Barry gives them some sweets to keep them
quiet.

– I want sweets an all, says Bella.

– You gotta share, says Barry.

My Tony blows his nose loudly.

– Ssh, I says.

– Don't ssh me.

– Ssh, I says.

So Tony lowers his head and butts me on my shoulder
what is his way to express what he wants to express
without going to no trouble to say it.

– Don't start, Dad, says Dawn.

– I ain't a kid, says Tony.

– Ssh, I says.

– What? Am I a cunt? he says.

– If the cap fits, I says.

– Don't, says Dawn. – Don't start. Not in here.

– See what I gotta put up with, says Tony.

– What? I says.

– Don't look to me for sympathy, says his mum.

– You what? says Tony.

– Shut it will ya? she says.

    I can hear him grinding his teeth how he got ticked off by his mum in front of me what ain't no surprise to nobody if that weren't his favourite feeling. And I feel sorry for him touching his skull and cross-bones thing to tighten his bootlace tie and them black boots he squeezes his self into what I'd been up to with Terry Harrison and my Tony trying to come it like Clint Eastwood.

– Can't say I never of warned you, says his mum.

– Change the record will ya, says Tony.

– Well! she says. –That's you all over. Why you always aimed so low. You could of done much better for yourself if you'd aimed a bit higher.

– You what, I says.

– I love Maureen, says my Tony.

– You what, I says.

– Me and Maureen's been together a long time now, Mum. We love each-other. When you gonna get your head round it?

    His mum opens her mouth to speak but nothing comes out. She turns away and snivels under her hat, then tries to catch up with the singing like nothing was said. I look at my Tony. He winks at me. I start to cry.

– Don't you start, says Tony.

– Do you mean what you said? I whisper.

– What? says Tony.

– What you said to your mum. How you feel about me.

– You know how I feel about you, Maureen.

– Do I?
– What is this?
– Tell me.
– Tell you what?
– Tell me, Tone.
He looks at me.
– I love you, Maureen, he says.
What weren't loud, but loud enough.
– Why treat me like shit then?
– You what?
– I can't take no more, Tone, I says. – I can't take no more.
   I sit down and pull Bella on my knee and press my face
in the back of her head. Her hair smells of nit shampoo.
– Will Nanny Nora get killed next now Tommy-Pop's
gone? she asks.
– Saints preserve us, says Tony's mum. – Can't someone
tell her to put a sock in it?
Dawn covers her face with her hands. I can't tell if she's
laughing or crying. The music stops. My mum coughs and
spits in a tissue.
– Please be seated, says the vicar.

He is smiling down on us from the pulpit. He raises his
arms in his droopy black sleeves and clears his throat. The
congregation settles down. Bella pipes up in the silence.
– If Mummy dies I want to be killed too.
My mum spins round and catches her by the collar.
– I'll fucking kill you in a minute, she says.
   Tony's mum goes like hem hem behind her hand and
gives Tony a look. Tony closes his eyes. The vicar's tired
voice comes over the tannoy about my dad what he never
knew from Adam. The vicar says my dad was a colourful
local character and it was a great tribute to him that so
many members of his large and close-knit family had
come on this most solemn day to pay their respects.

My mum is sobbing. The vicar is reading off of his stiff square of card how they don't make them like they used to. He smiles and looks out across the congregation, giving us permission to smile or laugh even, as if any of us felt like laughing.

Then the church door bangs behind us and we all turn round.

– Oh fuck, says my mum. – This is all we need.

Susan is tip-toeing into the church, handcuffed between two screws, in high shoes she must of borrowed off of some tart she was banged up with on the wing and bare legs thin as two streaks of piss teetering what she can hardly walk and her stretch skirt riding right up.

– Victor, she shouts.

So you can see her pale droopy knickers out of the bottom of it. And her skinny scarred arms and bruised shoulders and the black elastic of her bra straps dangling out of the big armholes of her vest.

– Victor!

Vic makes as if to stand up. My mum puts her hand on his arm and shakes her head.

– What a show-up, she says.

One of the screws flings a blanket over Susan and pushes her down in a seat. I am thinking the screws must of grabbed the blanket off of Susan's bunk where she never had no coat to cover herself if they was concerned for her welfare and her decency or just never wanted to look at her. But she shrugs off the blanket and stands up and wriggles to pull down her skirt.

– Jesus, says my mum, craning her neck to have a good look.

– I know, says Vic.

– She's only up the fucking spout.

– Never, says Vic.

– Look at her!

The screws pull Susan back down under the blanket. I am glad when she goes back under where the sight of all the damage inflicted on her and what she done to herself makes me think if I have a right to judge her or take offence at the obscenity of all the small wounds or if I just won't look and try not to love the baby they will take off of her. Where I had almost forgot she was pregnant with all what was going on in my head. But I did tell our Maggie to write to her and put her out of her misery. Not that Maggie was in the habit of obeying me.

I don't know how the screws subdued Susan if it was drugs they give her or what. But at least she is quiet now and not flaunting herself no more. Where the vicar's voice groans on out of the tannoy of Tommy's bravery in adversity whom you must all be very proud after a long illness may his soul rest in everlasting peace.

Georgina and Dennis is behind me with all of their kids scrubbed up and half decent for a change some stall down Hoxton what the stallholder never heard about my mum's win done her six outfits for twelve quid for the funeral. What was the first time them kids had something new since last Christmas we all put our hands in our pockets if Gina don't care who sees her up the top of Hoxton with the tinkers and all them what ain't got fuck all rummaging for bits off of the rag-yard I'd rather of seen my own kids go naked. And Alan is sobbing behind Gina and Dennis with his Sandra and a couple of her kids.

– Don't cry, Alan, says Sandra. – You're scaring me. Stop it.

Frankie gets up and reads from the bible. Raymond is snoring, his head on my mum's shoulder. He must of wore his self out. My mum can't stop crying. Victor puts his arm round her.

– Oh Vic, my mum whispers, sobbing in his neck.

– It's all right, says Vic. – It's all right my love.

Frank closes the bible with a slap and takes his place at

the head of the coffin. Alan rises slowly, shaking Sandra's hand off of his arm, and wipes his eyes with his sleeve. The heels of his shoes spark off of the tiled floor. Gina's Dennis gets up to follow our Alan, what is sobbing and carrying on at my dad's feet. Dawn digs her Barry in the ribs. He gets up and hurries after. Billy follows on. My mum wakes Raymond and shoves him off of the end of the pew. My Tony pushes past his mum and squeezes in next to our Billy.

My dad is lifted high on their shoulders in his box. I hear Tony grunt as the weight of the coffin settles on him. The men shuffle towards the church door, following the undertaker, the coffin balanced between them.

Billy don't look well. His legs is buckling and his face is an oily putty colour where he is too weak to manage the weight of the box. My Tony is all red with the strain where he is trying to take some of the weight off of Billy on his own shoulder.

But Billy's legs go out from under him. He stumbles and falls under Tony's feet. Tony nearly trips over him. The coffin lurches and you can hear the body slide inside it. You can hear my dad's head thud on the padding inside the coffin. My mum stands up, her hand over her mouth. A cry of misery goes up from the women in the church.
– Fuck me, says Victor.

The men struggle to steady the coffin but they can't move forward. Billy is still lying where he has fallen. Victor shoots out from my mum's pew and catches Billy by the feet. He drags Billy out of the way and goes to take Billy's place between my Tony and Raymond but Tony closes the gap and Vic is pushed out. Billy crawls back along the aisle towards the pew where his minder is waiting for him.

Victor shrugs and returns to his seat next to my mum.
– Only trying to help, he says.

Craig gets up and limps after the coffin on his crutches. The church doors open. My dad is gone.

Where she only had the two kids and I got four it feels all upside-down and back to front if you got more kids than your own mum. She was the only one I would ask if I never knew nothing when I first come home from the hospital and I was phoning her over every five minutes if Bella had a rash at the top of her legs or that time she drank a bottle of tea with lumps of bad milk in the teat what she found down the side of the chair and done projectile vomit all up the wall of my front room and Barry warned me not to tell no one.

But I already got more kids than she will ever have. Not that I ain't planning no more where I got my tubes tied for me while I was under the general anaesthetic last time they had to operate on me after I got that trouble underneath I thought while they was at it I might as well what weren't an easy decision to put myself through. Where I was snowed under with unsolicited advice I never wanted from all friends and family telling me what if my kids got killed in a car crash then I'd be sorry like people thought that if I got blessed with some more kids them new kids would make up for the pain of the loss of the ones I got now.

But it all made me feel sad. Even where the doctor assured me I can change my mind and he will untie the tubes again so the egg can travel to its destination when I see a young girl pushing a newborn in a pram I need to steel myself where I turn twenty-four on my next birthday and got all my kids already that life is all over for me now.

What ain't to say nothing bad about me like she underestimates me or nothing like that if she thinks I'm thick or what but she ain't got a clue it shines out of her face and she thinks I don't know. That lightness or sparkle ain't about my dad. Where she can't hide nothing from her own daughter whatever she might think of me.

And it ain't always easy to keep up with people once they change out of all recognition since all that weight dropped off of her from the back like a teenager as soon as she started over the bus garage in her new black trousers and a skinny-rib scoop-neck top and her hair is it a bob or all chunky at the back like that to show her nice neck. She don't look like my mum no more. When she was cleaning the school before she started over the bus garage in grey trackie bottoms and some peach or khaki t-shirt from a five-pack out of Asda what we all do it and her hair in a mauve scrunchie I borrowed her off of Bella scraped back off of her face so tight she was all chins. Not that I never loved her to bits if she could see all flab dented at the back by her bra like four tits through the fabric where I am just saying they make them cheap tops so thin you can see right through it.

Not that I can talk because they look quite nice from the front with the three buttons if you wear a smooth bra what ain't too tight if you need to go up a size and nobody ain't never said nothing to you about it out of tact or they just accept you how you are and it never made no difference to the way I felt about her.

Not that I never wanted to walk down Hoxton with her or nothing like that. Where she was always clean and put on a clean cardigan. She ain't never made me feel like that. What my Barry's mum belongs in a mental home if there was any justice in the world to get the care she needs where she is in danger to herself and can't help herself now she can't see herself no more since she has allowed herself to deteriorate Barry reckons she ought to stay indoors if she don't care. But my mum looks so lovely now she is working over the garage she is slimmer than me.

What ain't saying a lot after four kids you know how anyone would hoover up all what gets left over of crisp and chips and all that but when it comes to my own dinner I'm so knackered I can't hardly be bothered. Unless Barry picks up a kebab on his way back from work if he remembers Indian makes me heave ever since I fell for my Bella but I don't mind a bit of Chinese.

Where I ain't bitter and love my mum more than anyone else in the whole world almost as much as my own kids but since she changed I never enjoyed myself last week like we used to have a nice time down Hoxton. If she pushed the double buggy and I held hands with my Bella and little Jess and all them old girls what is friends with my nan from over the bingo and all what knows my mum where we have lived round here her whole life there ain't nobody what don't know us to say hello to. Bending over my pram and bunging me what they could spare folded in my babies' hands if I never whipped it off of them before they could swallow it and into my purse towards their milk and that and my mum smiling the proud smile she always had for me and my kids before Terry Harrison.

Not that she ain't proud no more but he took her mind right off of us. And she can't think about nothing else. What makes me sick how she is always thinking about him. What you can see it in her face if I would of guessed something was going on even if Auntie Linda never of said nothing.

With the babies in the double buggy. And the bag of carrots and onions hanging off of it where she always gives me a hand with my bits from Des what is the cheapest down there and the spuds stowed underneath to stop the pram tipping over. Or half the market would gawp how you ain't a fit mother what it could happen to anyone and you upright the pram and panic which one of them

babies to take out of it first if they are both screaming to
be lifted out where they banged their heads and only me
on my own to cope with it all if my mum ain't thinking
about me no more. And Bella and Jessica wandering off to
have a look at the toys on the toy stall however much you
scream at them to come back what just makes it worse. If
you ain't got your mum on you. How can you do it? If she
ain't nowhere up the market or indoors doing her work or
where the fuck is she when I need her to help me.

And after I got my spuds and that off of Des over the
cafe or the pie shop for a bit of dinner if you got all what
you need of spuds and that for the week to enjoy a nice bit
of dinner with your kids and your mum if she treats you
or you treat her if she's skint where they do a nice kiddie
meal with a drink and a scoop of ice-cream for afters what
I get one each for our Bella and Jessica. And a couple of
jars out of my bag for the babies what the lady warms up
for me and a ham omelette for my mum with salad and the
special of today for me or all day breakfast only a couple
of quid with tea and two slices what don't leave no room
for nothing off of the puddings although I do like a nice
sponge and custard if you can fit it in.

No, I never enjoyed my self like I used to. With my
pram and my mum down Hoxton or Dalston if I wanted
shoes for the kids but I can't do it on my own. With the
four kids if Barry is at work I just can't do it. How you end
up like you never wanted to end up screaming at them and
giving them a slap.

Where Big Sid on the knicker stall is having a laugh
and a joke with my mum about my babies in the pram was
her babies and made out like he thought we was sisters.
He tucks a pair of knickers in the top of her bag. But what
does that make me?

I never said she never come down Hoxton with me no
more. But we was so close before. I always phoned her

my Barry used to say if you don't get off of the phone to your mum you won't have nothing to say to each other in the pub later on what we all knew was not never gonna happen if he stayed in and looked after them for me.

So my mum stops the pram and flings the knickers back at Sid what scrap of black and red lace flies across the stall she would never of got her fat arse in all shiny and scratchy even if you was Kate Moss. What ain't no use to my mum. She ain't changed that much.
– What do you take me for? she says. – I only wear them big white ones.
What made me blush and grin where she shouldn't of told him that.
– I can't help you then, darling, says Sid, and puts the knickers on his head.
Bella and Jessica giggle and shriek.
– Clean out of big white ones, he says.
My mum laughs.
– Let's have another look at them ones then, she says.
So Sid takes the knickers off of his head and chucks them back at my mum. She holds them up and examines them.
– I reckon I'll give them a go, she says. – I ain't got nothing to lose now have I love? You got them in a size twelve?
– Yeah, says Sidney. – But you can't bring them back if he don't like them.

It's not like she ain't sad. But she hoots like no one would never of thought she only just lost her own father. How she is skipping along down Hoxton and swinging her shining hair. And after they lowered his box in the hole she took a handful of mud where it was all piled up in a heap by the slabs of cut turf and slung it at him. Not how my nan let it run through her fingers and shed tears over the coffin but my mum clenched her teeth and slung it.

And all the meat what we chipped in for my nan's golden wedding come out of Auntie Linda's chest freezer.

Over the community hall after we buried him where our
Linda done us proud. Where I am not trying to make out
like I am in floods over the loss but I feel sorry for my nan
and my mum, and I have a little cry and my Barry bungs
me a tissue and I pull myself together what with the kids
and that you can't afford to go into one.

And my nan and my mum have still got us. Where they
ain't never gonna be on their own. What was a good thing
I lent that run-proof mascara off of my cousin Tracie when
she was helping me to get the kids ready. Otherwise I
don't want to end up like a fucking panda where my Uncle
Raymond is upsetting his self he's starting me off again.
How he ain't never learnt to hold nothing inside and not
let it out if he can't help his self but it don't half grate on
me.

Where my Dad is playing cards in the corner of the
hall with Barry and our Craig. But what if he looks up
and clocks what she's up to? It's not that I don't love my
mum, I do want her to be happy. But not like Wendy
Lester I bumped into last week from my class at Burbage
over the baby clinic what told me if her mum charged for
it how she puts it about then at least they would all get
something out of it. Instead of giving it away for nothing.
What weren't a nice thing to say about your own mother.
But Terry Harrison is sitting in one of them grey plastic
chairs against the wall at the back of the hall and nobody
ain't talking to him like a wallflower if we was all dancing
over my nan's golden wedding but we ain't dancing. And
my mum keeps on glancing at him. He is leaning back
and nodding his head very gently against the grey breeze-
blocks of the wall behind him like he can hear soft music.
And above his head the tails of balloons dangle down
where kids must of let go of the pink strings and watched
the balloons bob out of reach at some party last week
they splashed out to give a bit of colour to the hall what

always looks stark in the strip lighting and never has no atmosphere whatever people dig deep on flowers and banners. And he can't keep his eyes off of my mum. What would of been sick if he was at the church service but I never saw him. I don't think he was in the church. What would of been sick.

I don't want her to give up on my dad. She is all he's got to keep him together, how he is if she bins him, he will go down the pan. It ain't right what she's playing at, it ain't right if all women got needs even if they was over the hill it should be my dad what is sorting all that out for her. What is my business if anyone is thinking it ain't none of mine because I am her daughter I think I got a say in what goes on. How I am supposed to feel when she is looking at Terry Harrison like that? If it's just flirting with him and that but it makes me feel bad. Where Wendy Lester started doing all them stupid things. Not that you'd catch me cutting myself or any of that. But I'm just saying it was Wendy what suffered over it.

So Auntie Linda never paid her respects when we laid Pop to rest. She was too busy carving the whole ham with cloves and mustard glaze over the hall while we was burying my grand-dad and that cold topside she does with pickles and fresh bread and jellied eels for my nan and all Linda had planned for the Golden Wedding of what my grand-dad was partial like pork-pie with egg what weren't like he was with us no more to enjoy it but still. And tubs of coleslaw and beetroot and two hundred volly vents hot out of the oven where we was allowed to use the big kitchen at the back of the hall if we left it as we found it and paid for the electric off of the meter, what my nan said she had hoped to be eating under happier circumstances but there weren't no point in letting it go to waste. With doileys and sprigs of fresh parsley to garnish and lemon wedges how Auntie Linda always does everything so nice.

And you should of seen the cake. Three square tiers on silver drums and white pillars, white icing with swags and white doves and white roses, all what my Auntie Linda modelled herself in her front room out of that sugar paste she buys by the block, all them fiddly little birds and petals for the golden wedding on a tray in front of the telly when my mum was up the hospital after work, each to his or her own to make a contribution. And I don't know how many pounds of flour and sugar and butter and dried fruit and almonds and black treacle and mixed spice and cherries and brandy to make the cake moist what was Auntie Linda's celebration recipe and two dozen eggs if that was the biggest cake I ever seen.

Where my mum ain't got a cake tin to her name. Nor does she feel the lack of it, cream the butter and sugar what we learnt in school until your arm drops off, like all the energy Auntie Linda got left over she bakes cakes where she ain't got no kids of her own. Not that I ain't saying nothing against my mum nor would I never say a word against her. But she never had no time for all that when we was kids, where she was doing outdoor work or scrubbing over the school how you let them scrape out the bowl with their fingers and lick the mixture off of the wooden spoon. Where it was me and Craig over Auntie Linda's in her hot kitchen helping her weigh out the butter and sugar on the scales and I used to think that one day she'd make someone a lovely mum.

But what was she supposed to do when my pop popped off a week before the big party? She draped the pillars of the cake with black ribbons. And took off the plastic bride and groom she stuck on top for Nanny and Pop to celebrate fifty years of married life through thick and thin whatever he put her through. And Auntie Linda says Nanny could give as good as she got when it come down to it. Where Linda is standing proudly by her beautiful

cake in the community hall. And turns round and tells
Julie she couldn't think of nothing but more flowers to top
the cake once she binned the bride and groom when the
old man died except a skull or a coffin to cover the bald
patch in the icing or the bride on her own if you cut off
the husband with a Stanley knife. What she winked at Julie
and said that wouldn't of been very nice.

And in the toilets the two screws are parked against the
row of hand basins waiting for my Auntie Susan. Where
she's six months gone and still can't hold nothing down
she asked me to go in with her why that girl ain't never
learnt to look after herself. She's puking in the cubicle with
the door wide open. I'm holding her hair for her out of the
toilet bowl and she's crying and retching until she's empty.
She asks me to help her wash her face.

– Wanna use some of my make-up? I says.

– If you don't mind, says Susan.

– Nah, I says. – Why should I mind?

The screws sigh and roll their eyes. Susan applies
mascara and lip-stick.

– What do you reckon? she asks, pouting at me.

– Yeah, I says.

Susan puts her head on one side and looks at herself in the
mirror.

– Do I look all right? She says.

– Yeah, I says.

– Borrow me your comb, Dawn, she says.

I watch Auntie Susan back-comb her hair. The front of
her hair is wet where I washed the sick off of it for her. She
looks like shit.

– Dawn, she says. – Do ya like Victor?

– Nah, I says.

– Why? says Susan. – Tell me why.

– I ain't never told no one, I says.

– What? says Susan.

– When I was a kid, I says. – He used to give me money and that. He tried to touch me.

– How old was you?

– Seven, eight maybe.

– Did you let him?

– Nah, I says. – You're joking ain't you? Why would I let him? I just took the money off of him and told him if he ever done it again I'd tell my mum.

– Got any hairspray? she says.

– I ain't got none, I says. – Sorry.

– Don't be sorry, darling, says Auntie Susan. – I hope you ain't never sorry for nothing.

– Ok, I says.

I look at her in the mirror. She is trying to smile.

– Why didn't you tell your mum? She says.

– Dunno, I says. – Did he touch you?

– Yeah, says Susan. – He loves me.

I look in her face.

– He loves you?

– Well I got him round my little finger, she says.

– What ain't the same thing, I says.

If my Tony had of known that Terry Harrison was in the hall he would of battered me earlier where I had wound him up in the church but he never knew until it was all over. If somebody must of said something to him at the bitter end and he weren't best pleased. What weren't no surprise to nobody when he totally lost it and come after me.

If it was malicious gossip against me from a member of my own family where they had to stir it for their own reasons or his name just got mentioned in passing how he found out ain't of no interest to me now. Of course I

never of asked Terry to come to the funeral or over the
hall where I ain't that fucking stupid or hoping to bring
trouble on myself like I weren't feeling bad enough already
over losing my old man. And never wanted nothing like
that off of my Tony if you are thinking I wanted it all to
kick off. But I just looked round and seen Terry at the
bar in the hall, taking a bottled lager off of one of Alan's
mates what was running the bar for our Linda. Terry was
talking to Frank where he used to work out of the same
garage and I am thinking maybe Frank must of invited
him or had Terry just decided to turn up for my sake what
he never should of done how things stood between us.
But I am glad he is here for me because he makes me feel
safe what must of been the 'reason he done it. Where I had
mentioned the arrangements to him not to invite him but
I had got used to telling him all what was going on for me
in my life and he was a good listener.

And of course I am trying not to look at him where
even Dawn is scoping me out and thinking her own
thoughts if she knows something and disapproves
where our Linda must of said something or maybe I
am dreaming when Dawn come out of the toilets and
looked at me and never smiled and I read too much into
her behaviour what would break my heart if she turned
against me.

Followed by Susan why she done her face and hair like
that in the toilets if Dawn helped her with the slap and
handcuffed to them screws again. What won't even take a
sandwich off of the buffet or a cup of tea like everything is
poison we got to offer and never showed much compassion
for her in her condition. What the fuck is Susan pulling
them across the hall to the little stage. And they just let
her do it even if they was smiling at each-other behind her
back. Not to offer encouragement to Susan but I thought
they was glad something was going to happen like it was

a day out for them and they was determined to milk something out of it or have a laugh at our expense whatever harm Susan done to herself in the process.

And stumbling up the steps in them high shoes with the double straps fastened with buckles round her ankles and the screws trying not to trip over or step on the oasis of white flowers what the old woman rescued to bring back from the graveside was a shame if nobody would get the beauty of them and the old man got so many he could spare us a few she reckoned for the wake if they all went to waste what was true he never had need of no flowers where he was going.

So on the narrow stage Susan grabs the microphone and fumbles for the switch. Her breath is broadcast over the system and she taps the top of the microphone to check if it is working. You can hear the voices of the screws out of the loud-speakers trying to talk her down now if they could see where this was heading and it weren't funny no more. Where she shouts in the microphone if anyone knows who is my real mum and who knows my real dad?

What we all turn to look at our Maggie. And I am thinking Maggie should of spat out her gum before she climbed on the stage because it looks bad if she ain't got no respect for her own daughter's pain but she just keeps on chewing. And Susan never shed a tear. Where she never knew her mum it makes you hard maybe, or all the drugs and that keeping her feelings at bay if Victor slipped her something and the screws looked the other way what must of made their job a bit easier for them. Not that I got any sympathy for them people but it must of been hard for them chained up to our Susan.

But if it was me up there I would of took her in my arms. But she weren't mine. And Maggie ain't like me.
– You? Susan goes. – You?

Maggie takes her big gold lighter out of her bag and sparks up a fag.
– Well don't sound so pleased, she says.
– Why didn't you of kept me? says Susan.
Maggie inhales and passes the fag to Susan. My mum is sobbing at the back of the hall, and Victor is holding her. Linda grins at me what a fuck-up the old man's funeral is turning out. In spite of all her hard work what she put in for our benefit.
– I was only a kid, says Maggie. – I thought it was for the best.
– Who's me real dad then? Asks Susan.
– You don't want to know, says Maggie.
– What, you forgot? says Susan.
– Nah, says Maggie. – I ain't forgot.
– You gonna tell me or what?
    Maggie shades her eyes with her hand where the lights is dazzling her and looks across the hall at my mum.
– Victor, says Maggie. – Victor is your real dad.
My mum blinks up at her friend.
– What, says Susan, looking puzzled. – My Victor?
Where we are all a bit slow on the uptake Susan cups her hand round her belly and grins at Maggie.
– How old was you? she says. – When you fell?
– Twelve, says Maggie. – I give birth to you when I was thirteen.
– We thought I couldn't have no kids, says Susan. – Where there ain't nothing of me, we thought it weren't never gonna happen?
    My mum is staring at Victor with her mouth open. He looks frightened but she takes him by the hand and leads him towards the door. Linda holds me back. I am screaming and trying to fight her but she has always been stronger than me. She won't let me go. Alan is laughing. I look round for Terry but I can't see him. Victor lets go of

my mum's hand and holds the door open for her.
– I'm gonna kill you, you nonce git, I scream.
My mum and Victor begin to run. Billy breaks away from
his nurse and runs after them.

Mother is on her landing with Billy. Victor is perched
on the balcony rail, his arse hanging out over the edge,
dunking a biscuit in a mug of tea. Billy is shouting, how
he can't understand nothing no more if the old woman
lives with a nonce and don't care her own kids and their
kids what he's interfered with as long as she gets her bit of
wages off of him on the nail for her bingo and that where
all she cares about is her bingo.

   My mum is crying but she ain't got nothing to say for
herself, what can she say? She is holding out her palms
to Billy, trying to show him that she is helpless. I am
hollering across the flats with Linda hanging off of my
coat.
– I'm gonna kill him, I shout. – Why did he fuck his own
daughter?
– Leave it, Maureen, says Linda. – The old woman's bin
through enough.
   I am so angry I am crying for Susan and Susan's baby.
Linda is holding me. Dawn is crying. Billy takes the old
woman by the shoulders and begs her.
– You gotta say something, Mum, he says.
– What do you want me to say? I never knew nothing. I'm
lonely, son. Vic is my friend.
   Billy pushes my mum out of the way and shoves Victor
off of the balcony. My mum screams and claps her hand
over her mouth. Vic's head cracks off of a bollard. I grab
Dawn and cover her eyes because I don't want her to see
no more.

My home is all smashed to fuck again.

– You cunt, says Tony, and bashes me up the side of my
head.
I back out of the front door and shout from the landing for
our Alan. He is in the crowd outside the hall with Sandra,
enjoying the last of the beer after the funeral and watching
the police screen off the area under my mum's balcony
where Victor's body is still laying on the ground. Alan
laughs as Tony comes after me.
– Help me, Alan, I scream, picking up a wooden chair
from the landing outside Aggie's where her Mick sits of an
evening.
– I'm gonna kill you, says Tony.
Alan shrugs. I hit Tony over the head with the chair. It
splinters. He staggers and falls.
– You cunt, says Tony, crawling towards me along the
landing. His little dog barks at me.
– Goodbye Tone, I says.

Terry Harrison is waiting for me over the hall where I'd
only popped home for five minutes to get some headache
tablets for Dawn after the shock of all what went on.
– What happened to you? he says.
– I'm okay, I says. – Where's Dawn?
– Barry said to tell you not to worry, Maureen, but he
thought it was best if he took her home.
– Oh, I says.
– Seems like a nice boy, he says.
– Yeah, I says.
– Go and have a wash, he says.
    When I come out of the toilets Terry is sat on the edge
of the stage with a bottle of beer in his hand. Linda is
sweeping through the hall with a wide broom. Raymond is
tidying Victor's records away.
– Go home, Ray, I says.
– Yeah? he says.

– Yeah, I says. – The old woman is all on her own up there. She needs you.

– Yeah? says Raymond.

– Yeah, I says.

– Maureen? he says.

– Yes, Ray?

– I knew what Victor was like, he says.

– Ok, I says.

– I won't miss him. It weren't just Susan what he…

– Ok Raymond, I says. –It ain't your fault. You know that.

– Better go home then, he says.

– Yeah, I says. – See ya.

I sit down on the edge of the stage next to Terry. He lights a couple of fags and gives one to me.

– I got plans, Maureen, he says.

– What? I says.

– For the future, he says.

– You don't have to sell yourself to me, I says.

– I always fancied driving a cab, he says.

– Yeah? I says.

– Yeah, says Terry.

He looks over at Linda wielding the wide broom.

– Wanna hand with that floor, Linda? he says.

– Nah, you're all right.

– Where's Billy? I says.

– Gone back in the clinic, says Linda. – The nurse said he'd had enough excitement for one day it was time to go home.

– And Susan?

– Shedding tears over Victor all the way back to Holloway I shouldn't wonder, says Linda.

– You reckon? I says.

– You gonna sit there all night? says Linda.

I look at Terry.

– Take her home, Tel, she says. – And you watch your

back, Maureen, do you hear me?
– Will do, I says.
Terry takes my hand and pulls me to my feet.
– Come on love, he says.
– See you, Linda, I says. – You done us proud.
– Yeah, she says. – Ain't nobody can't say we never give the
old cunt a good send-off.

They cuffed Susan to the bed during delivery like she
would of legged it between contractions if they give her
half a chance what she reckoned was a joke how come
nobody never told her the pain you have to suffer and she
ain't never having no more babies if she can help it.
– So it hurt then? said Linda.
– Never! I said.
– Where they had to cut me to get the baby out ain't no
picnic I can tell you, Susan protested.
– How long was you in labour? I asked.
– It felt like hours, she said. – I thought I was gonna die of
the pain. And the cunts only give me gas and air for all my
hard work and they was poking me where I never made no
progress I think it was their fucking fault they had to cut
me.
     Linda rolled her eyes and breathed out through her
mouth if she was regretting she even bothered to come
up the hospital what was her idea to ask me to keep her
company because Maggie said she was not ready or some
crap like that. And Susan went on in that flat whine out
of her nose the cuff chafed her wrist and she was lonely
in the side room off of the ward they put her out of sight
or harm's way to keep herself to herself like they was
expecting her to kick off if the other mums on the ward
was all blissed out over their babies and Victor never
come and held her hand how they had it all planned in
a letter she sent him from Holloway where she said she

kept on forgetting he fell off of my mum's flats. What I
knew was one way not to feel nothing of grief or loss if
you was full of love for a nonce what was your own father
if your milk was coming in and you was trying not to love
your new baby what she was a new beginning and yours
above and beyond anybody else in your life. With all that
pain of childbirth on her own in the delivery suite she
never signed up to without Victor holding her hand she
reckoned was worse in her case where she never wanted
no baby in the first place to look forward to at the end
what might of helped some people to get through it I
thought was a fair assessment of her situation. She said
Victor just let her down and not for the first time. How
he put his need on her until he was freed of it and she lost
her hold over him if she was too needy or what it was like
between them as she got older. She said it weren't just the
drugs he controlled her. What she will never understand
how he done that to her. But weren't no mystery to me
nor our Linda where it showed in Linda's face she was
thinking what Victor had done to our Susan was damage
beyond repair unless a miracle could be brought to bear
on her what was not very likely under the circumstances.
And me and Linda both felt angry with her for her
suffering how it goes sometimes with those people always
making a show of theirselves if they was conscious of
anything they was inflicting on their nearest and dearest
what nobody ain't trying to pretend was very fair on our
Susan.

– But where is the baby? I asked.

– In the special nursery.

– For how long? asked Linda.

– Six weeks at least. Where they gotta wean it off of the
drugs and that. What I never would of done no more if I
had of known I was like it.

– No, said Linda.

– Not at all, said Susan. – If I had of known how the baby would of suffered. But I never knew. I never heard nothing so pitiful, how it was trying to cry. I feel bad what I done to it.
– Ain't no point in crying, Linda said.
– I ain't crying, said Susan. – I wish I could.
– Yeah well, said Linda.
– I thought I couldn't never have no kids, Susan laughed.
    Linda took a handkerchief out of her bag and blew her nose.
– Mum told me it was a little girl, she said, her face softened and opening in spite of herself.
– And I had fifteen stitches, said Susan. – Nightmare!
– But what you gonna do? Linda asked.
– The old woman's been up to see me already.
– Don't tell me you ain't gonna give the baby to her? I shouted.
– She don't want it, said Susan. – She reckons she is too old to go through all that again.
– Don't you wanna keep her? Linda asked.
– The old woman says I ain't got a hope in hell giving a kid a good home the way I am. I thought Victor would of took her off of me.
– What, so he could of done to her what he done to you and your mum? I said.
– He was a loving person, Maureen, Susan said. – What do sound a bit hollow now, even to me.
    She smiled and looked at the clock above the door.
– Nearly time for my tablets, she said.
– Have you give her a name yet? I said.
– I ain't named her, she said. – I ain't hardly seen her.
– I thought you said you was gonna try and give up the drugs and that, I said.
– I don't even like kids, she said. – Don't you want her, Maureen?
– I can't, I said. – I ain't got it in me to take her. Not that I

ain't never thought about it. But I can't take no more pain in my life. As long as I don't see her.

– Shame, said Susan, and looked at the clock again.

Linda stretched her arms above her head and yawned.

– I'll take her, she said.

– Do what? I said.

– I'll take the baby, said Linda.

– You? said Susan. – I thought you never wanted no kids.

– How much do you want for her?

– I ain't selling her, darling. If you want her you can have her. Gratis and for nothing.

Susan pulled the covers up to her chin and closed her eyes.

– If you let me take her I ain't never gonna give her back, Linda said. – Do you understand that? She'll be mine, Susan. Like she come out of me.

Susan opened her eyes.

– But what would you tell her? she asked.

– The truth, said Linda. – That you was ill and I took her. Because I never had no kids of my own and was ready to give everything to her like she was my own daughter.

– Yes, said Susan. – And no money changed hands? Where you offered and I refused to make nothing for myself out of the transaction?

– If you think that's important, said Linda.

– Because I never want her to think she was sold by her own mother, said Susan. – What might do her head in if she found out.

Linda sat down on the edge of the bed and pushed her face in Susan's face.

– I would give her all the love I got to give, she said. – That I can promise you.

– All right, said Susan, shrinking back under the covers.

– What feels like a lot, said Linda. – A lot of love from me to her. I am trying to talk to you. Look at me!

– What?

– Do you understand what this means? said Linda. – You can't just turn round to me and say you've changed your mind if you want her back in the future. Whatever happens in your life.

– I ain't fucking stupid, said Susan.

– I'm just saying, said Linda.

– Well don't try and put feelings on me I ain't got. Where I ain't all that bothered? If you want her you can have her.

– And you don't want nothing off of me in return?

– Nah, says Susan. – We been through all that.

– You sure?

– Fuck sake, Linda, I said. – She don't want your money.

– So can I see her now?

– She's next door. Tell them I said.

– Cheers, Susan. You coming, Maureen?

– You go first, I said.

Linda got up off of the bed and turned towards the door.

– But you gotta be careful of her, said Susan, lifting her head off of the pillow. – Make sure you don't let her get in no trouble. You ain't gonna let her get in no trouble?

– No, said Linda. – She won't want for nothing.

– You gonna keep her safe for me?

– What can I say? said Linda. – I promise to watch her back like she was my own. I will do my best.

– Thank you, said Susan.

– Thank you, said Linda.

Susan let her head fall back down on the pillow. Her hair was tangled at the back and she was crying now, the tears pouring out of her like they would never stop. I passed her a box of tissues. Terry was waiting for me in his car to take me up the cash and carry but I was happy to sit with Susan while Linda went to see the new baby.

– Linda never wanted to hold me, Susan howled. – She

never wanted to hold me.

I sat on the blue chair by her bed and reached across and patted her on the upper arm. I was waiting for her misery to subside if I never showed how I was feeling for her where I had learnt to protect myself. Or I thought she would cry herself to sleep and might feel a bit better when she woke up and remembered that her baby was going to a good home. What was harsh if I never wanted to take her in my arms but was necessary for me. But a nurse came in and Susan sat up to swallow her medication.

– It's nice and warm in here, Susan said.

– Yes, I said.

– And clean, she said.

– Nice and clean, I said.

– You think I done the right thing, Maureen?

– Yes, I said.

– But what if she was a moany baby and cries all the time?

– Linda will cope, I said.